something heavy crashed into him. His head exploded and he looked around. A large pile of metal pipes was breaking loose and rolling over the deck. The pipes made a fearsome din, sweeping men and crates aside. Schulman glanced up and saw the towering derrick breaking up and collapsing. It was a terrible sight. The webbed beams were snapping free. They were bending and flying out and falling down and crashing into the drilling room. Schulman heard the demoniac noise, heard the screams of the dying men. The derrick platforms fell apart and dropped down between the legs, then the legs themselves buckled and broke and the whole thing collapsed. Schulman looked up in awe. The spectacle pinned him to the deck. There was a deluge of clanging steel and roaring wood and screaming men, and then the roof of the drilling floor caved in and the noise was appalling.

'– on your feet! Let's get going!'

W. A. Harbinson

The Oil Heist

CORGI BOOKS
A DIVISION OF TRANSWORLD PUBLISHERS LTD

THE OIL HEIST

A CORGI BOOK 0 552 10753 0
First publication in Great Britain

PRINTING HISTORY
Corgi edition published 1978

Copyright © W. A. Harbinson 1978

Corgi Books are published by
Transworld Publishers Ltd,
Century House, 61–63 Uxbridge Road,
Ealing, London W5 5SA

Made and printed in Great Britain by
Cox & Wyman Ltd, London, Reading and Fakenham

For Victor

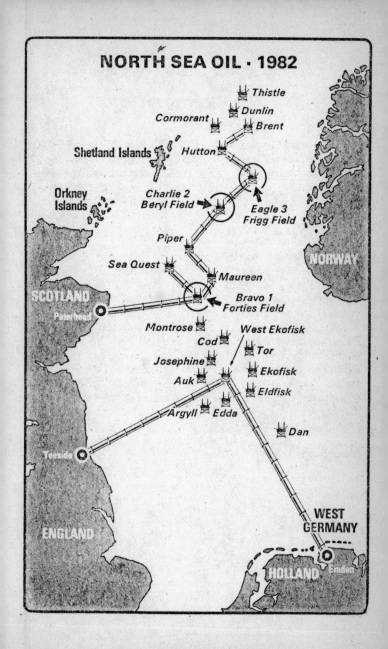

AUTHOR'S NOTE

THIS book is a work of fiction, and while all the oil fields mentioned herein actually exist, the rigs Eagle 3, Charlie 2 and Bravo 1 exist only in the author's imagination. The map shown opposite is therefore not descriptive of the North Sea oil fields as they are at present, but as the author thinks they could be by 1982. This concept was based loosely on a report in the *Times* of September 3, 1974, which stated: 'More than half of Britain's oil requirements in 1980 could be flowing from a single undersea pipeline linking five large oil fields in the northern part of the North Sea to the Shetlands.' Ignoring the Shetlands, the author has chosen to have such a pipeline flow directly into Peterhead, Scotland, where indeed much of the oil presently goes.

Research on the oil fields and rigs was supplied by the Hans Tasiemka Research Club, London, and the author is particularly indebted to an excellent book *The Oil Rush*, written by Mervyn Jones and photographed by Fay Godwin, and to Roger Chapman's *No Time On Our Side*, from which was gleaned invaluable information about submersibles. My thanks to Alan Earney for suggesting the idea and then promptly commissioning it.

Allen Harbinson

CHAPTER ONE

'Is it true the Prime Minister's in the V.I.P. lounge?' McGregor asked, wiping his lips with one hand and glancing idly around the crowded heliport lounge.

'That's right,' Ricketts said, studying the bottles along the bar. 'Why do you ask? You want to shake the bastard's hand?'

McGregor laughed sardonically and turned his head to grin at Ricketts. The Englishman was leaning against the counter, sipping his whiskey.

'Oh, aye,' McGregor said. 'I'd like to shake his hand all right. Then I'd push him off the edge of my drilling floor. For that I'd give my right arm.'

'You're a nationalist,' Ricketts said.

'Aye,' McGregor said, 'I am that. Me an' a lot o' other hungry Scots. Independence is coming.'

Ricketts didn't respond, his broad shoulders were slightly slumped, and he looked at the mass of waiting men with an air of impatience. The heliport lounge was packed, and the men in the chairs were surrounded by luggage. They wore jeans and anoraks, were mostly under thirty, and were now hazed in a fog of cigarette smoke. Outside, the weather was filthy; the strip was covered in a silvery drizzle. The helicopters had been grounded and they sat in metallic rows while the drifting clouds cast shadows on their perspex. Ricketts was annoyed: he wanted to get moving. All the men in the lounge had been sitting there for hours, and most were as impatient as himself.

'Look at 'em,' McGregor said softly. 'The scum o' the land.'

'Being one of them you should know,' Ricketts said.

McGregor smiled tightly, his eyes dark and obsessed. He had a rough wind-whipped face, a short wiry body, and the sort of restless energy that speaks of unreleased inner tensions. He snorted and drank some beer. His tongue licked along his lips. He kept the grin on his face, but his eyes showed resentment as he looked up at Ricketts' broken profile.

'I come from them,' McGregor said. 'I've no' forgotten that fact. I'm working-class and proud of it, but that dinnae mean I'm one o' this rubbish.'

'Rubbish?' Ricketts said. He glanced around the crowded lounge. He saw the young, unshaven faces through the haze of cigarette smoke, saw the suitcases and rucksacks, saw the blue jeans and anoraks framed by the windows that looked out on the cold, rainswept heliport. There was a storm over the North Sea, raging around the oil rigs, and the men in the lounge were all waiting to board the grounded helicopters. They had been here, in the Bristow Heliport in Aberdeen, for almost five hours.

'Aye, rubbish,' McGregor said. 'The scum o' the working-classes. They only work on the rigs because they can't find employment elsewhere.'

'*You* work on the rigs,' Ricketts said. 'And *I* work on the rigs.'

'Aye, but not because it's the only work we can find. The rigs attract the worthless, the North Sea attracts the debris. It's a job where yer not asked for yer past record or credentials, and that makes it very appealing to this scum.'

'This is 1982,' Ricketts said. 'There are approximately *three million* unemployed. That makes it very easy to be scum – as you so eloquently call them.'

McGregor picked up his glass and drank some beer. He put the glass down and lit a cigarette with abrupt, nervous movements. He didn't offer one to Ricketts, knew that Ricketts didn't smoke, knew that Ricketts liked the ladies, was a wizard on the oil rigs, and otherwise had no apparent interests. McGregor didn't like Ricketts because a lot of the rig-workers revered him. The Englishman was a toolpusher, one of the élite of the North Sea, and he was tough, efficient and ruthless. Ricketts could hire and fire. He was brutally impartial when doing so. He demanded hard work and obedience from the roughnecks and roustabouts, but he had an almost puritanical sense of justice. That was what bothered McGregor. For all his harshness, Ricketts was honest. He did not bend the rules, would not let others bend them, and let no one close enough to see his own weaknesses. For this reason he was respected ... and for this reason McGregor treated him warily.

'Aye,' McGregor said. 'Three million unemployed. That bastard's in the V.I.P. lounge while the rest of us starve.'

'You're not starving,' Ricketts said.

'I'm just a roughneck,' McGregor said. 'I'm not starving, but I could be any day now, just like the others.'

'It's not that bad,' Ricketts said.

'It's that bad and you know it. With three million unemployed, a man cannae risk his job, and the oil companies dinnae ignore that fact. We once had unions on the rigs. We still have, but they're useless. With the unemployment rising, the employers have the whip hand and the unions can't afford to take chances. You're an English toolpusher. That's a double advantage. You'll have a job as long as there's drilling, but we're not all so lucky. An' it's worse if yer Scottish. You know it and I know it. That oil's really in Scottish waters, but the Scots dinnae get a thing out of it – and now the Scottish National Party is getting close to a majority and the oil companies are startin' to get worried.'

'So,' Ricketts said. 'What's that got to do with your precious job? You're in charge of every roustabout on your rig. You should fall asleep laughing.'

'Tell me another,' McGregor said, snorting disgustedly. He had another swig of beer, inhaled on his cigarette and nervously drummed his fingers on the counter. 'The oil beneath the North Sea is estimated at about £2,000 million a year,' he continued. 'Why do you think we want an independent Scotland? If that revenue went to us it could meet our national budget and give us a healthy balance of payments surplus. That's what we're fighting for. That's why you have all this trouble. The terrorists won't stop until they've won us independence and all the oil rights that go with it.'

'You back the terrorists?' Ricketts said.

'No,' McGregor said. 'I'm not saying I agree with 'em, but that's how it is, and that's why it's not safe to be Scottish. They dinnae like us on the rigs. They think we're all sympathizers. They think all Scots back the terrorists, so if a man has to go they'll always pick a Scot before an Englishman. They're drilling less every month. There's fewer jobs for the taking. Men are being dropped left, right and centre – and few of them English.'

'I don't think that's true,' Ricketts said.

'It's true,' said McGregor.

Ricketts smiled remotely, put his glass to his lips, drank his whiskey and then ordered another. He knew what McGregor meant. He also knew that McGregor was right. The oil boom of the late seventies had given a lot of men employment, but not all that many had been Scots. While the oil, geographically, was in Scottish waters, ironically the Scots had had to take second place to an enormous influx of American, French, Spanish, Norwegian and British workers. Not only had there been little relief for Scottish unemployment – currently the highest in all of Britain – but the influx of the oil companies to Scottish coastal towns had sent rents and general prices soaring. Some of the most beautiful areas of Scotland had been devastated to make way for immense construction sites where the oil platforms were built; but most of the construction sites were financed and controlled by American companies – fast becoming multi-national conglomerates – and the majority of the rigs had been built in Europe and America, thus depriving even more Scottish workers of employment. To make matters worse, the British government, suddenly realizing that its own ineptitude had caused both jobs and remuneration to be handed over to foreign investors, had decided to recoup its losses by placing a crippling taxation on all North Sea earnings. This taxation, rather than bringing into the country a much needed revenue, had merely frightened the oil majors into reducing staff, cutting back on exploratory drillings, and keeping the oil under the sea; the anticipated revenue was therefore denied them, and the government, faced with massive balance of payments deficients, and with accelerating unemployment, was eventually also faced with a startling upsurge in political anarchy and violence.

Ricketts was aware of this. He had watched it building for two years. Since 1980, when the oil majors had pulled their horns in, there had been an enormous amount of opposition to Parliament, particularly from Scotland and the north of England, where unemployment was highest. Leading this opposition were the Scottish Nationalists, who were gaining more seats every year by selling the idea of Scottish rights to North Sea oil. McGregor therefore had a point. The oil companies were wary of Scottish workers. Of the numerous terrorist groups, the Scottish were the most ferocious in their activities against the British Government, putting even the revitalized I.R.A. in the shade with their assassinations, bombings and hi-jackings. Fearful of infiltration by members of such groups, the oil companies were becoming paranoiac about Scottish workers, and often used any excuse to get rid of them. Since most of the terrorist groups had plenty of English and Irish members, this antagonism towards the Scots served no purpose. None the less, McGregor had reason to be nervous.

'Maybe things will change,' Ricketts said. 'Rumour has it that the real reason the Prime Minister is paying this visit to Forties Field is to discuss the possibility of reducing taxes to encourage the oil majors to do more drilling. Everyone now knows that the oil companies are deliberately building up huge tax losses in the Middle East countries and setting the revenue against liability for tax in the U.K. They'll continue to do this until the British government reduces tax, and the Prime Minister is obviously aware of that fact.'

'Fuck dealing with them,' McGregor said. 'The government should nationalize the oil fields and *force* the bastards to drill.'

'They can't do that,' Ricketts said. 'It was the British government that originally granted exploration licences to the oil majors, selling them off by means of an auction with sealed bids. The British sector of the North Sea now belongs rightfully to the majors, and if the government stepped in and nationalized, it would cause an international scandal.'

'Aye,' McGregor said, glancing around the smoky lounge. 'They're desperate for money so they sell off the North Sea; now they're even more desperate and they can't get their hands on the oil. There'll be no sense in this country until Parliament's dismantled and a whole new legislation introduced. British governments, be they Labour or Conservative, are just capitalist lackeys.'

'You keep talking like that,' Ricketts said, 'and you *will* lose your job.'

McGregor finished off his beer. 'Aye, you're no' wrong there. A man on the rigs should be tight-mouthed. He'll go farther that way.'

McGregor put his glass down on the counter and wiped the beer from his lips. Looking up at Ricketts he saw a pair of grey eyes that were flatly surveying the crowded lounge. Following Ricketts' gaze, McGregor saw the mass of waiting men, the tables piled high with beer cans and crumpled papers, the ash trays overflowing, the cigarette smoke swirling above the heads of the men whose conversation was a constant, edgy murmuring. The men on the rigs worked a fortnight on and a fortnight off. Once on the rigs they would work twelve hours a day, seven days a week, in freezing wet weather and filth. Since smoking was allowed only in off-duty time, and since the only permissible alcohol was their allowance of two cans of beer a day, they were now doing as much smoking and drinking as possible before going back. Looking beyond their heads, out through the plate-glass windows of the lounge, McGregor saw the helicopters on their landing pads. The black clouds were low above them, the rain continued pouring down, and the wind was howling across the strip with considerable force. McGregor, feeling wet and cold, shivered. Right now, in the North Sea, there were winds of Force Nine, fifty miles an hour winds, hurling huge waves against the rigs. The weather ruled the North Sea. It made work costly and dangerous. The men were used to long delays, but that didn't prevent annoyance; and McGregor, like the rest of them, was getting edgy.

'I'm going for a piss,' McGregor said. 'That should help pass a minute or two.'

He picked up his bag, slung it over one shoulder, and moved off through the milling men towards the toilets. Ricketts watched him go, a small smile on his lips, then his grey eyes surveyed the noisy lounge. Most of the men were quite young. They were a rough-looking bunch. They had come from building sites, from the armed forces or the merchant navy, and they were generally the kind of men who, though possibly married, were used to spending a lot of time away

14

from home. Work on the rigs was rough and dangerous, it was not that highly paid, and its appeal was to men who could not get work elsewhere or who simply disliked the routine of on-shore life. It wasn't a nine to five job, you had to serve no apprenticeship, there was no attention paid to previous records or qualifications, and a man who had something to hide would have to answer few questions.

In a sense they were the last of the brigands. They weren't colourful, but they were distinctive. They were coming back now after two weeks on shore, where they would have visited families and girlfriends, buried themselves in their bed-sits, or infested the pubs of Peterhead and Aberdeen. They were an insular breed. They existed in a narrow world. They worked like navvies on the rigs, saw their relatives only fitfully, and had developed an underplayed *camaraderie* that gave them moral support. Ricketts particularly enjoyed the life. His military background had prepared him for it. He was fond of the ladies, but he was no family man; and the rigs, in their very isolation, had offered him freedom.

'A man deep in thought,' someone said. 'I do like to see that.'

Ricketts turned his head and grinned laconically at Robert Barker, who was leaning on the bar to his left. Barker, who looked younger than his thirty-eight years, was chief security man of British United Oil, the conglomerate for which they all worked. Well-built, boyishly handsome, blue-eyed and blond-haired, he wore a jacket of pigskin, the fur collar turned up, and blue jeans that emphasized his long legs.

'Gin and tonic,' he said to the barman. 'And one for my friend here. The best toolpusher in the business needs his breakfast.'

'It was whiskey,' Ricketts said.

'I know that,' Barker said. 'And the barman obviously knows who you are; he's just poured you a large one.'

Ricketts grinned as the barman set the drinks on the counter. Barker gave him two pounds, waited for his change, put the money in his pocket and sampled his gin.

'Very nice,' he said. 'Very nice. A day like this, a man needs it.'

'I thought you'd be in with the Prime Minister,' Ricketts said.

'I was,' Barker said. 'He's having brandy and potato crisps. The brandy's a sign that he's an ambitious Prime Minister; the crisps denote that he's still one of the lads. It's what you'd call politics. He's appealing to both sides. He wants to convey to the oil barons that he believes in the good life, but he also wants to woo the rig workers.'

Ricketts smiled again. 'I'm surprised you're not still in there. I thought you were our top security man.'

'How can I protect him?' Barker said. 'He's already surrounded by bodyguards and military police, and if they can't do the job, no one can.'

'It's a sign of the times,' Ricketts said, sipping his whiskey. 'If all this terrorism continues, we'll soon be forced to turn the country into a police state.'

'Right,' Barker said. 'And we're almost there already. You go to Heathrow or Gatwick and it's almost like walking into an army parade. Have you seen the police around Downing Street? Have you seen the soldiers around the House of Commons? I sometimes think it might be safer in Belfast; and that's the sad truth.'

Barker sipped his gin and tonic, put the glass down, and smiled at Ricketts.

'Anyway,' he said, 'my real job is to protect the Forties Field. Our venerable Prime Minister is spending two days and one night on Bravo 1, and I've had that platform checked from top to bottom. I also have men all over the place, and I'm praying to God I haven't left a loophole. I believe you won't be joining us this time.'

'No,' Ricketts said. 'I'm flying out to Eagle 3 in the Frigg Field to start closing it down. We'll soon be towing it away to another site.'

'Frigg's finally dry, then?'

'Yes, it's pretty dry. We concentrated on Frigg during the boom years, and now it's all gone.'

'I would have come across sooner,' Barker said obliquely, 'but I didn't want to interrupt your conversation.'

'You mean McGregor?'

'Yes.'

'A prick,' Ricketts said. 'A real pain in the ass. But he also happens to be a good worker.'

'He's a trouble maker,' Barker said. 'He backs the unions

16

to the hilt. Two years ago, when we were having all those strikes, McGregor was up to his neck in it.'

'So he's a union man,' Ricketts said. 'A lot of the men are in the union. I don't give a bugger as long as they get on with their work. McGregor's all right. He's just a bit obsessed, that's all. If he catches you at the bar he's a pain, but he *does* do his job.'

'I suppose you're right,' Barker said. 'I just can't stand the bastard.'

Ricketts smiled gently. 'You don't have to work with him,' he said. 'And neither do I.'

'*Touché*,' Barker said.

They touched glasses and drank, and then the both of them studied the crowded lounge. To the casual eye the men would have looked like a solid mass, but the more experienced eye saw segregation. The rig workers, who felt separate from the outer world, were also separated by the particular hierarchy of the oil fields. Packed together in the grey haze and smoke of the lounge, they had nevertheless formed into their own groups. The majority of them were roustabouts, the general labourers who worked on the lower decks of the rigs, unloading the supply boats and moving the machinery or steel pipes in and out of the storage space and up to the drilling floor; they did this and every other unskilled job on the rigs, and in general were the lowest paid on board. The second largest group was comprised of the roughnecks, the men who worked on the drilling floor, usually around the roaring shaft, changing the bits that had broken on rocks eleven thousand feet beneath the ocean bed and extending the drills by adding lengths of heavy steel piping. It was skilled, exhausting, dangerous work, and the roughnecks were therefore paid more than the roustabouts. These two very different groups formed the backbone of the rigs, but their jobs usually kept them apart. Working seven days a week, twelve busy hours each day, they weren't given enough spare time to strike up close friendships with anyone outside their immediate environment. Thus they stuck to their own kind; they formed two distinct groups. Now, in the smoky lounge, they seemed all of a part, but a practised eye could pick out the groupings.

Even more remote were the key men, the toolpushers like

17

Ricketts, the men who kept a tight check on the roustabouts and roughnecks and were directly responsible only to company supervisors. The toolpushers were the élite; they had total authority over the other men. If their status could be equalled, only the divers could come close – not because they had authority, but because their high fatality rate placed them near to the top of the wage structure. The divers were the most insular; their way of life made them that way. During their time on the rigs they would either be diving or suffering the harrowing isolation of decompression. It was a bizarre way of life. It was like the life of an astronaut. Either under the sea or in the decompression chamber, enduring the danger and monotony of relentless saturation diving, they would not be in physical touch with their fellow human beings for the whole of their two weeks on board. So, they remained strangers, they hardly knew the other men, and in this lounge, in the smoke and the grey haze, they were a group well apart.

Listening to the men's murmurings, to the sudden outbursts of laughter, to the rattling of beer cans and the restless scuffling of feet, to the howling of the wind around the distant helicopters, Ricketts felt that he had truly come home. The conversations were a mixture of the profane and the technological, coming at him in fragments, disembodied, without direction, and they brought back the feel and the taste of a world that was as far removed from the normal world as the moon. Ricketts liked the words. They had a masculine thrust. They conjured up a world without history or future, a way of life that had no fixed direction and reinvented its own rules:

'—still drilling for Complex, but expect to complete the current and final hole shortly. Then the rig'll be towed to Hamburg for the demobilization of diving equipment and a lengthy refit. Then God knows where else ...'

'—they call them "rig-worker's widows". They say they never see their men. The divorce rate's going up and they say there's too much booze going down. I just can't take much more of it ...'

'—definitely a hell of an improvement. Unscrambled speech facilities from the diver back to the bellman; processed speech side tone speaker for clear speech between diver and bellman; diver tape connections plus tape con-nections for playback in all chambers; and a good ten hours life in the power pack. Comex, of course ...'

'—lots of saturation dives and bounce dives, and a fair bit of surface orientated diving on the platform recording equipment. Bloody exhausting, but pretty good experience. Just hope ...'

'—it can't go on much longer. She keeps coming to the boarding house. Says I picked her up in the Granada in Peterhead and then made her pregnant. Lying cow! I don't even know her name ...'

'—wind of a hunnerd an' thirty miles an hour, waves ninety feet high. Fucking tanker crashed into the platform an' all hell broke loose. Five of the crew were killed, a two-mile oil slick on the sea, then the fucking well-head exploded an' I woke in the hospital. What the hell am I doin' here?'

'—in the mud room, for Christ's sake. Listen: the mud is pumped down as far as the drill goes, right? It keeps the pressure in the shaft higher than in the water outside it, right? Then the mud circulates and comes up again with the cut-tings, fragments of rock millions of years old, and the cuttings come to me and I examine them under a fluoroscope and ...'

'—rig was blown off location, but we're back now. Drilling ahead and think we'll do at least one more well before Texaco put us out to grass ... bloody D.T.I. inspection last month, but the diving equipment passed A1 ...'

'—Sidko 803 just returned to Rover Oil after drilling a well for B.P.; now on permanent contract to Rover since B.P. no longer seem interested in the rig. Meanwhile Beta 45 is in the Netherlands for the replacement of its Comex 1000 system and will soon be operating for ...'

'—hell of a storm. Stupid bastard fell down the moonpool. Another hit in the face with a bolt from the shaft and a load fell on the crane-driver's cab. They tried to burn through the metal. The storm came back again. The crane broke loose and was swept into the sea. It was four degrees centigrade ...'

'—I can't go home again. It's all over for good this time. She said it was the North Sea or her, and I picked the North Sea ...'

19

'—fucking rain.'

'—and a beer, mate.'

Ricketts listened to the words and felt his instinct for work creeping back to him. The words made him think of the Army, of the Suez Canal and Aden, of that world in which men without women looked to hard work for comfort. It was an unstated *machismo* code, removed a man from the normal, and gave rise to a feeling of freedom that was not quite definable. The North Sea held that attraction. The oil rigs were a world apart. The rigs encouraged competitiveness and a chauvinistic pride that had long since disappeared from on-shore life. Ricketts liked the male world, enjoyed a life of hard action. He had married once and been divorced three years later, simply because he couldn't stay home. Ricketts wanted his freedom, as did a lot of the rig-workers. The men who drilled the North Sea, who braved the sweat and the storms, were pioneers of the most ordinary cut, but they did stand apart.

'I think the Prime Minister's leaving,' Barker said. 'Let's go take a look.'

Glancing up, Ricketts saw a general movement of the waiting men towards the windows that overlooked the landing pads. Following Barker, he pushed through to the windows and looked out at the silent helicopters. The rain was still pouring down. The wind blew it across the strip. The sky was dark and the greyness was bleak, the view chilly and desolate. Farther along the strip, emerging from the bunker-like entrance to the V.I.P. lounge, were the first of the military police. Bulky in boots and helmets, carrying Sterling Light Automatic rifles, they came out in two lines that formed a protective path for the Prime Minister. Beyond them were two aircraft hangars, the rain pouring down their walls, and on top of them were more Army marksmen, scanning the heliport. Then the Prime Minister came out. He was wearing a black overcoat. A man in a grey suit was holding an umbrella over his head while other men in similar suits poured out around him. Ricketts watched them carefully. The whole scene was terribly depressing. The men moving across the strip through the rain and the howling wind seemed like fugitives from some bygone age. There was no ceremony here. There was simply a watchful, nervous advance. The military police with their weapons fanned out towards the helicopter while the Prime Minister and his entourage hurried between them.

'It's still filthy weather,' Barker said. 'That's a pretty strong wind out there.'

'It must be dying,' Ricketts said. 'It's probably passed over the rigs. They wouldn't let him take off otherwise. We'll probably all take off soon.'

'A lot of armour,' Barker said. 'I never thought I'd see the day. There's enough weapons and ammunition in this heliport to start a whole war.'

'He needs it,' Ricketts said. 'The assassination list is growing. There's even a rumour that they found a bomb in the House of Commons. The whole country's a war zone.'

'Happy days,' Barker said.

Ricketts looked at the distant hangars, saw the glint of binoculars, saw the barrel of a machine-gun moving back and forth in slow, searching motions. Ricketts smiled a little and returned his gaze to the helicopters. The Prime Minister was at the last one in the row, being helped up. He disappeared inside, his large entourage followed him in, and the military police formed a circle around the helicopter as it roared into life. The rotor blades whipped the wind up. They blurred and merged into a single line. The military police stood beneath them with their clothes beating furiously and their weapons pointing out in all directions. The helicopter roared louder, vibrated and rose a little, then it turned towards the east and climbed higher and disappeared through the grey clouds.

The men around Ricketts relaxed. They went back to their chairs. The conversation became louder, more ebullient, as if a crisis had passed. Ricketts stayed at the window. He was still standing beside Barker. McGregor came up between them and gazed out at the grey, cloud-filled sky.

'He's left,' Ricketts said.

'Aye,' McGregor said. 'I saw that. Now maybe we can all get out o' here and get back to our work.'

'It won't be long,' Ricketts said.

CHAPTER TWO

THE Prime Minister gazed through the window of the helicopter and saw, far below him, through the haze of thinning cloud, the choppy grey desolation of the North Sea. It made him shiver slightly. He felt cold and a bit unreal. The sea stretched out as far as the eye could see, and then was lost in the drifting clouds.

'It looks terribly cold down there,' he said. 'I would not like to work there.'

'No, Prime Minister,' the Under-Secretary said. 'And neither would I.'

The Prime Minister chuckled, and offered a fleeting, sardonic smile. He had a florid, well-fleshed, stubborn face, with cold blue eyes and greying hair. The Under-Secretary, beside him, had the appearance of a young executive; unlike the Prime Minister, he had not come up the hard way, and the differences between them often showed. Now the Prime Minister sighed, kept his gaze on the North Sea, and his large body shifted uneasily as the clouds drifted past him.

'Yes,' he said. 'It's not a job for the likes of me. It's a job for the sort of man my father was. It must be a rough life.'

The Under-Secretary was opening his brief case, and he glanced up with surprise. His accent, unlike the Prime Minister's, was public school English.

'You sound almost nostalgic, Prime Minister. That world died a long time ago.'

'Did it, lad?'

'Didn't it, sir?'

'I'm not so sure it did. Those lads aren't paid as much as they're worth, and the both of us know it.'

'I thought they were paid quite well.'

'You think the miners get paid well.'

'And don't they?'

'They get paid well, but they don't get paid enough for

22

what we ask them to do. And I believe the North Sea's worse. I'm told the fatality rate is high. In fact, according to my reports the chances of death are ten times as great as in coal-mining.'

'And fifty times as great as in general industry, Prime Minister.'

'Precisely.'

The Prime Minister sounded annoyed, and the Under-Secretary, smiling slightly, picked some papers out of the brief case on his lap. The Prime Minister turned his head, saw the papers, returned his gaze to the sea below.

'Where are the guards?' he said.

'Up front.'

'This is a very big helicopter.'

'Quite.'

'And I have to stay till tomorrow night?'

'Yes, Prime Minister.'

'I hope I don't get seasick.'

'You won't, Prime Minister. You'll be staying on the concrete platform, not a rig.'

'I thought they were all rigs.'

'No, they're not. It's the rig that would make you seasick. A rig is used for test drillings, to actually check if there's oil in a given spot. Most of the rigs are semi-submersible, having most of their weight below water, usually in the shape of enormous pontoons, and held down by fourteen-ton anchors. They are, in a sense, like floating factories, and they *do* pitch and sway just like ships. However the platforms are different. Once a rig finds an oil field, a platform is sent out to replace it. The rig drills to find oil; the platform houses the production machinery when they actually start to bring the oil up. Made of concrete, its main deck about the size of Trafalgar Square, its legs firmly planted in the seabed, the platform is more an island than a floating factory, and it probably doesn't sway as much as high-rise flats. We're going to the new Forties Field platform. It's the largest platform in the North Sea. All the oil from the other fields now flows through the Forties Field and goes back through a single pipeline to Peterhead. This platform is really huge. It's almost a self-contained refinery. We won't feel a tremor, and I really don't think you'll be seasick.'

The Prime Minister nodded, studied the North Sea far below him. There was nothing down there but that grey sheet of cold, deadly water. The helicopter roared and shuddered. There was still a wind outside. Inside there were forty-four seats with not one of them vacant. The Prime Minister sighed, felt tired and aggravated. The last three years had been terrible, a general election was being called for, and the importance of this trip weighed upon him.

'What do you think?' he said.

'About the oil companies?'

'Yes.'

'I think we'll have to tread with some care. They're not easy to deal with.'

'No,' the Prime Minister said. 'They're not easy to deal with. I sometimes wonder who really runs the country – the conglomerates or us.'

The Under-Secretary smiled. He knew what the Prime Minister meant. He gazed at the reports in his hand and he learnt nothing from them.

'They're a problem,' he said. 'They're almost beyond all jurisdiction. We have to think of the voters, of the House of Commons, of our British interests, but the conglomerates are nearly all multi-national and don't recognize boundaries. They're not tied to any one country. They simply trade amongst themselves. If they have problems with one country they move their assets to another, and each can conveniently offer the other a tax haven. That's why we're in trouble. They're not willing to pay our taxes. They've now practically stopped work in the North Sea and, instead, have turned their attentions to the Middle East countries where they enjoy tax-free profits beyond belief.'

'These are British companies, lad.'

'No, Prime Minister, they're not. They're multi-national conglomerates with their roots overseas, and the so-called British companies are merely subsidiaries. The *British* companies, as we know them, are simply sitting on their oil, claiming they can't afford to invest any further, and patiently waiting for us to lower the current oil tax.'

'Naturally you approve.'

'I don't think there's a choice, Prime Minister. Like yourself, I'm a socialist, but three million unemployed is what counts. At the moment the oil companies are making enormous, virtually tax-free profits of thousands of millions of pounds, and none of it is coming into this country. They're not extracting and selling here, but they're extracting and selling overseas. Indeed, only recently the Parliamentary Accounts Committee reported that the only revenue from a large number of North Sea operations is the royalty and licence payments. It also reported that the oil companies are continuing to run up deliberate tax losses in Middle East countries – now running at approximately £6 million for the major operators – and that they might, if we don't do something, siphon off our oil scot-free and leave us with nothing but our balance of payments crisis.'

'Bastards,' the Prime Minister said.

'Exactly,' the Under-Secretary said. 'Still, we have to negotiate. We no longer have a choice. Back in 1977 we bought international confidence by promising to restore our balance of payments through North Sea oil. That promise has not been kept. We were too eager for the revenue. We made the oil tax too high because we desperately needed the money and the oil companies reacted by simply cutting back on drilling and setting up more profitable operations elsewhere. Thus we gained nothing from the North Sea, our balance of payments deficit soared, the economic crisis deepened, more and more private enterprise collapsed, and unemployment, which is officially at three million, is actually higher and growing every week. I don't think there's any doubt about the matter: the oil companies have whipped us.'

The Prime Minister shuddered. He had been feeling older recently. He sometimes felt that he had been at the game too long, that he could no longer handle it. There were no more simple answers, the ground was shifting all the time, and the politician had to share all his decisions with the unions and businessmen. Who ran the country indeed? It was a question he frequently asked. There were forces beyond the reach of mere governments that could make and break policies. The politicians had lost confidence, they no longer knew where they stood, more and more they felt like pawns in a game that had no standard rules. The business world controlled the economy, the trade unions controlled all labour, both sides had the sort of power that transcended mere legislation, and between them they created situations that the government could not ignore. The House of Commons was becoming a farce. The politicians were becoming redundant. Increasingly the government's function was simply to make legal those policies which had been shaped by big business and the unions to suit their own ends. The government was merely a mouthpiece, a focus for public attention. Behind the scenes, in private boardrooms and on faraway continents, the real decision-makers ruled the world.

'All right,' the Prime Minister said. 'So what are they asking for?'

'They're asking for a larger return on their investment. At the moment they're only getting a minimum return of 19 per cent and they claim they can't operate on that. They've been fighting for three years for a minimum return of 25 per cent, and they're sitting tight on the rigs until they get it.'

'Twenty-five per cent is a lot,' the Prime Minister said dryly.

'Well,' the Under-Secretary said, 'we have to bear in mind the enormous expense of these operations and the astronomically high minimum return needed. Their argument will be based on these facts. A single semi-submersible rig costs about £14 million to build and £40,000 a day to operate. A platform costs anything from £22 million to £65 million. Establishing a well-head costs anything from two to four million, and a single field will have twenty or thirty wells. Undersea pipelines cost £800,000 a mile, and then of course there are the enormous towing charges, wages, boat and airfreight charges and so forth. It's a whole new form of industry, Prime Minister, and in general the costs are quite unbelievable. The oil companies' argument is that so far their investment has not been returned, and that they can't commit themselves further until a return on investment has been guaranteed. The only way we can guarantee it is to alter the tax structure to ensure that their future returns are greater. They expect, and we'll have to give them, twenty-five per cent.'

'And what about the unions? Do you think they'll take that quietly? They'll accuse us of collusion with the capitalists, and they'll have a strong point. We're doing what the Conservatives have threatened: we're letting the oil companies dictate to us. They're laying down the law **and we're** surrendering, and that's all there is to it.'

'I don't think the unions will say much. They won't like it on principle, but they know as well as we do that without a return to full investment in North Sea operations our economy will simply collapse beyond repair. We've lost international confidence. No one wants to invest in Britain. We have three million unemployed, and without the North Sea we can't correct our balance of payments and revive international confidence in this country. The unions are aware of this. They won't like it, but they'll accept it. They'll grumble in public, but in private they won't make an issue out of it.'

'God, it's a dirty business,' the Prime Minister said. 'Just whose side are we on?'

He rubbed his chin with his left hand and then turned to gaze out the window again. The North Sea was unchanged, remained choppy and desolate, and the Prime Minister, straining to see a rig, saw nothing but greyness. The very sight of it made him shiver. He felt cold and strangely lonesome. It was odd to realize that the future of Britain depended on the men who worked in those arctic wastes.

'How far out is Forties Field?' he asked.

'Just over a hundred miles.'

'It's not near Shetland, then?'

'No. Frigg and Beryl are near Shetland; about halfway between Shetland and Norway.'

'Still, it should be cold there.'

'Yes, Prime Minister, it will be cold.'

'I hope they don't get any gales.'

'They get a lot of gales, Prime Minister. They even get gales in summer. Work on the rigs is totally subject to weather, and the North Sea is terrible that way. Again, it makes things costly; it wrecks schedules and destroys rigs. Supply boats often toss at anchor for days, sometimes weeks, just waiting until unloading is possible. They often can't tow rigs away, men are frequently swept overboard, and rigs are sometimes blown off their sites and then have to be towed back. Yes, Prime Minister, they get gales all right.'

The Prime Minister's large body shifted uneasily in the seat, and he massaged his ruddy chin with one hand.

'The Scots won't like it,' he said. 'They'll say we're giving it all away. They're getting close to a majority, they want independence, and they'll want the oil to be there when they succeed.'

'*If* they succeed, Prime Minister.'

'I don't think we can discount the possibility. The Scottish National Party is growing stronger all the time, and Scottish terrorism is the worst in all Britain. If we can't control the terrorists – and our record to date is lamentable – there'll soon be pressure to give them what they want. It's the same with Northern Ireland. The situation's out of control there now. The public are frightened, they want all terrorists out of England, and they'll soon be demanding independence for both Ireland *and* Scotland.'

'All the more reason to reach an immediate agreement with the oil companies. With the economy of this country in ruins, Scotland – or indeed anyone else – could really bring pressure to bear. I think it imperative that we come to an equitable agreement with the oil companies – now, while we still have the chance. At least this way, if the crunch comes, we'll have the oil companies on our side and will therefore have a stronger bargaining position. We'll worry about Scotland when the time comes; right now we should be worrying about ourselves.'

The Prime Minister sighed. He knew the Under-Secretary was right. The British economy was hanging on by its finger-nails, and only North Sea oil revenue could possibly save it. Yet he had good reason to worry. The whole of Britain was in a mess. The Irish saga continued, unemployment was shockingly high, overseas investors were pulling out every week, and the possibility of economic collapse had become public knowledge. The whole country had changed dramatically. There were daily strikes and demonstrations. Radical politics and terrorism had reached terrifying proportions and were draining the resources of both the army and the police. The I.R.A. had returned in strength, there were bombings and shootings in Wales, and in the North of England, where the unemployment was monstrous, terrorism was growing. Worst of all were the Scots. British oil was in Scottish waters. The terror groups in Scotland, while despising the Scottish National Party. were ferocious in their attacks against

England. London had become a siege city with the police and army everywhere. There had been bombings in stores and railway stations and airports, and politicians of all parties had been murdered. Yes, there was cause for worry. The British Isles were on the verge of anarchy. The wealth of the North Sea could give the government a reprieve, but compromises would have to be made.

'We're going down,' the Under-Secretary said. 'I think we've reached Forties Field.'

The Prime Minister looked through the window, saw the bleak, windwhipped sea. There was a derrick on a platform far below, looking terribly desolate. Then the helicopter dropped lower. He saw another rig, then another. One of the rigs was burning off its waste gas, and the smoke billowed sideways. The helicopter dropped lower. The rigs started to look bigger. He saw a square, concrete platform with huge legs and crossbeams, and with two or three frail-looking derricks. The platform didn't move. The sea poured between its legs. They dropped lower and the platform grew larger and took shape and dimension. It was indeed very large. It was like a giant Meccano set. There were towering derricks and cranes, steel catwalks and metal tanks, piles of crates and a plethora of small huts and prefabricated buildings. The Prime Minister was impressed; he felt an unusual, childish awe. The helicopter dropped lower, dropped below the tallest derrick, and then suddenly the massive platform was spread out to his right like some monolith from a new, unborn world.

The legs were incredibly wide. They were webbed with thick steel beams. The sea surged up and smashed against the legs and fell back and poured in again. The Prime Minister held his breath. He saw the helicopter pad. It was circled in blue and white, was on the edge of the platform, and loomed nearly 200 feet above the sea, just above the main deck. The helicopter dropped towards it. The steel-webbed derricks grew taller. He glanced up, but he couldn't see their tops so he looked down again. The landing pad rushed up towards him. The sea surged far below it. The monstrous steel maze swung around him and then towered above him. The Prime Minister licked his lips. He heard the helicopter's roar. There was a bump and he was bounced up and down

29

and then came to a rest. He heard the engine tapering off. The rotor blades separated. He stared out at a huge factory, saw men hanging from metal girders, saw prefabricated buildings and ladders and soaring piles of steel pipes. Then he looked down. He saw the sea far below. An enormous concrete leg plunged down towards it and made him feel dizzy.

'Home and dry,' someone said.

CHAPTER THREE

THE rotor props were still spinning as Ricketts jumped out of the helicopter and stood on the landing pad of Eagle 3. The wind whipped his face, he felt the fresh, freezing sea air, and a man in red overalls waved at him and he grinned and waved back. The chopper's motor tapered off. The rotor blades finally stopped. Two men in yellow overalls placed blocks around the wheels as the pilot jumped down behind Ricketts. The pilot combed his brown hair, chewed gum and grinned lazily. Ricketts looked at the floating factory that soared up to the grey sky and listened to the savage roaring of the drilling shaft.

It never failed to impress him, was too big to be normal; it was a factory built for giants, and the men were like ants beneath huge structures. The men were working on the muddy deck. The deck itself was a maze of equipment. There were raised cranes and loading bays, countless lamps and antennae, and mountains of three-ton pipes and pre-fabricated buildings. The deck was a quarter mile wide and swayed gently from side to side. Beneath the deck there were two other floors; beneath those, the pontoon legs.

'Shall I get 'em out?' the pilot asked.

'Yes, get them out. The holiday's over.'

Ricketts looked down at the sea. It was 200 feet below him. It was grey and quite rough, washing around the pontoon legs, and it stretched out to the distant horizon, now couched in a dismal haze. This was a semi-submersible rig. It had four main pontoon legs. They were thirty feet wide and 280 feet long and they plunged eighty feet below the sea to the massive pontoons. The pontoon legs were hollow. They were webbed with steel ladders. The pontoons were filled with water and attached to the sea-bed with anchor chains that weighed fourteen tons.

'All right!' the pilot shouted. 'Shake your asses!'

Ricketts looked around and saw the first of the replacement crew jumping out. Beyond the helicopter, stretching out to the horizon, was the featureless grey mass of the North Sea. The helicopter rose and fell. The deck was swaying to and fro. The men were jumping out and piling up their luggage on the vibrating landing pad. The whole rig was vibrating. The central shaft continued roaring. The jib of a distant crane swung out over the sea and its thick chain rattled over the side. There were other rigs in the distance. They were hazy and faraway. They were still drilling the Frigg Field, but now Eagle 3 was closing and preparing to be towed away to another site.

Ricketts shivered and slapped his hands. The wind was constant and always icy. Eagle 3 was 200 miles north of Aberdeen, halfway between the Shetlands and Norway. Originally the oil from Eagle 3 had been piped down through Beryl to the Orkneys; but violent terrorism in the Orkneys had put a stop to that, and now the oil went on through Beryl to the Forties Field. Ricketts grinned at the thought of Forties Field. The Prime Minister would be there now. Ricketts' supervisor, Keith Turner, would be acting the diplomat and quietly cursing under his breath.

'Okay,' Ricketts said to the men grouped around the chopper. 'Sort your own gear and take it down to your quarters and then report immediately to your supervisors. You new men, take your gear and go down those steps over there. When you get down the steps walk across the main deck to those prefabricated buildings you can see. Go in any door and ask anyone to show you where the canteen is. Have something to eat and drink and then stay there until I come down. I'll just remind you once again to watch your step. Don't trip on anything, don't fall off the edge, and don't let the wind blow you away.' Some of the men laughed at this, but they soon stopped when Ricketts gave them a cold look. 'I'm not kidding,' he said. 'These rigs are very dangerous. The decks are slippery with mud and oil, machinery often breaks loose, and the wind can unexpectedly turn fierce and blow men off the catwalks. The sea's two hundred feet below. The temperature's five degrees centigrade. If you don't break your neck when you fall, you'll freeze to death in five minutes. Okay, let's get moving.'

The men sorted out their gear and started walking towards the steps that led down from the landing pad to the deck below. The deck was swaying to and fro, dipping slightly towards the sea, the waves growling and smashing against the pontoon legs and sending spray shooting upwards. Ricketts looked up at the derrick. The grey clouds moved above it. It was 150 feet tall, its tapering legs webbed with steel, and its square base rested firmly on the roof of the semi-enclosed drilling deck. The drill shaft was rotating. It made a godalmighty roar. Around the shaft, on the edge of the massive deck, the cranes shrieked and turned back and forth.

'You gonna sign for this lot, Ricketts?'

The pilot, chewing gum, was standing beside Ricketts and holding out the passenger list. Ricketts grinned and signed it, and the pilot winked and spat his gum out. He put his hand in a pocket and pulled out another stick and popped it into his mouth and started chewing.

'Why did you bring those new kids?' he said. 'I heard this rig's closing down.'

'It is,' Ricketts said. 'We're towing it away next week. The work on board will be light and we can teach the new ones easier that way.'

'Hi ho,' the pilot said. He had a broad Montana accent. 'I got another load to go back. What time are they leaving?'

'About an hour,' Ricketts said. 'One hour, maybe two. I've got to check the new ones in and then check the old ones out, so just hang on to your balls and we'll get there.'

'Old fireball Ricketts,' the pilot said. 'You sure are some operator.'

The pilot zipped up his flying jacket. His brown hair blew in the wind. He glanced around at the huge derrick, at the screeching cranes, the roaring drill room, at the men who moved like ants up and down the metal catwalks and hung from the girders hundreds of feet above the sea. The noise was almost deafening. The whole rig was vibrating. With the steel pipes and oil drums and prefabricated sheds, it looked more like a refinery than a rig, and it swayed like a ship. The pilot grinned and chewed his gum. His flying jacket was bright red. He glanced beyond Ricketts' head and saw the sea stretching back to the grey sky.

'A nice place to work,' the pilot said with a grin. 'Sweet music and all the amenities. It sure beats air-conditioning.'

Ricketts grinned at him. 'You're getting soft, Jack,' he said. 'It's the curse of being born an American; your bones have gone soft.'

'Oh, yeah,' the pilot said. 'Don't I know it? I do know it. Now you, Ricketts, you're just a monster. You got no sensitivities.'

'I eat breakfast,' Ricketts said. 'I try not to masturbate. I'm a clean living, all British lad, and I work for my tuppence.'

'You were in the army, Ricketts.'

'Yes, I was in the army.'

'I hear you was a hot-shot in the army, that you picked up some medals.'

'Is that right?' Ricketts said. 'Well that was a long time ago.'

'How'd you get to be a toolpusher?'

'I worked for my tuppence.'

'Come *on*, Ricketts. Most of the toolpushers are American, so how did you do it?'

'Why ask me? I just work around here. I just take what I'm given.'

'Shit,' the pilot said. 'You're just giving me a snow job. I heard you started as a roustabout in the fields out in Texas shortly after you got out of the British army.'

'That's about the size of it,' Ricketts said. 'It's a glamorous story.'

'You climbed fast,' the pilot said. 'You musta been pretty good. The oil companies don't normally think so highly of Limey rig-workers. Yeah, you musta been good. You musta been pretty fucking sharp. Now you're one of the top tool-pushers on the rigs, and you're no man to mix with.'

'Thank you, Jack Schulman, for those kind words.'

'You going down now?'

'Yes, I'm going down.'

'I'll go down for a coffee.'

Ricketts picked up his bag and they both walked away from the helicopter. The landing pad was above the main deck, and was joined to the deck by a steep catwalk. Beneath the catwalk was nothing but a dizzying plunge down to the sea. Ricketts stopped halfway across, looked out over the sea. There was a rig on the horizon, burning off its waste gas, barely distinguishable except for the smoke that coiled skyward obliquely. Then Ricketts looked down, saw the huge, slanting leg. Hollow supports, three foot thick, formed a web beneath the decks, and angled down about 140 feet to join the massive pontoon legs. The sea smashed against the legs, made a hollow, drumming sound. The shifting shadow of the rig turned the grey water black and made it look ominous, almost frightening.

'Hey, Ricketts! What the fuck are you doing? You planning a swim?'

Jack Schulman was on the deck. He was waving up at Ricketts. He seemed small and he was shouting against the noise as the wind beat about him. Ricketts waved and walked on down. He kept his right hand on the railing. He stepped on to the deck with some care, saw the oil and the mud.

'Fucking filthy,' Schulman said. 'It's goddam filthy. I don't know how you stand it.'

They started across the open deck. The oil and mud had made it slippery. From their right, at the centre of the deck, came the roar of the drilling room. They passed stacks of iron piping, went under a raised crane. The crane was rumbling forty feet above their heads on a broad, round steel base. Ricketts stopped and looked up. The crane was picking up some crates. They were large wooden crates and some men stood on top of them, holding on to the thick chain of the jib. The crane roared and turned around. The men swung out on the crates. They swung out beyond the deck, two hundred feet above the sea, and then they shouted and the crates were lowered down to the supply ship below.

'Goddamned roustabouts,' Schulman said.

'Yes,' Ricketts said. 'We're taking off some of the heavier equipment before we move on.'

'When does the tow start?'

'Weather permitting, next week.'

'You any idea where you're going?'

'Down to Beryl, I think.'

They started walking again, a yellow forklift roared past them, and the driver shouted a greeting at Ricketts and waved one dark-stained sleeve. Ricketts waved back, passed some cursing roustabouts. They were leaning on a spanner that was bigger than a human being, straining to disconnect two massive pipes. A heap of pipes towered above them. The pipes were forty-five feet long. Each stack weighed three tons and the chain of a crane was dropping towards them. The men cursed and strained. The wind lashed across the deck. The deck constantly vibrated, swayed slowly from side to side, and ricocheted with insane metallic screeching and the roar of the drilling shaft.

Around all this was the sea. It swept about the oil rig. It smashed monotonously against the steel pontoon legs and made them reverberate.

Schulman reached one of the modules, opened the door and bowed to Ricketts. Ricketts grinned and stepped in and Schulman followed him and then closed the door. They heard a deep, muffled rumbling.

'Just show me the bar,' Schulman said. 'I could do with a drink.'

Ricketts unzipped his jacket. 'No liquor allowed,' he said. 'We *do* permit two cans of beer a day. You can take it or leave it.'

Schulman grinned and chewed his gum. 'Fucking hot in here,' he said. 'Yeah, I'll take you up on that offer. It'll help me to fly straight.'

They were in a narrow, low-ceilinged corridor. The electric lights were very bright. It was just like a ship, with steel steps and iron doors and sharp corners leading off in all directions. It was a prefabricated building. Such buildings were generally called modules. They were erected after the rig had been towed to its site, and they could easily be dismantled and off-loaded.

'It's a morgue,' Schulman said.

'The living quarters,' Ricketts said. 'The living quarters and the operations rooms.'

'Jesus Christ, I feel buried.'

Ricketts walked along the corridor, turned the corner at the end, walked along another corridor, the metal walls painted white, and stopped when he came to an open door. Ricketts' head disappeared. He said, 'Peace!' and stepped inside. Schulman followed him in and found himself in a small, cluttered office. There was a porthole in one wall.

Schulman saw the grey horizon. Another white wall was covered with a huge map of the North Sea, and a third was covered with various charts and graphs. There was a man behind the desk, very heavy and suntanned, and Schulman, who recognized a redneck when he saw one, knew that this Yank was a redneck.

'How are you, Ricketts?' the redneck drawled. 'You been getting your oats?'

'Dipped it once or twice,' Ricketts said. 'An academic endeavour.'

'Jesus,' the redneck said, 'you goddam English. Always quick with the comeback.' He scratched his nose and looked at Schulman. His eyes were green and analytical. 'Who the hell's that?' he said to Ricketts. 'He looks like Jack Nicholson.'

'Jack Schulman,' Ricketts said. 'You got the first name right. He's the pilot come to take your crew back. What time do they leave?'

The American yawned and stretched himself, his gut tight and his muscles bulging. He rubbed his face with his hands and stood up and glanced out through the porthole.

'They're waiting in the canteen,' he said. 'They've been cleared to take off.'

'Any problems?' Ricketts said.

'No problems,' the American said. 'Apart from the fact that most Limeys are lazy cunts, it's all been hunky-dory on Eagle 3.' He turned back to face Ricketts. His grin was lazy and full of charm. He was wearing grey trousers and a shirt that advertised Twentieth Century Oil. 'We're off-loading the heavy machinery. We're extracting the blow-back preventer. We'll soon be putting the locks on the cranes and then we're ready to go. It'll look like a ghost ship.'

He yawned again and rubbed his eyes, then he lazily surveyed the room. Schulman noticed that his shoes were covered in oil and a thin slimy mud.

'Are you going back?' Ricketts said.

'Yeah, I'm going back. I'm having two weeks on shore and then I'm taking over a rig in Forties Field.'

'There'll be a lot of work there shortly.'

'There hasn't been in the past. That fucking government of yours has just killed it, and we're not playing ball.'

'It's going to change,' Ricketts said. 'The Prime Minister's there right now. I think he's going to reduce the oil tax. If he does, we'll start drilling.'

'I hope so,' the American drawled. 'I sure hope so. I don't want pensioned off.' He grinned again at Ricketts. 'I better get ready to leave,' he said. 'Go and get your new boys organized – and send mine up to the chopper.'

Schulman stepped out of the room and Ricketts followed him out. He led Schulman down a flight of steel stairs and into the canteen. It was a functional room and the electric lights were very bright. There were white-plastic tables, blue-leatherette chairs, and the plates were covered with huge T-bone steaks. The replacement crew were eating the steaks. The departing crew were at the bar. Hard liquor wasn't allowed on the rigs, so they were all drinking beer.

'Hey, Ricketts!' one of them shouted across the room. 'When the fuck are we leaving?'

'Leave?' Ricketts said. 'You want to leave? I just don't understand that.'

Most of the men laughed. 'I need cunt!' someone shouted. 'Just let me see the pubs of Aberdeen! I'm in need of a quick thrill!' Another burst of laughter followed. The men were obviously eager to go. 'Two weeks on shore!' someone added. 'What's the delay, Ricketts?'

Ricketts grinned and put his hands up. 'Hey, back off,' he said. 'The helicopter's being refuelled and then you can go.' The men at the bar cheered and Ricketts waved them to silence. 'Okay,' he said. 'I want you to wait in the rec room. You can take your beer with you, and we'll call you when we're ready to leave.'

The men applauded, bawled remarks, slapped each other on the back, then started picking up their luggage and beer cans and moving out of the canteen. The men at the tables had stopped eating. They were grinning at the departing men. Remarks were bandied back and forth until the last of the departing crew had walked out.

'Okay,' Ricketts said to the men at the tables, 'put your knives and forks down and listen. You regular crew members know what I'm going to say, but you'll just have to wince and bear with it. You new men, please note these facts. Most of you have probably worked in factories before, and an oil rig resembles a factory. However the resemblance is deceptive. An oil rig is very different. For one thing, it floats. That means it's always rolling. The decks are slippery and it's easy to lose your footing and slide right off the edge. It's a two-hundred foot drop. That sea freezes men to death. If you survive the fall, you won't survive the sea, so try not to fall. A rig is also exposed. The North Sea is very dangerous. An average wind can be something like fifty miles an hour, and it often reaches a hundred or a hundred and fifty. We get waves the size of large office blocks. They wreck machinery and swallow men. Even a modest gale can cause chains to snap, and then all hell breaks loose. Watch out for flying bolts. Watch out for sliding equipment. It's easy to be crushed between crates when they slide on the decks. And be careful on the catwalks. Keep your hands on the railings. When a man gets too cocky he gets careless, and that's something we can't afford. Men have been swept off the catwalks. They've fallen down the moonpool. They've been hit by flying bolts, they've been crushed between machines, and they've been killed by equipment falling from the cranes or the platforms above them. Believe me, this happens.'

Ricketts stopped and studied the men. They were all lis-tening very carefully. They were impressed by the sound of his voice, by his air of authority.

'About your work,' Ricketts continued. 'It's two weeks on and two weeks off. What you do when you're ashore is your own bloody business, but on the rig you'll obey all the rules. Work on the rig goes on all around the clock in two shifts. You work twelve hours a day, seven days a week. You sleep four to a room, but since you all work in shifts, there'll only be two of you sleeping at any one time. Work is hard on the rigs and you'll find you need your sleep and you won't want to be disturbed by the other two men. Bear this in mind if you have to go to your room, and try not to disturb whoever is sleeping. If you do and a man complains you'll be dismissed, and that's all there is to it. There's a recreation room. There's a film show every evening. You're only allowed to smoke in off-duty space and off-duty time; and the only alcohol permitted is your free allowance of two cans of beer a day. Anyone caught breaking these rules will be flown back on the next available helicopter – and they won't be given a chance to appeal.'

Ricketts looked at all the men, his face firm and uncompromising, standing with his hands on his hips, his two legs outstretched.

'Another point to remember,' he continued. 'Most of these rigs are actually hired from drilling companies and are indirectly under their supervision. Now although you men are employed by the oil company, you'll find yourselves dealing with men employed by the drilling company, a geological company, repair and maintenance companies and a catering company. Don't mess with these men. Avoid all disputes with them. If you've any complaints go direct to your foreman and let him investigate the matter. Anyone breaking this rule, whether for good reasons or bad, will be rewarded with instant dismissal.'

Ricketts turned to the wall behind Schulman and picked up the telephone receiver. 'Hello, Segal? Ricketts here. Get yourself down to the canteen. I've got some new men here.' He put the receiver back on its hook and then turned to the men again. 'In a minute you're going to be shown to your quarters. On your beds you'll find maps of the rig. Study them carefully, have a good look around, and then report to the foreman named on the map. His location will be marked. He'll tell you when you have to start. He'll get you overalls and he'll show you what to do and he'll keep his eyes on you. Once you're working, don't piss around. Make sure you do as you're told. If you cause any trouble you'll be sacked – and I'm tone deaf to arguments.'

A man came into the canteen. He was wearing overalls and boots. His brown hair was dishevelled and he was covered from top to bottom in mud and oil. He grinned and nodded at Ricketts and waved one grimy hand. He glanced at the men at the tables, but he didn't say anything.

'I've just given them the briefing,' Ricketts said. 'Show them down to their quarters and then tell Delaney they're here.'

'Right, chief,' the man said.

The men shuffled out of the canteen as Ricketts and Schulman went to the bar. Ricketts asked for two beers, snapped the lids of both cans, then pushed one of the cans across to Schulman.

'There,' Ricketts said. 'Have some vitamins.'

Schulman rolled his eyes, drank some beer and put the can down, wiped his lips with the back of one hand and then gasped with mild pleasure.

'That was a pretty good speech, Ricketts,' he said. 'It almost made my flesh creep.'

Ricketts grinned. 'I'm glad it got through to *someone*. It's a pity you can't practise what I preach. Why not stay for a fortnight?'

'No, thanks,' Schulman said. 'I feel safer in the chopper. The only thing you've got to offer is beer, and that isn't enough.'

'I'd keep you busy,' Ricketts said.

'I bet you would,' Schulman said. 'You'd run my ass ragged and then send me back home in a box. No thanks; I'm a growing lad.'

Ricketts drank some more beer, put the can on the counter, glanced casually around the empty canteen, then stared back at his beer can.

'What about those guys I'm taking back?' Schulman said. 'I think they're still waiting in the rec room.'

'Not yet,' Ricketts said. 'I've got a few things I want to check. When the men know they're shore-bound they sometimes get careless and leave foul-ups that cause a lot of damage. I want a quick look around. I want to check that it's all okay. I want to check that none of the bastards have made mistakes before they take off.'

'And what if they have?'

'Then you can take them to Aberdeen and leave them there. I won't want them back again.'

'You're a fucking tough nut.'

'Yes, Schulman, I am. And now you know why your American friends appreciate me.'

They finished their beer and left the bar. Ricketts walked on ahead. They went up the steel steps and along some narrow corridors, passing offices and living quarters and storerooms. All the corridors were brightly lit; all the ceilings were very low. There were portholes overlooking the sea, the grey, hazy horizon. The muffled rumbling never stopped. There was a constant vibration. The rumbling grew louder as they climbed down more steps, and then it suddenly

41

turned into an awesome roar that shattered the senses.

They were on the drilling floor. The massive derrick towered above them. The drilling floor was walled in, but it was open to the sky and there was a very large square hole in the deck. The hole was called the moonpool. The sea was two-hundred feet below it. Enormous lengths of piping plunged down through the hole and travelled over four-hundred feet to the sea-bed. The central shaft was roaring and spinning. The men were working all around it. They wore overalls and helmets and all of them were filthy with oil. The central shaft roared. The whole deck vibrated violently. Men were standing on girders directly over the sea, tied securely to the structure with rope.

Schulman wanted to cover his ears. He glanced down the moonpool. He saw the linked pipes plunging down two-hundred feet and disappearing in grey sea. It almost made him dizzy. It wasn't like being in the helicopter. He saw the men tied to the structure with the ropes, hanging over that awesome drop.

Ricketts was shouting at someone. He was trying to make himself heard. He was waving and then Schulman saw him grin and walk over towards him.

'What are they doing?' Schulman shouted.

'They're extracting the blow-back preventer. It's a twenty ton cube, but it's down four-hundred feet and that makes it about four hundred tons. They're trying to bring it up. They do it in forty-five feet sections. They have to disconnect each pipe as it comes up, and it's a hell of a job.'

The roaring suddenly stopped. The shaft whined to a standstill. The men on the girders fixed huge clamps to the pipe and then attached thick chains to the clamps. The chains rattled and banged, and the clamps made a screeching sound. The men were fixing large handles to the clamps as Ricketts walked from the hut.

Schulman followed him out, felt the blast of an icy wind, saw the main deck with its network of huge oil tanks and catwalks and silver pipes. The derrick soared up above him. The grey sky moved beyond it. There were three platforms inside the derrick, and the highest was smallest. There were more men working up there. They seemed tiny and unprotected. The wind was howling between the girders of the derrick and making their clothes flap. Schulman looked across the deck, saw more stacked pipes and tanks. Like everything else they were immense, towering above him. He followed Ricketts across. A crane roared and screeched above him. A stack of monstrous wooden crates swung out over the sea with men hanging from the chains and waving arms.

Ricketts waved Schulman forward. They were nearing the edge of the main deck. They both stopped when they got near the rim, and then Schulman looked down. He grabbed a metal rail beside him. He held it very tight. The wind was tearing at him, trying to push him off the edge, and he felt nervous. The sea was very far below. He was looking down at a supply ship. It was long and very thin and it looked very small from up here. Schulman felt a bit dizzy. It wasn't like the helicopter. The massive legs of the rig, running outwards and down, emphasized that awesome drop to the sea.

The crane was lowering the wooden crates; they were swinging backwards and forwards. They swung under the decks and out again and dropped down and grew smaller. The roustabouts were still on top. They were like ants on the chains. They were now at least a hundred feet down, and they were shouting and waving. Schulman felt respect then. He felt a tingling, childish pride. His eyes fell upon the void between the men and the sea, and then he saw the sea washing over the long, bobbing bulk of the loading ship. Schulman really felt strange. He turned away from those frightful depths. There was a sudden, savage roar from the drilling hut, and the derrick towered over him.

Ricketts was grinning at him, had walked off the deck, was framed by the sea and the sky as the wind howled around him. Then Schulman saw the platform. It was thrusting out from the main deck. It was standing out over the sea and Ricketts stood on the edge. He was at a bottle-shaped metal tank. There was a diving bell on top of it. The diving bell was clamped into the tank and the tank had round windows. It was a decompression chamber. Ricketts was at one of the windows. He was gesturing at someone inside, and then he put one thumb up. Schulman didn't want to go out there. He felt queasy at the very thought. He didn't want to go out there and be picked up by the wind and hurled down two-hundred feet to the sea.

Another man walked past Schulman. He walked straight up to Ricketts. He had a white helmet on his head and his overalls were covered in oil. He grinned and shouted at Ricketts, glanced up and waved his hands. Schulman heard the screeching roar of a crane and saw a chain swinging towards him. It stopped above Ricketts' head, above the decompression chamber. The toolpusher waved a hand and two roustabouts rushed forward and clambered up the sides of the diving bell. There was a huge clamp on the chain. It was like a monstrous, metal claw. It closed around the steel ring at the top of the diving bell, and the roustabouts tightened screws all around it. Ricketts waved and left the platform, walked back up to Schulman. The men on the decompression chamber were checking the diving bell while the toolpusher below shouted orders.

'It's the divers,' Ricketts explained. 'They're on saturation diving. We're going to lower them down there again, to check out the drilling point. They go down in the diving bell.'

'How deep?' Schulman asked.

'Four hundred feet,' Ricketts said.

'Jesus,' Schulman said, 'that's pretty deep. How do they stand it?'

'It's a tough job,' Ricketts said. He was watching the decompression chamber. 'That chamber's only ten foot long,' he added. 'And there's six men inside it.'

'How long have they been in there?'

'They've been in there two weeks. There's six bunks in there. They go down in the diving bell, it's hauled up when they're finished, it's attached to the top of the decompression chamber again, and they go straight into the chamber from the bell.'

'You mean they *live* in that fucking thing for two weeks?'

'That's right. In the old days they would dive, undergo decompression, have a long break and then go down again. Now we can't afford that. We simply can't afford the time. Instead of bounce diving, we have saturation diving, which is what these men do. The diver comes up and stays in the chamber until he needs to go down again. Since he doesn't step out into normal pressure at all, he doesn't have to be completely decompressed before he goes down again. He eats and sleeps in there. Food is sent in through the air-lock. He reads books or plays cards, the pressure turns his voice girlish, and the helium even destroys his sense of taste. He lives and works there for a fortnight then he spends another week there decompressing. It's a hell of a life.'

Schulman looked at the platform. The roustabouts were still there. They were on top of the decompression chamber, surrounding the diving bell. One of them put his thumb up. The toolpusher waved them down. They slid down the side of the metal chamber and walked back to the main deck. The toolpusher looked through a window, then grinned and put his thumb up. He walked away from the platform and looked up and then waved his right hand. The crane above roared into life. The winch clattered ferociously. The chain straightened and went very taut and then it picked up the diving bell. The bell swung from side to side, over the decompression chamber, was dangling in the grey void of the sky with the sea far below it. It began dropping down. It bounced gently against the deck. It dropped lower and had half disappeared when the sea started roaring.

'*Jesus Christ!*' Ricketts hissed.

The roaring started far below, then spread out and enveloped them. They all automatically rushed to the platform and grabbed hold of the railings. The whole deck suddenly tilted. They heard the roar and saw the sea. They saw the waves leaping up and curving down and smashing over the loading ship. Then the roar became an explosion. Water geysered up and outward. It was exploding out from under a pontoon leg and turning the sea wild.

Schulman couldn't believe it. The deck tilted to the left. The rig shook and he heard the exploding sea and saw a white wall of water. The water soared out and upward. It soared a hundred feet high. It spread out like a fan and crashed down and the loading ship disappeared. Schulman glanced around at Ricketts, saw Ricketts' wide eyes, saw Ricketts' white knuckles on the railings that slanted down to the left. The whole deck was slanting downward. It jumped up and dropped again. It was a quarter mile long and it was tilting and screaming insanely. Schulman saw the diving bell. It swung out and in again. It crashed into the deck with a dreadful chilling bang, and then Schulman saw the sea and the sky and found himself on his back.

'The diving bell! Get it in!'

Schulman felt himself sliding, heading feet-first towards the edge. He couldn't breathe and he felt his heart pounding and he clawed at the air. His hand found something solid, his fist closed around a chain. His head was spinning and the roar was in his ears and he heard Ricketts shouting. Schulman licked his lips and blinked, gazed along his own body. His feet were hanging over the edge of the deck and he saw the thin platform. The platform was tilting downward. He saw the decompression chamber. It was nearly on its side and it was hanging out over the sea. Schulman heard the shriek of metal, saw the metal clamps splitting. He heard men shouting all around him and he looked down and saw the diving bell. It was swinging out from the tilting side. Ricketts was looking up and screaming. The crane was trying to winch up but the diving bell swung in and smashed once again against the deck.

'Jesus Christ! It's the crane!'

Schulman rolled on to his stomach. He was hanging down the tilting deck. He pulled himself towards the crates that were piled up above him and he heard the shriek of metal and heavy clanging. He pulled himself to his feet, saw men running in all directions, looked up and saw the crane high above, twisting round and then tilting. It was making a fearsome sound. It was being torn from its support. The huge support was leaning over to the right with the crane sliding off it. Schulman couldn't believe it. It was forty feet in the air. It was monstrous, a huge crane and its jib, crashing down to the deck. Men screamed and then scattered, metal shrieked and the crane fell. It seemed to hang in the air, the jib buckled and broke apart, then the whole mass of metal and chains exploded over the deck.

Someone screamed and Schulman blinked and saw the spinning diving bell. The chain snapped and it disappeared from view as it plunged towards the sea. Then the noise became overpowering. The falling crane had smashed through the deck. A huge chain shrieked through the air and the jib fell apart and enormous jagged pieces of steel pipe started bouncing and clattering. They rolled off the deck's edge, plunged down towards the sea. They smashed into wooden crates and the wooden crates exploded and were torn

46

from their moorings and crushed men and dropped over the side. Schulman heard the awful screams. The deck shuddered beneath his feet. He looked up and heard the oil derrick groaning and saw the frame bending. 'Oh, my God!' Schulman cried. *'Schulman, move!'* Ricketts bawled. Something grabbed him and tore him from the crates and pushed him forcefully forward. Schulman knew it was Ricketts, but he didn't stop to look around. He raced away from the derrick and ran straight for the landing pad and heard bawling and insane metallic screeching and saw chaos on all sides.

Something heavy crashed into him. His head exploded and he looked around. A large pile of metal pipes was breaking loose and rolling over the deck. The pipes made a fearsome din, sweeping men and crates aside. Schulman glanced up and saw the towering derrick breaking up and collapsing. It was a terrible sight. The webbed beams were snapping free. They were bending and flying out and falling down and crashing into the drilling room. Schulman heard the demoniac noise, heard the screams of the dying men. The derrick platforms fell apart and dropped down between the legs, then the legs themselves buckled and broke and the whole thing collapsed. Schulman looked up in awe. The spectacle pinned him to the deck. There was a deluge of clanging steel and roaring wood and screaming men, and then the roof of the drilling floor caved in and the noise was appalling.

'—on your feet! Lets get going!'

Schulman jumped up and ran, was running up the sloping deck, saw the helicopter pad in the distance, sloping down towards the sea. A sudden panic whipped through him. He saw the helicopter moving. It was sliding towards the edge of the landing pad, turning around slowly. Schulman sobbed and kept running. He didn't look back for Ricketts. He heard screams and passed other running men and saw a huge tank collapsing. The tank smashed through its supports, hit the deck with a fearsome sound. It was forty feet wide and it rolled across the deck and crushed men and crashed into the modules and swept them over the side. Schulman didn't stop to look. He saw the helicopter slipping. A large wooden crate was racing towards him, shaking and shrieking. It hit a tank and fell apart. The wood exploded in all directions. The yellow forklift inside it spun around and crashed into a catwalk. The catwalk didn't stop it. The forklift tore it from its moorings. It buckled down the middle and bounced up in the air and rolled shrieking across the careening forklift and then was trailed along with it. Schulman saw waving arms, heard a terrible, dying scream. A decapitated body was mangled up in the catwalk, limbs jerking in a last bloody dance spinning over the side.

Yet Schulman kept running. He ran up the sloping deck. He saw the helicopter slipping towards the sea and he wanted to scream. Another roar, another crash. More explosions and colliding pipes. He heard screams and saw the vague shapes of men and then he reached the catwalk. The landing pad was tilting down. The near-side was rising up. It was tearing the catwalk out of the deck and Schulman heard the bolts snap. He leapt forward without thinking, grabbed hold of the railing, glanced down and saw a sickening void, two hundred feet to the sea. Then Ricketts slapped his back. He heard Ricketts screaming at him. The catwalk shuddered and he heard the metal shrieking as he started to climb.

'It's broken loose!' Ricketts bawled.

Schulman dived at the landing pad, hit the deck and rolled over, heard the mangling of metal as the catwalk broke loose, and then something fell across him and rolled off and he saw Ricketts lying there. Schulman jumped to his feet, saw the catwalk disappearing, saw the quarter-mile length of the rig tilting down towards the sea. He turned away from it and ran. He saw Ricketts at the helicopter. The helicopter was sliding close to the edge as Ricketts pulled the door open. Ricketts hauled himself up. Schulman raced up behind him. Ricketts disappeared inside and Schulman hauled himself in and went blank until he found himself sitting behind the controls.

He heard the roar of the engine. The props were picking up speed. He glanced out and saw the deck sloping down, the edge curving away from him. He worked the controls, felt a feverish, frightened clarity, glanced down and saw the sea far below, the upturned ship, the drowning men.

Schulman frantically gave full power, but the chopper swung towards the edge. The deck disappeared beneath him, he felt himself start to scream, then the helicopter dropped into space and fell down and rose up again.

'Jesus Christ,' Ricketts said.

They climbed to eight hundred feet. They hovered there and surveyed the wreckage. The great rig was sinking down on one corner, slipping into the sea. The massive deck was a hideous mess of tangled steel and crates, and a deluge of men and equipment was pouring over the sides. The north-east corner of the rig sank. The sea danced and swirled around it. The rest of the deck was pointing at the sky, swaying to and fro, sinking. It sank slowly and horribly. They saw two huge pontoon legs. They rose up three hundred feet in the air and then slid under the water. The water boiled and danced above them. They disappeared and the water swirled. A black hole materialized and it turned into a whirlpool that imprisoned the men and machinery and sucked them all down. It was a ghastly, silent spectacle. It was a dark, eerie dream. The whirlpool swirled and sucked everything down and then collapsed on itself.

Eventually the sea settled. It was calm and utterly desolate. They both looked down and saw that there was nothing but those grey, arctic wastes.

'Head for Forties Field,' Ricketts said.

CHAPTER FOUR

THE first interruption came in the middle of the Prime Minister's opening remarks, and Keith Turner, sitting thoughtfully at the long table in the boardroom of Bravo 1, looked exasperated as he picked up the phone. 'Excuse me, Prime Minister,' he said. 'I have to leave this line open.' He put the receiver to his ear and saw the Prime Minister watching him. He had never met the Prime Minister before and he found him intimidating.

There was some static on the line and Turner flushed with annoyance: he had told them specifically not to call him unless it was urgent. Now he heard the radio operative, and the man was obviously quite upset. 'I think you better get up here right away. Eagle 3's in bad trouble.' Turner coughed into his fist and glanced apologetically around him. The Prime Minister had his chin in his hands and was staring straight at him.

'Trouble?' Turner said. 'What kind of trouble?'

The boardroom was crowded. It overlooked the Forties Field. There were lonely oil rigs in the distance, burning off their waste gas. Turner couldn't stop looking at them. They suddenly filled his whole vision. The Prime Minister and his executives and the oil men and their secretaries disappeared from his eyes and his thoughts as his heart started racing.

The operative's voice was high-pitched. It sounded almost hysterical. It kept talking about a message from Eagle 3, and Turner knew it was serious. He said something to the operative, put the phone down gently, glanced at the men all around him, and shook imperceptibly.

'Excuse me, gentlemen,' he said, 'but I'll have to leave. I think we have an emergency.'

'Emergency?' someone said. It was Sir Reginald Mc-Millan. He was the Chairman of British United Oil and he was drumming his fingers. 'What *kind* of an emergency?'

'I'm not sure, sir,' Turner said, standing up and rubbing his beard. 'We've just had a call from Eagle 3 and I'll have to attend to it.'

He didn't wait to discuss it further. He wasn't sure of his information. He smiled nervously and rushed from the room and headed straight for the radio hut. It took him quite a while to get there. Bravo 1 was immense. It was a platform with five drilling units and numerous decks. Turner raced across the catwalks, felt a warm, southerly wind. He saw the sea far below and all around him, and it gave him no comfort. Was Eagle 3 sinking? Could it possibly be true? The questions rang in his head as he raced across a deck and wove his way between forklifts and modules. He felt the pounding of his heart, felt unreal and disbelieving, saw the radio hut and thought of the operative gibbering into the phone. Turner raced towards the hut, saw the antennae soaring skyward. He thought briefly of Ricketts and then he pushed the door open and rushed in to see the pale face of the operative.

The man was sitting before the radio, trying to contact Eagle 3. He was cursing as he looked up at Turner and took off his earphones.

'I can't get a response,' he said.

The radio hut was small and cluttered, terribly hot and badly lit. The operative had his two sleeves rolled up, and was covered in oil.

'They said they were *sinking*?' Turner said.

'That's right,' the operative said. 'That guy on Eagle 3, he was screaming, and he said they were sinking. There was a hell of a lot of static. His radio wasn't working properly. I asked for confirmation of the message and he sounded demented. He just screamed that they were sinking. He said they were going down fast. I tried to get some more details, but the line just went dead, and I haven't been able to get him back since.'

'It was the operative?' Turner said.

'That's right, chief, the operative.'

'And you didn't get any other calls?'

'No, chief. Not a one.'

Turner bit his lower lip and glanced blindly around him. It was something he didn't want to accept; it just seemed quite impossible. How could it suddenly sink? What the hell had gone wrong? A rig didn't just suddenly sink in a matter of minutes. Turner rubbed at his black beard, his broad bulk shaking slightly, then he blinked and looked down at the operative, trying to gather his thoughts.

'Any other calls from Eagle 3 this morning? Any messages at all?'

'No,' the operative said. 'We've been keeping the lines clear. All the rigs had instructions not to call except for emergencies.'

'No messages from Ricketts?'

'Swear to God, chief, not a thing. The first call I got was from Eagle 3 – and he said they were sinking.'

'I don't believe it,' Turner said. 'It just doesn't seem possible. An accident, yes, I see that; but I can't see it sinking.'

'It sounded like it,' the operative said. 'That fucking guy was hysterical. And his radio was really in a mess, and then it cut off.'

'Bloody hell,' Turner said.

He reached for a telephone, dialled a number, bit his lip and glanced out through the door and saw a stretch of grey sea.

'Hello, Jackson? Turner here. I think we've got an emergency. I want a helicopter over the Frigg Field to survey Eagle 3. No, not from here. I think that's going to take too long. On second thought, I'll get in touch with Beryl and get them to fly out. What's the closest rig in Beryl Field?' He drummed his fingers on the deck, then nodded and put the phone down. He looked at the operative and said, 'Okay, ring Charlie 2. Tell them to get their helicopter to Eagle 3 and check out what's happening.'

The operative nodded and put on his earphones. Turner walked out of the hut and looked up at the sky and wondered what the hell was happening out there. The afternoon light was hazy. The southerly wind was turning cold. He suddenly thought of the conference in the boardroom, and his stomach turned nervously. Could the rig have gone down? Could it actually have happened? The possibility was enough to make him shiver with a fearful fatigue. He wouldn't tell anyone yet. He would keep it quiet until he knew. The very thought of having to announce such a catastrophe was beyond comprehension.

He heard the operative's voice, saw him standing in the doorway. The operative was staring at him with wide eyes and seemed very confused.

'I can't get them,' he said.

'What?'

'I can't get them. I can't get in touch with Charlie 2. I can't get a response.'

'What the hell do you mean?'

'I can't get them to reply. The line's open, but I can't get an answer. They just won't reply.'

Turner couldn't believe his ears. He glanced around at the choppy sea. He turned back to the operator and saw his wide eyes and white, confused face.

'You mean there's no one at their *radio*? You mean the operative isn't there? Are you trying to say there's no one on duty? Is that what you're saying?'

The operative threw his hands up. 'I can't get a reply,' he said. 'I'm simply saying that the line's definitely open, but they just won't reply.'

'That's crazy!' Turner said.

'Yeah, it's crazy. I know.'

'For Christ's sake, keep on trying,' Turner said. 'What the *hell's* going on?'

The operative disappeared and Turner paced up and down. He saw the modules that were piled up on modules as this platform grew bigger. He was dwarfed by this immensity. The five derricks towered above him. The grey sky swam beyond them and the sea was all around him and the silence of the platform was strangely eerie. None of the drills were in operation; they hadn't been working for weeks. Nevertheless, the enormous platform was busy, working as a refinery. Men were hurrying across the catwalks. Cranes and forklifts were roaring. New buildings were still being erected, and that work hadn't ceased. Turner looked all around him. He surveyed his immense domain. He thought about Eagle 3 and Charlie 2 and they just didn't make sense.

He went back to the radio hut. 'What the hell's going on?' he snapped. The operative lifted one hand and waved him to silence.

'Okay,' the operative said. 'Roger and out.'

He went on to Receive, placed his earphones on the table, swivelled around in his chair and looked at Turner.

'Charlie 2?' Turner said.

'No,' the operative said. 'Ricketts.'

'Eagle 3?'

'No. In the helicopter. He says he's coming in now.'

Turner felt confused and fearful, tugged his beard and glanced around him, looked out through the door, at the sky, saw no sign of the chopper. He sighed and looked down at the operative, at his pale, confused face.

'Did he *say* anything?' Turner asked.

'Yes, he asked if you were here.'

'Did he say anything about Eagle 3?'

'He said to tell you to be here.'

That wasn't like Ricketts. It actually sounded like a command. Turner cursed and walked up and down the hut and tried to order his thoughts.

'What about Charlie 2?' he said.

'They won't reply,' the operative said.

'What the hell's going on?' Turner said. 'I don't get the connection.'

He walked out of the radio hut, climbed down some steel steps, crossed the deck between towering blocks of modules, around the soaring steel derricks. The wind was growing colder. He saw the sea's rise and fall. He passed some men on a huge pile of pipes, walked beneath a raised crane. Turner felt his heart pounding. He didn't like to feel this nervous. He reached the end of the deck, climbed back up another ladder, then mounted the steel catwalk to the landing pad.

The rig's helicopter was there. There was another landing pad beside it. The helicopter was clamped to the deck and there was no one about. Turner went to the phone. It was in a booth near the landing pads. He rang through to a tool-pusher and told him to send up two roustabouts. When this was done he put the phone down and went back to the empty pad. He looked up at the sky and saw the helicopter high in the clouds.

Turner cursed and paced the deck. He watched the approaching helicopter. The two roustabouts came up the catwalk, wearing bright yellow overalls. They nodded at

Turner, then looked up at the sky. The helicopter was dropping towards them, sounding muffled and distant, and the roustabouts unlocked the clamps. They worked smoothly and efficiently. When they were finished they stepped back beside Turner and looked up at the helicopter.

It was roaring right above them. The props whipped the wind around them. They held on to the railings of the catwalk and watched it descend. It landed with some precision. It rose up and sank down. The engine stopped and the props turned more slowly and then the door opened.

Ricketts jumped down first. The pilot followed him rather quickly. The broken features of Ricketts' face were like granite and his brown hair was windblown. He came quickly towards Turner. Jack Schulman was close behind him. Turner noticed that Schulman was white-faced and seemed a bit dazed. The roustabouts went to work. They started blocking up the wheels. Ricketts walked right up to Turner and looked at him with his eyes strangely anguished.

'Eagle 3 has gone down,' he said.

Turner didn't know what to say. It seemed incomprehensible. He licked his lips and then he looked at Jack Schulman who seemed physically ill. Jack Schulman shook his head. He shook it slowly from side to side. There was shock and disbelief on his face and he was visibly shaking. Turner stared hard at Ricketts. Ricketts nodded and turned to Schulman. He told him to go down to the bar and wait for him there. The kid did as he was told. He simply left without a word. They watched him go along the sloping catwalk and enter one of the modules. Then Ricketts went to the phone. He rang through to the doctor. He told him to go down to the bar and have a look at Jack Schulman. When he had done this he put the phone down and turned back to Turner.

'What happened?' Turner said.

'It went down,' Ricketts said. He took Turner by the arm and led him away from the listening roustabouts. They stopped beneath the catwalk, heard the murmuring of the sea, and Ricketts ran his fingers through his brown hair and glanced sharply around him. 'We were bombed,' he said simply.

Turner felt a little dazed. He also felt a creeping chill. He tried hard not to think of the Prime Minister, of what he might have to tell him.

'Jesus,' Turner said.

'Fucking right,' Ricketts said. 'Some bastard put a bomb in the forward leg – and it was under the water.'

'A *bomb*?' Turner said.

'That's right. A fucking bomb. It blew a hole in the leg, the rig tilted, and the whole place went crazy.'

'It's totally gone?' Turner said.

'That's right, it's totally gone. The whole rig fell apart and then it sank and took everything with it.'

'No survivors?'

'No survivors.'

'My God,' Turner said.

'A fucking bomb. I just couldn't believe it. But that's what it was.'

Turner looked at Ricketts' eyes. They were anguished and angry. They kept flitting back and forth around the deck, as if searching for clues.

'Who the hell . . . ?' Turner said.

'I don't know,' Ricketts said. 'The Prime Minister . . . I don't know . . . I thought about it. It just doesn't make sense.'

'It had to be someone on the rig.'

'You're pretty smart,' Ricketts said.

'A fanatic. Not caring if he went with it. A political gesture.'

'Perhaps,' Ricketts said. 'But he didn't have to go down with it. He might have primed it with a long delay timing device; he didn't have to be there.'

'*Why*?' Turner said.

'The Prime Minister,' Ricketts said. 'The time and date can't have been accidents. It's just too close for comfort.'

'But why *Eagle*?'

'I don't know.'

'It's a hundred and fifty miles north.'

'I know. It just doesn't make sense. There must be something else coming.'

Turner glanced all around him. He heard the sea's distant murmuring. He kept looking at the roustabouts and roughnecks crawling over the platform.

'They're still in conference?' Ricketts said.

'Jesus Christ, just don't mention it.'

'Do they know?' Ricketts said.

'No, they don't,' Turner said. 'They know there's an emergency, but they don't know what it is, and I doubt that they suspect the extent of it.'

'What about the radio operative?'

'Well, he knows it went down. He knows that, but he doesn't know what happened. Your man didn't get that far.'

'Okay,' Ricketts said. 'We better make him stay quiet. We can say there's been a very bad accident. We needn't say what it was.'

'A bomb,' Turner said. 'Jesus Christ. Do you think it's us next?'

'I doubt it,' Ricketts said. 'I mean I really can't believe it. This whole platform was checked from top to bottom – and I *mean* top to bottom. The divers were down there today. We've got cameras on the sea-bed. We've X-rayed every crate and every pipe, and the boardroom's well guarded. I don't think it's here. I don't think so. But I can't work it out.'

'Why *Eagle*?' Turner said. 'They must have *known* it was closing down. What the hell are they doing putting a bomb on Eagle? They must have been crazy.'

'I can't figure it,' Ricketts said.

'Charlie 2,' Turner said. 'When we heard what had happened, we tried to get in touch, but they simply wouldn't answer our calls.'

Ricketts' head jerked around. He stared very hard at Turner. 'You got no reply from Charlie 2? You think *they* might have sank?'

'No,' Turner said. 'The line was obviously open. Their radio was definitely on Receive, but they just wouldn't answer.'

'Oh, my God,' Ricketts said.

He suddenly started walking. Turner blinked and rushed after him. They walked across the main deck, past the stacked pipes and crates, beneath the cranes, around the derricks and modules, to a vertical steel ladder. Ricketts started to climb it, went up it with practised ease, and Turner followed and stood beside him on the platform, where the wind softly moaned. Ricketts stopped and rubbed his forehead, blinked his eyes and looked around him, glanced at the grey sky and the sea, then stared at the radio hut.

'Let's keep it quiet for now,' he said. 'The last thing we want is panic. Let's just say there was a very bad accident and we're working it out.'

'An explosion,' Turner said. 'We'll say the well-head exploded. We'll say a couple of oil drums went with it and caused complete chaos.'

'Charlie 2,' Ricketts said. 'There must be a connection. They simply don't leave the radio open. They just don't walk away.'

'Jesus Christ,' Turner said.

'It's on the pipeline,' Ricketts said. 'The main pipe runs from Frigg down to Beryl and then on to Forties.'

'You mean terrorists?'

'I mean terrorists.'

'Jesus Christ, that's impossible.'

'There's no security on Beryl or Frigg. The security's here.'

'The *Prime Minister's* here.'

'That's right. He's right here.'

'Then why Beryl? Why Frigg? I don't get it. It doesn't add up.'

'It just might,' Ricketts said, glancing vaguely around him. 'There's a floating refinery on Beryl, and the pipe runs to here.'

'Then why Frigg?' Turner said.

'The Frigg supply runs through Beryl. The oil extracted from Frigg goes to Beryl and then on to here.'

'But Frigg's drying up.'

'That's right. It's drying up.'

'Then why would they want to cut off Eagle if the field's drying up?'

'I don't know,' Ricketts said.

He started walking again, heading straight for the radio hut. He disappeared through the door and Turner followed him in and saw the operative looking up in surprise. The operative was white-faced and confused. He stared at Ricketts and he opened his mouth to speak and then he coughed and then stuttered.

'I've got Charlie 2,' he said. 'They want to speak to you, Ricketts. I asked for the message and they wouldn't give it and they told me to find you.'

58

'There's been an accident,' Ricketts said.

'They sounded weird,' the operative said. 'It wasn't the usual guy – it was McGregor – and he sounded real weird.'

'What did he say?' Ricketts said.

'He said nothing,' the operative said. He looked nervously from Ricketts to Turner. 'He just said go get Ricketts.'

'Nothing else?'

'Nothing else. He was weird; he sounded angry. I said what's the message and he said there's no message, just go and find Ricketts and make it quick. What's *happening* out there?'

'There's been an accident,' Turner said. 'There's been an explosion on Frigg. We're still trying to find out what caused it, so we want it kept quiet.'

The operative looked relieved. He gave a sigh and licked his lips. He shook his head and grinned nervously at them both and then he slowly stood up.

'Oh,' he said. 'I see. I mean, I thought it was me. I thought maybe I'd done something wrong and I just couldn't figure it.'

'It's classified,' Ricketts said. 'Accidents like this are always classified. We have to check it all out and then put in a report, and it has to be strictly confidential.'

'I understand,' the operative said.

'Make sure you do,' Ricketts said. 'If I hear the slightest word from the crew you'll be out of a job.'

The operative licked his lips. He was young and he looked nervous. He glanced at Ricketts and then he looked at Turner and nodded his head.

'Go outside,' Turner said. 'Close the door when you leave. Stand outside and don't let anyone in. Now is that understood?'

The operative nodded quickly and stepped out of the crowded hut. The door slammed and Ricketts sat at the table and put on the earphones.

'Bravo 1 to Charlie 2,' Ricketts said. 'Are you receiving me?'

Turner heard the crackling radio. He couldn't hear what was being said. He heard Ricketts, but he couldn't hear Charlie 2; he just heard the crackling.

'Bravo 1,' Ricketts said. 'Yes, it's Ricketts. Let me speak to McGregor.'

Turner paced up and down, feeling dazed and quite ill. He was nervous and he looked down at Ricketts with a singular sympathy. Ricketts listened a long time. His hands were steady on the table. He had large hands and long calloused fingers, and they didn't move once. Turner thought the hut was stifling. It was dimly lit and airless. He paced up and down the short, narrow space and tried to empty his mind. Then he heard Ricketts curse, saw him put the earphones down. He saw him swivelling around in the chair and look up with bright eyes.

'It's McGregor,' Ricketts said. 'He's got a terrorist group on board. He says they've also got a plutonium bomb on board – and they're willing to use it.'

'Jesus Christ,' Turner said. 'Oh, my God. What the hell do they want?'

'They want the Prime Minister.'

CHAPTER FIVE

RICKETTS and Turner were both sitting by the radio when Robert Barker walked into the hut. He saw the sweat on Turner's forehead and the tension in Rickett's face. He had never seen Ricketts tense before, so he knew it was bad.

'Okay,' Barker said. 'What's the emergency?'

'It's pretty bad,' Ricketts said.

'I gathered that,' Barker said. 'I'm supposed to be protecting the Prime Minister. Now what the hell is it?'

'We were bombed,' Ricketts said. 'Eagle 3 has been sunk. Now the Clan has taken over Charlie 2, and they've got a plutonium bomb.'

Barker looked at him. He couldn't quite believe his ears. He saw a strange anguished rage in Ricketts' eyes, and he knew it was true.

'Bombed?' he said. 'The Clan?'

'That's right,' Ricketts said. 'They bombed one of the legs of a pontoon and they sank Eagle 3.'

'Oh, my God,' Barker said.

'It was the Clan,' Ricketts said. 'There's a foreman on Charlie 2 called McGregor, and the cunt is a terrorist.'

Barker shook his head a little. He suddenly felt claustrophobic. The radio hut wasn't well lit, and it felt like a Turkish bath. He glanced from Ricketts to Turner. He saw the sweat on Turner's forehead. The supervisor was drumming his fingers on the table, studying the radio.

'Why Eagle?' Barker said.

'I don't know yet,' Ricketts said. 'I didn't get the chance to ask questions. They want the Prime Minister.'

'The Prime Minister?' Barker said.

'That's right. The Prime Minister. They say they'll blow up Charlie 2 – and if they have to they'll go with it – if we don't let them speak to the P.M. They have a plutonium bomb on board. McGregor said they would use it. I don't know how they managed it, but they've taken over the whole of Charlie 2.'

'You mean they've hijacked the rig?'

'I think that's what I'm saying.'

'How many?'

'I don't know.'

'There's eighty men on that rig.'

'I know. I don't know how they did it. But they've certainly got it.'

Barker whistled, patted the blond hair on his head, shook his head gently from side to side, trying to take it all in.

'God,' he said, 'that's bad. That's pretty fucking disastrous. The Clan are the worst terrorists in Scotland, extreme, quite fanatical.' He shook his head again, feeling hot and a little shaky. 'They're the type, if they could blow up the world, they'd just go on and do it.' He shook his head more vigorously, scuffled his feet on the floor. 'I don't even want to consider it,' he said. 'It just seems impossible.'

'It's McGregor,' Ricketts said. 'McGregor seems to be the leader. He said, "This is an official announcement from the Clan: We've taken over your rig." He also claimed credit for Eagle. He didn't bother to explain it. He said he wanted to speak to the Prime Minister, but he'd speak to you first.'

'Bastard,' Barker said.

'He's not kidding,' Ricketts said. 'He could be bluffing, but he certainly isn't kidding – and he *did* blow up Eagle.'

'How?' Barker said.

'A pontoon leg,' Ricketts said. 'They planted a bomb in a pontoon leg. They probably used a long delay timing device with the primer on Charlie 2.'

'Some of the crew,' Barker said. 'The rig-workers aren't checked out. I've been wanting to check the bastards for years, but they just wouldn't let me.'

'They will in future,' Turner said.

'Fucking great,' Barker said. 'In the meantime it costs us two rigs, and now they want the Prime Minister.'

'That's right,' Ricketts said.

'It's impossible,' Turner said. 'We can't even let him know that it's happened. We can't let the word out.'

'It'll get out,' Barker said.

'Not immediately,' Turner said. 'The Prime Minister's in conference and we'll let him stay there until we manage to sort this mess out. We can't tell him till then.'

Barker looked down at the floor. 'Let me get this straight,' he said. 'The terrorists have bombed Eagle. They've taken over Charlie 2. We don't know how, but they've managed to gain control, and now they've got a plutonium bomb. Where the hell did they get the bomb? How on earth did they take the rig? There's eighty men in that crew, and you don't buy plutonium bombs for jam. Have they got any proof?'

'I don't know,' Ricketts said. 'McGregor wouldn't discuss it with me. He just said he wasn't kidding, that he wanted the Prime Minister, and that he was willing to speak to you first.'

'The Prime Minister's impossible.'

'That's what he wants, Barker.'

'It's not feasible,' Barker said. 'He must be bluffing. He's just trying it on.'

'Maybe,' Turner said.

'Maybe not,' Ricketts said. 'The only way you're going to find out is to get on that radio.'

Barker glanced up and smiled. He chuckled softly and shook his head. He paced up and down the small hut and kept pursing his lips.

'Okay,' he said, 'I'll talk. Let's hear what they've got to say. Let's hold them off as long as we can and keep the Prime Minister out of it.'

He looked down at the radio. 'Has that got an open line?' Turner nodded and reached out and flicked a switch. 'Now we'll all hear,' he said. Barker nodded. 'That's what I want,' he said. Ricketts sat forward and spoke into the mike, and he kept his voice level. 'Bravo 1 to Charlie 2. Bravo 1 to Charlie 2. Are you receiving me?' There was the crackling of static, swelling up and fading out. 'Charlie 2 to Bravo 1, we're receiving. We don't want Ricketts. We want Barker.' Ricketts grinned up at Barker and got out of his chair. Barker patted the blond hair on his head and sat down at the microphone.

'Okay,' he said, 'it's Barker. Give me McGregor.'

There was silence for a moment. They heard nothing but the crackling receiver. Barker placed both his elbows on the table, and put his chin in his hands. Turner got out of his chair. He stood close beside Ricketts. Their eyes met and then they both looked at the radio, feeling tense and defeated.

'Barker?' McGregor said.

'Yes, this is Barker.'

'This is McGregor speakin'. I'm speakin' on behalf of the Clan. I'm notifying you officially that we've requisitioned Charlie 2 on behalf of the People's Army for the Liberation of Scotland.'

'Cut the shit,' Barker said. 'What do you want?'

'Our demands will only be given to the Prime Minister. We won't settle for less.'

'You can't speak to the Prime Minister. It's impossible and you know it. There's no way I'm going to bring him into this, and that's all there is to it.'

'You'll give us what we want,' McGregor said, 'or you'll suffer the consequences.'

'What consequences?'

'The Clan's captured Charlie 2. We've got a plutonium bomb on board. We'll no' hesitate to set the bomb off if we aren't satisfied. Dinnae attempt to assault the rig. Dinnae try to win it back. If we see any ships or helicopters, we'll just set the bomb off.'

'Do that and you'll blow yourselves up as well.'

'We dinnae care,' McGregor said. 'We're all willin' to go down with it. And you all know enough about the Clan to know we mean what we say.'

'I don't believe you,' Barker said. 'You couldn't find an A-bomb. If you did, you couldn't transport it to the rig without being detected. I think you're just bluffing.'

'Eagle 3 was no bluff. It was a demonstration and warnin'. It was a much smaller bomb on Eagle 3, but this one is the real thing. We didn't find it, we made it. They're surprisingly easy to make. The finished product is thirty-six inches long, and it doesn't weigh much. It was easy gettin' it on the rig. It's been on the rig for months. It only weighs half a ton and it was put in a packing crate and shipped out from Aberdeen with the regular equipment. I'm the foreman on this rig. Yer toolpushers are all Clan members. We shipped it in with the regular supplies, and now it's all set to go.'

'I don't believe you,' Barker said.

'You don't have to,' McGregor said. 'We've left the proof for you to find. Get yer on-shore security men to check out the Aberdeen heliport. Tell 'em to check the toilet. Tell 'em to look behind the cistern. I left a brown envelope there an' it contains a full breakdown of the design and construction of the bomb. Get them to check it out. They'll soon confirm that it's authentic. When they ring you back with this confirmation, we'll be able to deal.'

Barker studied the microphone. He covered his face with his right hand. He rubbed his eyes and he looked up at Ricketts and shook his head wearily.

'Okay,' he said. 'We'll check it out.'

'You have an hour,' McGregor said. 'I'll no' give you longer. If I dinnae hear back in that time I'm gonna blow up the rig. You know what that means, Barker. The blast will destroy the whole Beryl Field. It'll wipe it out completely, and it'll also cause a lot of damage to the Forties Field. The supply pipes will go with it. You'll lose two-thirds of North Sea oil. There'll be enough contamination to make sure you can't work the sea for years. Think of that while yer waitin'.'

Ricketts looked at Turner. His supervisor was visibly shaken. He was leaning against the door of the hut, wiping sweat from his brow. Ricketts thought about the Clan. He knew what the Clan were like. They were vicious and ruthless and suicidal, and he knew they would do it. The Clan had hijacked aircraft, had assassinated politicians, had set off bombs in airports and chain-stores, killed civilians and policemen. The Clan believed in publicity, in putting on spectacles. Ricketts knew that if they had a plutonium bomb they would willingly use it. He glanced down at Barker. The security chief was worried. He was tapping the table gently with his fingers as he studied the radio.

'How many men have you got?' he said.

'I've got sixty,' McGregor said. 'They were all regular crew members. We've been working on this plan for eighteen months, so we'd plenty of time. Yer chief toolpusher's my man. He's been with us from the start. He's the man who hires and fires, and he's gradually been replacing your men with ours. It's one of the attractions of the work, Barker. Rig-workers aren't asked questions. Any man who's willin' to work on a rig will be hired without question. You never approved of it. Too bad yer supervisors didn't listen. It's taken eighteen months, but now we've sixty men on board and we've executed most of the remaining crew.'

'You bastard,' Barker said.

'We spared two,' McGregor said. 'I thought you might want a few witnesses, so there's two still alive. One's John Griffith, your geologist. He's standin' beside me right now. You want proof, so I'm gonna put him on and you can ask what you like.'

Ricketts felt himself burning with a murderous rage, smacked a fist against one hand and turned away and stared out through a window. The afternoon light was dull. The North Sea was quite calm. It stretched out to the horizon, towards Beryl Field, and then was lost in a misty haze. Ricketts started to tremble with rage and frustration, turned around when he heard the voice of Griffith coming over the radio.

'Barker?'

'Yes, Griffith.'

'It's true, Barker. It's all true. They've got about sixty men on this rig and they've taken it over.' Griffith sounded very shaky. He actually sounded close to tears. His voice was trembling and it seemed almost girlish: high-pitched and confused. 'They killed the remaining crew,' he said. 'They took them up to the deck and shot them. They just shot them and threw them over the side, and they made us two watch it.' Griffith stopped and seemed to sob. They heard him trying to control himself. Ricketts clenched his fists and looked at the radio and he wanted to smash it. 'They're serious,' Griffith said. 'They mean every word they say. They spared me and Sutton, but they killed all the others and then they threw them over the side. Oh, dear God, I just don't ...'

Barker put his head down. They all listened to Griffith sobbing. Ricketts clenched his fists while Turner closed his eyes and hissed 'Bastards!' and looked away. Barker kept his head down. His fingers drummed on the table. Griffith's sobbing faded out and then McGregor started talking again.

'Is that enough for you, Barker? Are you satisfied? Or do you want to hear more?'

'No,' Barker said. 'That's enough. I don't want to hear more.'

'You have one hour,' McGregor said. 'You can check out our drawings. The photographs and drawings will convince you that we're no' playing games. You have one hour, no more.'

McGregor said nothing else. Barker turned off the receiver. He drummed his fingers on the deck and pursed his lips, and then he slowly stood up. He surveyed the small hut, looked at Ricketts and Turner. He shook his head despairingly from side and side and gazed down at the floor.

'Well?' Ricketts said.

'We'll have to check,' Barker said. 'I can't believe they've made a working A-bomb, but we'll just have to check. I'll ring Andy Blackburn. He's the best man I have. I'll tell him not to use the local police, to use the company labs. We have to keep this thing private. We don't want the army or police involved. If word got out that the terrorists had managed to do all this, the repercussions internationally would be disastrous. Jesus, it's so *stupid*! We've no security on these damned rigs. We've actually *hired* sixty terrorists over the past eighteen months, and I don't think we'd ever live that down. We *can't* let the news out. We've got to solve it on our own. We've got to check if that bloody bomb works and then take it from there. I'll ring Andy right now.'

Barker picked up the telephone and rang through to the heliport. He spoke to Andy Blackburn, told him what to look for, and then told him not to ask any questions and to keep his mouth shut. Ricketts stood there and listened. Barker gave nothing away. Ricketts gazed out the window and tried hard to control his boiling rage. His hands opened and closed, clutched the air and released it. He looked out at the sea and thought of Griffith and Sutton on that rig. The terrorists had sunk Eagle. The whole crew had gone down with it. The terrorists had murdered twenty men on Charlie 2 and thrown them over the side. Ricketts felt like exploding, like smashing the radio hut. He heard Barker speaking into the telephone, sounding calm and collected. Then Barker rang off. He turned around and looked at Turner. The bearded supervisor was chewing a matchstick and sweating profusely.

'Okay,' Barker said, 'he's going to check. In the meantime, we wait.'

CHAPTER SIX

CONVINCED that the situation should be kept secret as long as possible, Turner decided to return to the boardroom. Walking across the main deck, seeing the rig-workers all around him, he felt himself succumbing to panic. His stomach seemed to be in knots, he found it hard to think clearly, and he felt a terrible, almost lacerating pity for the men who had died. Yet beyond this was the fear. It was cold and intangible. It was tied up with the thought of the terrible repercussions if this awful situation came to light. Turner saw the flat grey sea, the clouds on the horizon. Beneath the clouds, beyond that horizon, was Charlie 2 with its terrorists. They had simply applied for jobs. Their backgrounds hadn't been checked. For eighteen months, as men had left, they had arrived, and now they owned the whole rig. They had a plutonium bomb. They could obliterate Beryl Field. The bomb could also devastate Forties Field and set them back a good ten years. The results would be catastrophic. The whole of Britain could collapse. Turner thought of the men in the boardroom, and he felt like a drowning man.

He reached the end of the deck, started climbing the steel steps, saw the grey sky passing over the sea as if nothing had happened.

Turner didn't want to do it. The thought of the boardroom made him ill. He would have to go in there and lie, and this thought made his heart pound. He wished that Ricketts were here with him, knew that Ricketts could do it, wished that he, instead of Ricketts, was at the radio, waiting for Blackburn. And what would happen when Blackburn called? What could they do if the bomb worked? Turner desperately tried to find a way out as he climbed up the ladder.

He reached the upper deck, opened the door of the nearest module, stepped inside and closed the door behind him and took a deep breath.

He didn't think he could face them. He was trembling when he reached the boardroom. The guard opened the door and Turner felt himself smiling, putting on a casual mask as he walked in. Then the panic disappeared. It simply fell away from him. He walked over to the table and sat down and gazed calmly around him.

'Sorry, gentlemen,' he heard himself saying. 'A spot of bother on Frigg Field.'

The Prime Minister, who had been talking, went quiet and glanced up. Turner noticed that his eyes were very blue, with a cold, hard intelligence.

'Oh,' he said. 'I'm sorry to hear that. Anything serious?'

'We're not sure,' Turner said. 'We think a well-head exploded. We don't know how much damage it caused, but we're having it checked out.'

Sir Reginald McMillan looked at him. He was drumming his fingers on the table. He was slim and grey-haired and distinguished, with a pale, remote face.

'An explosion?' he said.

'Yes, sir,' Turner said.

'Deary me,' Sir Reginald said. 'What rig was this?'

'Eagle 3,' Turner said.

Sir Reginald glanced at the Prime Minister. The news obviously hadn't pleased him. He picked up a pencil and started doodling, then looked over at Turner.

'What happened?' he said.

'We don't know, sir,' Turner said. 'They're still trying to sort it out. Apparently some oil drums exploded, which has made it all worse. We're waiting for further news and they're ringing us back as soon as possible. I've left Ricketts in charge, but I'll probably have to go up there again. I hope you'll excuse me.'

'Of course,' Sir Reginald said. 'Who's this Ricketts?'

'A top toolpusher,' Turner said. 'He's one of our very best men. He's handled lots of things like this before, and he knows what he's doing.'

Sir Reginald sighed. He was obviously very annoyed. Such accidents could happen, but it was dreadful to have one right now. He glanced at the Prime Minister, saw the blue eyes staring at him, a certain accusation in the eyes, a sly, suppressed triumph. Of course the Prime Minister would enjoy it. He would try to use it as a weapon. He would strengthen his party's bargaining position with suggestions of negligence.

'An explosion?' the Prime Minister said. 'Is this sort of thing common?'

'No, Prime Minister,' Turner said. 'It does happen, but not often. The North Sea's very deep and the pressure is tremendous and that obviously leads to the unexpected. It's happened before and it'll happen again – but it isn't that common.'

'I see,' the Prime Minister said.

'It's on Frigg,' Sir Reginald said. 'Luckily the explosion was on Eagle, which was closing down anyway.'

'Closing down?' the Prime Minister said.

'Yes, Prime Minister, closing down. Eagle 3 was drying up and was due to be towed away to another field. The blow-up therefore won't be as bad as it might have been, since to all intents and purposes the rig was closed. Had she been operating, it might well have been worse.'

'That *was* lucky,' the Prime Minister said.

'Yes, Prime Minister, very lucky. That no oil was coming out of Eagle 3 was very lucky indeed.'

Sir Reginald smiled at the Prime Minister, but the Prime Minister did not return it. Instead, he looked around at the other men, who were all sleek and well-fed. These were the oil magnates. They represented the conglomerates. They headed individual companies that were part of larger companies, and the source of all their power was quite elusive. They were an international crew, lived in airports and hotels, reported behind closed doors to unknown superiors, and weren't intimidated by mere politics. The Prime Minister didn't like them because they had made his government impotent. They used the laws of one country against the other, and they couldn't be stopped.

'Anyone hurt?' the Prime Minister said.

'We don't know yet,' Turner said. 'I would anticipate casualties, but we won't know until they ring back.'

'They seem slow,' the Under-Secretary said.

'They're fighting the fire,' Turner said.

'I trust we'll receive a full report.'

'Of course, sir. That's our policy.'

The Under-Secretary smiled at him. He thought that Turner was very calm. He knew that accidents on the rigs were handled by the oil companies and that the reports were written up by their own men. The Under-Secretary didn't approve. He knew the reports couldn't be trusted. He felt that the Department of Energy should be called in at such times to conduct an independent investigation. He had been fighting for that for years, but it was a fight he hadn't won. The oil companies had resisted all attempts to uncover their skeletons.

'What's happening now?' he said.

'We're simply waiting,' Turner said. 'I've left Ricketts in the radio room with instructions to call me.'

'Excellent,' Paul Dalton said. He was smiling encouragingly at Turner. He was a rough-looking, suntanned American with a shock of red hair. 'That Ricketts is good,' he said. 'He worked with us in New Mexico. We've used him in more than one emergency, and he's always been excellent.'

'American?' Sir Reginald said.

'No, British,' Dalton said. 'But he's been in Kuwait and the Gulf of Mexico and Texas, and there's no one in the business who's better. He's a very good man.'

Turner looked at Dalton. He had great respect for him. Dalton was one of the Americans' top dogs, and his word carried weight. He was also an expert, knew every trick there was, had worked as a roustabout, as a roughneck and toolpusher, then had taken over security in Saudi Arabia and New Mexico and was now one of the most powerful of the executives. A lot of the men were frightened of Dalton. They weren't too sure of his specific function. They only knew that he was free to roam around the world at will, dropping in on any oil field or office. He did so frequently. They knew he put in tough reports. His presence here, at this top-level conference, had put them all on their toes.

'Ricketts is good,' Dalton said. 'He's really good. I've no doubt we can trust him.'

'I agree,' Turner said. 'Ricketts has been through this before. And he knows what to do when they call: he'll send someone to fetch me.'

'Will they need help?' Sir Reginald said.

'I don't know,' Turner said. 'We won't know until they call back; in the meantime, we'll sit tight.'

'Fine,' Dalton said.

'Most unfortunate,' Sir Reginald murmured.

'So,' the Prime Minister said. 'Let's get back to business.'

The conference continued, the voices arguing back and forth, the smoke from cigars and cigarettes drifting over their heads. Turner heard himself talking, hardly knew what he was saying, kept looking through the portholes of the boardroom, at the rigs in the distance. Was Forties Field safe? Could Barker be sure of his security? Could they be certain that there wasn't a terrorist right here in their midst? He heard the Prime Minister's voice, heard Sir Reginald and then himself. His own voice seemed to come from far away, but it was calm and assured. Turner gazed through the portholes. He saw some rigs near the horizon. They were miles apart and seemed very small, very lonesome and desolate. Turner shivered a little. He tried to focus on the conference. He thought bitterly of the terrorists on Charlie 2, and he wished that the phone would ring.

When it rang, he felt paralysed.

CHAPTER SEVEN

ROBERT Barker knew the news wasn't good when he saw Turner's face. Turner was back in the radio hut, standing opposite Ricketts, his broad shoulders slumped and his fingers tugging nervously at his beard. Ricketts didn't look happy either. His broken features were like granite. He turned around when he heard Barker enter, and he gave him a tight smile.

'Well?' Barker said.

'Blackburn thinks the bomb would work. He found the photographs and plans and he took them to our lab and they phoned him five minutes ago and said they thought it would work.'

'Jesus,' Turner said, smacking a fist into one hand, glancing down at the radio and looking away and gazing out through the window. 'I don't believe it,' he said.

'And they're sure?' Barker said.

'They're not sure, but they're pretty certain. It's about the size of a tea chest, it weighs approximately a quarter ton, it's got everything it needs, they're all in the right place, and with a minimum of luck it would work.'

'Jesus,' Turner said again. He kept staring through the window. He was looking at the faraway rigs, at the darkening Forties Field.

'Okay,' Barker said. 'It's a workable design for a plutonium bomb. But that doesn't mean the bastards could actually *make* it. They're terrorists, they're not scientists; they're a bunch of damned killers. To design an A-bomb is one thing; to actually make it another. Where did they get the materials? How did they put it all together? And how the hell would they manage to test it? The drawings don't mean they've got one.'

'You'd be surprised,' Ricketts said. His grin was humourless and tense. 'According to Blackburn, they're relatively

73

easy to make, and they're not that expensive. He says they're becoming more common. He says that schoolkids have made them. He says that all of the materials can be bought in the open market, and that a large bomb, a workable A-bomb, is not beyond credibility. The plans McGregor left were perfect. The lab thought the bomb could work. True, we don't know if he made it, but I still don't feel too good.'

Barker lightly smacked his forehead, shook his head from side to side. He walked to the door of the hut and turned around and came back again.

'I'd like to know for sure,' he said. 'I'd like to know if they actually made it. I'd like to know if they've got a bomb on that rig or if they're just trying to bluff us.'

'Blackburn's on to it,' Ricketts said. 'He's trying to find out right now. He's going to check out McGregor's movements over the past few months and try to come up with more positive information. In the meantime, we'll have to accept that they might have that bomb.'

'The bastards,' Turner said.

'A fair description,' Ricketts said.

'We'll have to go to a higher authority,' Turner said. 'I don't think we should handle this.'

'Not yet,' Barker said. 'We don't know what they want yet. We only know they want to talk to the P.M., but we might coax them out of that. Let's talk to McGregor. Let's try to sound him out. Let's try to stretch it out a bit more, and give Blackburn more time. They may not have made the bomb. It's just possible they haven't got it. If that's true, and if we can find out for sure, we're on far better ground.'

He looked at Turner. Turner nodded and stepped aside. Barker sat down at the radio and turned it on, engaging the open line. He got in touch with Charlie 2. An unfamiliar voice answered. The voice asked him who he was and he said, 'Barker. Now get me McGregor.' There was quite a delay, they heard the crackling of static, there was the sound of distant laughter in the background, then they heard someone coughing.

'Is that Barker?' McGregor said.

'Yes, McGregor, this is Barker. You told me to call you back in an hour, and I'm calling you back.'

'I'm glad you listened,' McGregor said. 'I'm glad yer no'

without some sense. I dinnae like the thought of what would happen if you didn't show that.'

'How are Griffith and Sutton doing?'

'The prisoners of war are doin' fine.'

'They're not prisoners of war, they're fucking hostages. So let's cut out the horse-shit.'

McGregor chuckled. 'Aye,' he said, 'yer a sharp one. You can call 'em what you like, but we've got 'em – and that's all that matters.' Barker didn't reply. There was a very long silence. There was static and then they heard McGregor chuckling, a soft sound, triumphant. 'So,' he said, 'you've called. I assume you've done what you were told. I assume you know this bomb of ours works and we can now discuss business.'

'It might work,' Barker said. 'It might and it might not. We're not interested in whether it works or not; we want proof that you have it.'

'Eagle 3 was your proof.'

'You didn't use an A-bomb there. That blast didn't come from an A-bomb and both of us know it.'

'It dinnae matter,' McGregor said. 'It was proof of our intentions. It was proof that we could get a bomb on board and that we mean what we say. We've already destroyed one rig, Barker. We've managed to hijack another. We've already lost you two whole crews and now yer trying to convince yourself that we're bluffing. Pull the other one, Barker. Yer shit-scared and sweating. You've seen a photograph of this bomb and the drawings of its construction and now yer trying to say we don't have it. Well, we have it, make no mistake; we have it and we'll use it. If you really want proof try to take back this rig or simply refuse to meet our demands. You know what'll happen, Barker. If this bomb goes off, yer finished. It'll wipe out Beryl Field, devastate half of Forties, and destroy the main pipeline to the refineries. That's over half of Britain's oil. It'll take years to repair the damage. And even when you repair it, the oil companies probably won't want to touch it. We'll wipe the North Sea off the map. You'll see Britain sink with it. Think of that before you say any more about the Clan tryin' to bluff you.'

Barker sighed, rubbed his forehead with his hands, glanced up at Turner and Ricketts and then looked down again. The radio hut was very quiet. Only the crackling static spoke. It was turning dark outside, and they heard the sea washing around the rig. Barker stared at the radio, put his hands beneath his chin. He seemed pale and the shadows fell over him, making him ghostlike.

'What do you want?' he said.

'The Prime Minister,' McGregor said.

'You want me to let you talk to the Prime Minister?'

'No,' McGregor said. 'More than that.'

Barker almost stopped breathing. He leant back in his chair. He stretched his hands out on the table and studied his fingernails. He didn't move for a long time. There was no sound from the radio. Barker finally sat forward and looked at the radio and spoke softly.

'What do you mean?' he said.

'The Prime Minister,' McGregor said. 'I'll only give my demands to the Prime Minister. Until then, you'll know nothing.'

'You mean, *in person?*' Barker said.

'Aye, I mean in person.'

'And where do you plan to have this great meeting?'

'On Charlie 2,' said McGregor.

Ricketts suddenly clenched his fists. Turner sat in a chair. He put his elbows on his knees, then put his chin in his hands and looked down. Barker didn't move a muscle. He just kept staring at the radio. It was crackling and it seemed to hypnotize him, to draw him towards it. Ricketts glanced through the windows. Shadows swooped across the sea. He saw the afternoon turn into evening, heard the wind, felt the cold.

'You're kidding,' Barker said.

'No, I'm not,' McGregor said.

'You don't think we'd actually fly him over there?'

'I don't think you've a choice.'

Barker didn't say anything, didn't know what to say, just sat there and listened to the static and thought he was dreaming. He really couldn't comprehend it. It went beyond the bounds of reason. He had been in the army, in the police and in private security, but he had never come across anything like this. The demand was impossible. The alternative was unthinkable. He couldn't face it, so he tried to stretch it out, crawling dumbly from silence.

'I can't do that,' he said.

'Yer gonna have to,' McGregor said.

'It's crazy and you know it. There's just no way you'll get the Prime Minister. They just won't let him go.'

'I'll get 'im,' McGregor said. 'I'll get 'im by 1900 hours. Fifteen minutes after that, if the Prime Minister isn't here, I'll set the bomb off.'

'You'll go with it,' Barker said.

'You've already said that,' McGregor said. 'And I'm sayin' again we don't mind. We're all committed to do it.'

'Why do you want the Prime Minister?'

'I want to give 'im our demands.'

'Why not let me pass on the demands?'

'I want him as collateral.'

'Collateral?' Barker said.

'That's right, Barker, our collateral. We need a guarantee as big as our demands, so we want the Prime Minister.'

'What are you trying to pull, McGregor?'

'I only represent the Clan.'

'Then what the hell are those bastards trying to pull? I want to know their demands.'

'You won't be told,' McGregor said. 'I'll only tell the Prime Minister. He's the only man who's got the authority to get what we want.'

'You might kill him,' Barker said.

'Aye, I might kill him.'

'Then you know we can't possibly agree.'

'Yes, you will. You've no choice.'

Barker broke all the rules by lighting up a cigarette. He inhaled and leant back in his chair and looked up at the ceiling. Ricketts looked down at his face, which seemed thin and very pale. There were beads of sweat shining on his forehead, just beneath the blond hair. It was quiet in the hut. They heard the murmuring of the sea. Turner scratched at his beard and looked at Ricketts and shook his head and looked down again. Ricketts remained standing, opening and shutting his large hands. He saw Barker sit up and lean forward and look straight at the radio.

'No arguments,' McGregor said. 'No delays and no tricks. If anything comes anywhere near the rig, the whole thing will go up. We want the Prime Minister. We want 'im at 1900 hours. We want him to arrive by helicopter with no police or security. You and Ricketts can come. I want Ricketts to fly the chopper. If we find another pilot on board he'll be instantly executed. You'll land at 1900 hours. We'll give you fifteen minutes' leeway. If yer not here by 1915 we'll blow the whole place to hell.'

'I refuse,' Barker said.

'You can't refuse,' McGregor said.

'I won't do it,' Barker said.

'I don't care,' McGregor said. 'It's your choice.'

Barker opened his mouth to speak. The line went dead before he could do so. He stared for a long time at the radio and then he leant back.

'Jesus Christ,' he said quietly.

Turner still sat in his chair. He raised his eyes and stared at Ricketts. He saw Ricketts looking out of the window, at the darkening sea. Bravo 1 wasn't drilling. The sea whispered all around them. They heard the isolated roar of a forklift, the shouting of men. The radio continued crackling. Charlie 2 was not receiving. Barket sat before the radio and quietly studied it, smoking his cigarette. Ricketts turned and looked at him. Ricketts' granite face was shadowed. The low ceiling made him look quite enormous, and he seemed to be shaking.

'We just can't,' Turner said. 'It's just out of the question. We can't possibly give this news to the Prime Minister. It's just too much to ask.'

'What else is there?' Barker said. 'The decision isn't ours to make. We can't take a chance on that bomb. We'll have to let *them* decide.'

'Oh, my God,' Turner said.

CHAPTER EIGHT

EVERYONE in the boardroom looked around them as if suffering from shock. They looked first at Turner. They then looked at Ricketts and Barker. The news seemed so preposterous that they couldn't quite take it in, but gradually, in the grim silence following Turner's level recital, the awful reality was hammered home. They started looking at one another. They glanced back up at Turner. Their eyes wandered back and forth as if blind, and never really stopped wandering. Sir Reginald glanced at the Prime Minister. He saw the blue eyes and turned away. The Prime Minister's blue eyes swept the table and went back up to Turner.

'Well, lad,' he said, 'that's quite a tale.'

'Yes, sir,' Turner said. 'I'm afraid it is.'

'Nineteen hundred hours?'

'Yes, Prime Minister,' Turner said.

'That's seven o'clock this evening?'

'Yes, sir.'

'Then we have ninety minutes.'

Turner didn't reply. He glanced at Ricketts and Barker. They were standing at the head of the long table, their eyes wandering back and forth. Sir Reginald stared down at the table, drumming his fingers on one knee, desperately trying to throttle his own fury, his horror and outrage. He glanced across at Paul Dalton. The American was smoking a cigarette. His eyes were grey and they roamed back and forth with their well-renowned fearlessness. They came to rest on the Prime Minister. His bulky frame filled his chair. He was nicking the ash off his cigar and looking at Turner.

'You can't do it,' Sir Reginald said. 'We can't expect you to go over there. We can't hand over the Prime Minister of Great Britain to a bunch of fanatics.'

'I agree,' Paul Dalton said. 'That request is just crazy. I'm all for trying to meet their demands, but I stop short at this.'

'Ludicrous,' Sir Reginald said. 'It's quite simply ridiculous. I think they must be utterly insane. I just won't accept this.'

The Prime Minister leaned forward. The cigar burned between his fingers. His florid, well-fleshed, stubborn face held a shrewd native cunning.

'Yes,' he said. 'It's ludicrous. That's exactly what it is. Now what *I* want to know is how it happened. That really does interest me.'

He was looking right at Turner, then he glanced briefly at Sir Reginald. The Chairman flushed and coughed into his hand and kept drumming his fingers.

'Well, lad?' the Prime Minister said.

'I'm not sure,' Turner said.

'All right, you're not sure,' the Prime Minister said. 'Now let's ask our security chief.'

He turned his blue eyes on Barker, picked up his cigar, inhaled and blew the smoke to the room and then sat back and waited.

'It seems irrelevant—' Sir Reginald began.

'It's not irrelevant,' the Prime Minister said.

'No,' Paul Dalton said, 'it's not irrelevant. It's a goddamned disgrace.'

The Prime Minister looked at Barker. 'Well?' he said quietly. 'I'm being asked to go out on that rig and I want to know why.'

Barker sighed and shrugged his shoulders in defeat. 'Well,' he said, 'it seems we simply hired them. We've been hiring them for months.'

There was silence in the boardroom. Sir Reginald kept his head down. The Prime Minister sat forward in his chair and kept his eyes fixed on Barker.

'You *hired* them?' he said.

'That's right, sir, we hired them. They signed up back in Scotland. They signed up just like all of the others and were shipped out the normal way.'

'Sixty terrorists,' the Prime Minister said.

'Yes, Prime Minister, sixty terrorists.'

'You're trying to tell me you signed up sixty terrorists without checking them out?'

'They didn't all come at once, sir. They signed on over

80

eighteen months. They came out of the dole queues and factories just like all of the others.'

'I appreciate that, Mr. Barker. I'm well aware of that fact. What I want to know is how a damn terrorist can walk on to an oil rig.'

'You don't check them?' Dalton said.

'No,' Barker said, 'we don't. There's so many unemployed we never bother checking credentials, so we don't know too much about their past.'

'This is incredible,' the Prime Minister said. 'I think it's utterly scandalous. Any fool, any madman can apply and get a job on the rigs.'

'It's not *that* bad,' Sir Reginald said.

'It's bloody scandalous,' the Prime Minister said. 'These oil rigs are the life-blood of this country, and you don't check who works on them.'

'I didn't realize,' Sir Reginald said. 'I must say, it is appalling. I shall, of course, order an investigation and demand a complete report.'

'It's Barker's area,' Dalton said. 'Barker's in full charge of security. I'd like to know how the hell he got his job if this is any way typical.'

'I won't take that,' Barker said. 'I don't work in the employment office. My job is security on the rigs. I can't check out the men.'

'Right,' Dalton said. 'So no one does.'

'I've been wanting checks for years.' Barker glanced down at Sir Reginald. 'An inspection of my files will confirm that. My requests were denied.'

'Why?' Dalton said.

'It's just the policy,' Turner said. 'The North Sea isn't the most popular of places, so it isn't easy recruiting workers.'

'So you don't ask many questions.'

'That's right, Mr. Dalton. We ask the minimum of questions and that makes the job a bit more appealing.'

The Prime Minister glared at Sir Reginald. 'This is scandalous,' he said. 'You won't let the government touch the oil fields, and this is what happens.'

They all glared at one another. The air was smoky and smelt of brandy. Through the windows they could see the falling darkness, the lights winking on.

'Eighty minutes,' Ricketts said. 'We have exactly eighty minutes. I think we should be talking about Charlie 2. I think we'll have to decide.'

'Decide what?' Sir Reginald said. 'There's simply nothing to decide. The Prime Minister's not going on that rig and that's all there is to it.'

'I agree,' Dalton said.

'They have an A-bomb,' Ricketts said.

'Correction,' Dalton said. 'We don't know that. We don't know if they have it.'

'Right,' the Prime Minister said. 'We don't know that they have it. Nor can we be sure that they haven't. I wouldn't like to take chances.'

'But your life's at stake, Prime Minister.'

'The North Sea's at stake, Sir Reginald. Britain's future and the lives of countless men. I think that's worth considering.'

There was no immediate reply. They were all looking at the Prime Minister. His bulky frame filled up the chair and his blue eyes were thoughtful.

'We'll take the rig back,' Dalton said. 'We've no choice but to try it. We can't let you go to the terrorists. We don't know their intentions.'

'And the bomb?' the Under-Secretary said. 'What happens about that bomb? They've said they'll set it off if we attack. They might actually do it.'

'I think they'd do it,' Ricketts said. 'I'm pretty certain. I don't think they'd be shy.'

'We could still try,' Dalton said. 'We don't have to announce we're coming. We could use the two-man Pisces submersibles and come up right beneath them.'

'What are those?' the Under-Secretary said.

'Miniature submarines,' Dalton said. 'We could use a whole fleet of them and surface right beneath that damned rig. It's already dark now. It'll be darker by seven. We come up under the rig and scale the legs and take them all by surprise.'

'I don't think so,' Turner said. 'I wouldn't bank on that at all. That McGregor's a foreman, he obviously knows the rigs well, and he'll know about the television in the drilling room. There are cameras on the sea-bed. They're operated from the drilling room. Anything that goes on under the water will show up on that screen. McGregor won't forget that. He'll have the screen on all the time. He'd see the submersibles coming in, and then he'd set off his bomb.'

The Prime Minister rubbed his forehead, stubbed out his cigar, clasped his hands under his chin and gazed around him. He did not look at Sir Reginald. He looked carefully at Ricketts. His eyes finally came to rest on Paul Dalton who was pursing his lips.

'We're still assuming,' Dalton said. 'We're still assuming they have that bomb. The fact that they had a photograph and a workable drawing doesn't mean they've actually managed to make the thing.'

'That's true,' Sir Reginald said. 'It seems a bit far-fetched to me. I don't think it's all that easy to make an A-bomb. It seems a little bit ludicrous.'

'It's been known, sir,' Ricketts said. 'Our on-shore men think it's possible. They say the materials can be bought on the open market and that they're easy to make.'

'That's preposterous,' Sir Reginald said.

'No, it's not,' Dalton said. 'There's kids making them in their backyards in the States. They're pretty crude, but they work.'

'Not A-bombs,' Sir Reginald said.

'Pretty close,' Dalton said.

'It would help,' Ricketts said, 'if we had proof. And Blackburn's trying to find it.'

'Blackburn?' the Prime Minister said.

'Our on-shore security,' Turner said.

'And have the police or the army been informed?'

'We didn't think that advisable, sir.'

The Prime Minister looked at Turner and raised his bushy grey eyebrows. His cold blue eyes flicked around the room, returning once more to Turner.

'You didn't think it advisable?'

'No, Prime Minister, we didn't.'

'That strikes me as extraordinary, Mr. Turner. I simply cannot accept that.'

'In certain cases—' Turner began.

'In *what* cases?' the Prime Minister said. 'This isn't simply an oil company matter – it involves national security.'

'That's correct,' the Under-Secretary said. 'I find this secrecy reprehensible. The future of the North Sea and the whole of Britain is at stake, and you attempt to keep the civil authorities out of it.'

'It was a temporary measure,' Turner said. 'We just thought it best this way. We were simply trying to find a way out before—'

'Rubbish!' the Under-Secretary said, glaring at Sir Reginald. 'It's been the oil companies' policy for years and damned well you know it. I find this whole thing appalling. I am appalled by the negligence, by the lack of security, by how far you've let this go, by the fact that you've tried to keep it secret to save your own faces.'

'That's not true, sir,' Barker said. 'We have our standing instructions. The reporting of such matters to civil authorities is not in our hands.'

'This is scandalous!' the Prime Minister said.

'There's a reason, sir,' Dalton said. 'Although the oil fields are licensed to private companies, their work involves your whole country.'

'Exactly!' the Under-Secretary said. 'Your work involves our whole country. That's precisely why we should be informed. I find this quite reprehensible.'

'We don't want panic,' Dalton said. 'We think the public shouldn't know. The whole future of Britain now rests with the North Sea, and the news of a disaster could be fatal. You must understand, Prime Minister, we think only of the general good. We do not think that the general public is ready for such things.'

'I am not concerned with the public, Mr. Dalton. I am concerned with this government.'

Dalton started to reply. The emergency telephone rang. Every head in the room turned towards Barker as he picked the phone up. There was a very brief silence. Barker covered one ear. He nodded and then he lowered the phone and looked all around him.

'It's Blackburn,' he said. 'They're putting him through now. I think he should speak on the open line. I think we'll all have to hear this.'

'I don't think—' Sir Reginald began.

'I certainly do,' the Prime Minister said. 'I think we

should *all* be kept informed as from this moment on.'

Barker glanced at Sir Reginald. The Chairman nodded his head. Barker flicked a switch beneath the telephone and they heard a soft hissing sound.

'Blackburn?'

'Yes, Barker. We've managed to check out this McGregor. It wasn't very difficult at all. He didn't cover his tracks.'

'Good,' Barker said. 'Go ahead.'

'Is this line on scramble?'

'Yes, Blackburn, it's scrambled.'

'Good. I wouldn't want to be overheard. I think it's all pretty dicey.'

There was a very short pause. They heard the shuffling of papers. They were all studying the speakers on the wall, waiting for Blackburn.

'It was easy,' Blackburn said. 'It took no time at all. A quick check of the rig-workers' pubs in Aberdeen was enough to tell us where he spent his free time. McGregor lived in a boarding house. It's near George Street in Aberdeen. He's been using the same house for years, every time he's ashore. A pretty normal boarding house. A typical rig-workers' retreat. McGregor used to have a lot of friends in; apart from that he was normal. Naturally we searched his room. He hadn't attempted to hide anything. The search revealed correspondence between himself and various members of the Clan. McGregor was obviously high up in the hierarchy. The correspondence was about various plans. They were plans about bombings and assassinations and hi-jackings – and we know that quite a few have been carried out.'

Sir Reginald McMillan coughed. The Prime Minister glanced at him. Sir Reginald offered a smile that was rejected, so he looked at the floor.

'Also found,' Blackburn said, 'was a notebook with various addresses, including the address of a local garage workshop. Also found were invoices from various specialist libraries and bookshops, all of which were rather unusual. Included were the National Technical Information Service of the U.S. Department of Commerce, the U.S. Atomic Energy Commission, the Science Reference Library of Chancery Lane, and the Office of Technical Services. A subsequent investigation of the local garage workshop revealed various books

– all openly available from the sources I've just named and all filled with unclassified and declassified – but extremely dangerous – information. Amongst these books were both volumes of *The Plutonium Handbook*, another book called *The Science of High Explosives* – this one written by Melvin Cook, Professor of Metallurgy and director of the Explosives Research Group at the University of Utah – and, finally, the *Source Book on Atomic Energy* and *The Los Alamos Primer*; the last one mentioned consisting of notes made during the production of the first A-bomb in Los Alamos, New Mexico, and published openly by the Atomic Energy Commission.'

'Did you say *published openly*?' Sir Reginald said.

'That's right, sir,' Blackburn said. 'These are treated as information libraries. This information, which our laboratories have already said is extremely dangerous, is either unclassified or declassified and is therefore freely available to the public. You just walk in and pay for the books and that's all there is to it.'

'I think that's scandalous,' Sir Reginald said.

The Prime Minister stared at him. Sir Reginald stared up at the speakers. The rest of the men didn't say a word; they were waiting for Blackburn.

'Anyway,' Blackburn said, 'this is interesting. Also found in that garage workshop were traces of plutonium oxide – which I'm told can be easily converted into concentrated plutonium nitrate – an electrical induction furnace, a sealed glove-box of the type used to avoid contamination, high temperature crucibles, hydrofluoric acid, oxalic acid, metallic calcium, crystalline iodine, quartz glassware, and a cylinder of argon and nitric acid – all available on the open market; all ingredients for a workable plutonium bomb.'

Blackburn let this sink in. None of the men in the boardroom spoke. Finally, after what seemed a long time, Barker asked him a question.

'What does all this mean?' Barker said. 'It doesn't mean they could make it.'

'Yes, it does,' Blackburn said. 'All the information needed to put those materials together into a working bomb can actually be found in the books I've named – and the bomb could be made with that equipment. According to our lab boys, any particularly complicated calculations could be done simply by using hired computer time with any legitimate computer firm. The computer operative, probably innocent, would be shown nothing other than a set of partial differential equations and a written request for a particular programme to be run; the operative therefore wouldn't have a clue what it was for. Also, suitable explosive lenses are now commercially available just about anywhere; and the initiator and other materials can be bought over the counter from any university supply firm. In short, they could have, and appear to have made their plutonium bomb.'

Dalton gave a low whistle. Turner wiped sweat from his brow. Sir Reginald coughed into his right fist while the Under-Secretary stared at him. The Prime Minister was immobile. He simply stared up at the speakers. Ricketts turned his head and looked across at Barker as he started to speak.

'Okay,' Barker said. 'So they made their damned bomb. But could they actually test it without setting it off?'

'Dead easy,' Blackburn said. 'A piece of pie, really. They only have to test the detonating circuits for simultaneity, and the equipment for this is also available commercially. Apart from ordinary metering equipment, this would comprise a double beam oscilloscope with long stay traces, a pulse height analyser, and an accurate recording digital timer – all available commercially. My lab boys tell me that they've previously come across arming devices made from cooker timers and second-hand servo-motors, and that the detonation circuits can actually be linked to a device known to every Post Office engineer – an arrangement which allows detonation of the bomb by telephone on any line using STD codes. So they could have – and probably have – tested their plutonium bomb.'

Turner sat down in a chair and covered his face with his hands. The Prime Minister looked at him and then glanced across at Sir Reginald. The Chairman seemed shocked. He was staring harshly at the Under-Secretary. The Under-Secretary was looking down at the floor, his brow creased in thought.

'I can't believe it,' Sir Reginald said. 'I can't believe my own ears. I am told that the materials and the instructions for an Atom bomb are freely available to the general public. I find the whole thing appalling.'

The Under-Secretary didn't reply. He shuffled some papers on his knees. He glanced once at the Prime Minister, but the Prime Minister was staring at the speakers.

'Any more?' Barker said.

'A bit more,' Blackburn said. 'We traced the names that we found in McGregor's notebook and we managed to find some. A few are in prison, a few have disappeared, and a fair amount are working on the oil rigs. I assume that's your problem.'

Turner uncovered his face. He looked up at Sir Reginald. Sir Reginald was leaning back in his chair, staring up at the ceiling. Barker looked across at Turner. Turner noticed him and nodded. Barker glanced first at Ricketts, then at Dalton, then he started to speak again.

'Yes,' he said, 'that's our problem. It's a very big problem. I'm classifying this whole item top secret and I want it to stay that way.'

'Right,' Blackburn said.

'Put a seal right across it.'

'I will,' Blackburn said. 'It's as good as done. Will there be anything else?'

'No,' Barker said. 'Nothing else. That's enough for one evening.'

'Best of luck,' Blackburn said.

The line went dead. Barker put the phone back. He turned around and stared into space, and then he just shrugged his shoulders.

'That's it,' he said quietly.

They all sat there in silence. Someone coughed and someone sighed. They heard the sound of the sea around the platform, a remote, rhythmic murmuring. It was now dark outside. The platform lights were all blazing. They threw shadows across the tiered decks and reflected off the antennae. Turner climbed to his feet, wandered slowly back and forth, brushed gently past Ricketts and glanced up to see his grim, granite face. Ricketts was immobile. He simply stared into space. Dalton looked at him and then looked at Barker who was rubbing his forehead. They heard the murmuring of the sea. They heard the roar of a forklift. Men were shouting as they got on with their work, oblivious to all. Sir Reginald picked at his trousers, threw some fluff to the floor. The Under-Secretary watched the movements of his fingers and then turned away. He glanced at the Prime Minister. The Prime Minister seemed thoughtful. The Under-Secretary sat up in his chair and surveyed the whole room.

'So,' the Under-Secretary said. 'They probably have a working bomb. They may use it, but they may just be bluffing, and there's one way to find out. Are we willing to take that risk? Can we possibly afford to do so? All in all, I don't think we can risk it. There's too much at stake.'

'And if we don't?' the Prime Minister said. 'If we wait till seven-fifteen? What happens if we wait and it goes off? Can we possibly live with that?'

'It's your life at stake, Prime Minister. We don't know what they want. These men are assassins, they've killed before and will again, and of all the political targets they could find you're the biggest there is. I don't think you should do it. I don't think we should take that chance. I think we'll have to try and take that rig before they set the bomb off.'

'That's impossible,' Ricketts said.

'Why?' the Under-Secretary said.

'Because, as we've explained, they're bound to see us well before we get there. All the rigs have got radar. That means we can't use boats. They've got cameras and sonic beacons beneath the water, so we can't use submersibles. There's no way we can surprise them. It's simply out of the question. We either sit here and pray that they're bluffing or we do as they say.'

'I see,' the Under-Secretary said. 'You want to risk the Prime Minister. You're willing to risk the life of the Prime Minister on a mere speculation.'

'They're not bluffing,' Ricketts said.

'We don't know that,' the Under-Secretary said.

'And what if they're not?' the Prime Minister said. 'I don't think we can chance that.'

'You can't mean that,' the Under-Secretary said. 'You're the head of the British Government. You can't give yourself up to these terrorists in the hope that they'll spare you.'

'Is there a choice?' the Prime Minister said. 'I can't see that there's a choice. A bomb like that will finish the North

Sea, not to mention Great Britain. I don't think there's a choice. I think we'll have to go along. We'll just have to see what they want and hope it isn't my neck.'

'It's just pointless,' the Under-Secretary said. 'We've no guarantee at all. They could kill you or fly you out of there and then *still* set the bomb off.'

'We'll have to chance it,' the Prime Minister said. 'They haven't left us any option. They've got the whole of Britain in their hands and we can't let them drop it.'

'I don't care,' the Under-Secretary said. 'I still think it's a futile gesture. Once you're there, there's not a thing we can do – and they can do what they want.'

'I think the Prime Minister's right,' Ricketts said. 'I don't think we have a choice. And I think we should at least get on that rig and find out just what's cooking.'

'And then what?' the Under-Secretary said. 'What if that's all they want? What happens if all they want is to kill the Prime Minister? What good if they're going to set the bomb off anyway?'

'I take your point,' Ricketts said. 'But we still don't have a choice. And at least, if we get on that rig, we might be able to do something.'

'*Do* something, Ricketts?'

'That's right, sir, do something. It's a long shot, but at least we'll be aboard and that does count for something. I might be able to get away. I don't know how, but I might. I might be able to disappear long enough to find out where the bomb is. If I do, I can dismantle it. I know how these things operate. I can make sure it won't work again and then we'll take it from there.'

'They'll kill you,' Dalton said.

'At least they won't have their bomb. And if they don't have their bomb, then the only thing they have is the rig.'

'They'll kill you,' Dalton repeated. 'They'll kill you and the Prime Minister. If you take their bomb apart they're going to kill you. I'm certain of that.'

'It's our only chance,' Ricketts said. 'It's our only possible hope. It's a long shot, but it's the only one we've got so we might as well take it.'

'It's suicide,' the Under-Secretary said. 'Either way, it's just suicide.'

'It's a chance,' Ricketts said.

The Prime Minister looked at him. It was a hard and searching look. The Prime Minister saw a rough worker's face, a pair of grey, ruthless eyes. He saw that Ricketts was looking back. He saw no sign of intimidation. He saw intelligence and a growing frustration and a fierce, burning anger. There were no other exits. There were no escape routes. While they talked the bomb was ticking away and the future was shrinking. The Prime Minister didn't like it. He didn't really want to do it. He looked at Ricketts and he wondered what would happen if they waited it out. The bomb might go off. The oil fields would be destroyed. His own future, and the future of Britain, would go down with the rigs. There were no other exits. There were no escape routes. He looked at Ricketts and he saw that granite face and he knew it was madness.

'We've no choice,' the Prime Minister said.

CHAPTER NINE

THE black sky was all around them. Below was nothing but darkness. The helicopter rose and fell on the wind as it headed for Beryl Field. Ricketts was at the controls with Barker sitting beside him. The Prime Minister, sitting behind them, coughed lightly and then gave a loud sigh. He glanced down towards the sea. He saw a dark, vitreous void. He heard the roar of the helicopter and he shivered with fatigue and some nervousness. He didn't like to look down there. It was the black vale of a dream. They were fifteen-hundred feet above the sea, but they still couldn't see it. The Prime Minister shivered again. He felt the tingling of his nerves. Mixed with fear was a certain sly excitement, a child's ultimate disbelief. It all seemed too incredible, too bizarre to be real. The situation, which in fact was quite fearful, was also out of a comic book. The Prime Minister glanced around him. He saw the black void everywhere. There was no moon, but he did see the clouds as deeper stains on the darkness. He shivered once more, felt excitement and tension. The helicopter suddenly dropped down and lurched and then it rose up again.

'Are we close?' the Prime Minister asked.

'Yes, we're close,' Ricketts said. 'We should be seeing their lights any minute now. We'll be going down soon.'

'What time is it?' the Prime Minister asked.

'Eighteen fifty hours,' Barker said.

'Ten minutes,' the Prime Minister said. 'I trust they'll feel pleased.'

Ricketts didn't reply. His brain was racing with possibilities. He was exploring Charlie 2 in his head and trying to think of a way out. He wondered where they would be held, wondered where the bomb was hidden, wondered if he could make his escape and stay out of sight long enough. It wouldn't take long to dismantle it; the time spent would be in

92

searching. He had to elude his captors long enough to locate and destroy the bomb. Yet what if he succeeded? What would happen then? He tried to think of a way of escaping, but he just couldn't figure it. There was Barker and the Prime Minister. He had to think of them as well. He simply couldn't dismantle the bomb and run away and leave them trapped with the terrorists. His head was racing as he thought this. His eyes were scanning the black sky. He looked down and saw some distant, winking lights, and he knew they were close.

'That's it,' Barker said.

'Yes,' Ricketts said, 'I see it.'

'I feel trapped,' Barker said. 'I feel useless. What the hell can we do?'

The Prime Minister looked ahead and saw the distant, winking lights. They were pinpoints of light in a black void, stars swimming in outer space. There was something chilling in that sight, something awesomely mysterious. The Prime Minister suddenly felt quite alone, floating free in the cosmos. He blinked and licked his lips, felt excitement and dread, felt his worldly skin falling away, revealing something more naked. It was not all that uncomfortable. It softened his dread with curiosity. He felt totally dislocated from his past, felt a strange incandescence. It wasn't himself watching the lights. It was the young man he had been. He suddenly felt a cold, competitive rage against the men on that rig. They had to beat them somehow. They had to deprive them of victory. His own future, and the future of his country, was what hung in the balance.

'I'm going down now,' Ricketts said.

'I'm glad,' the Prime Minister said. 'I want to get this over and done with. I don't like not knowing.'

He saw the lights in the distance. They were pinpoints in the void. He wondered where the moon was and then he saw some nearby clouds and then he saw the moonlight stippling the water. The Prime Minister strained to see. He felt a strange, calm acceptance. The helicopter, shaking visibly, dropped lower and he saw Charlie 2. There was no coherent shape. There was a pyramid of lights. The lights seemed to be floating in the sky above the moon in the water. The water was very dark. It was a black, alluvial pit. The lights of

Charlie 2 shone out above it, danced and jumped in the lapping waves. The Prime Minister blinked his eyes. The helicopter dropped lower. He had a vision of the lights of Manhattan, sweeping out, soaring skywards. It was singularly beautiful. It almost took his breath away. He looked down and saw the silhouetted derricks, the black mat of the platform.

'There they are,' Ricketts said. 'The bastards are waiting. Now let's find out what's happening.'

The helicopter turned around. It started to fall down towards the rig. The Prime Minister looked down at the landing pad, a large circle of bright lights. And now he saw the whole rig, saw the derricks and the modules, saw a quiltwork of shadow and light, of stark black and white brilliance. There were dots in that mosaic. They were moving back and forth. They took shape and became human beings and surrounded the landing pad. The helicopter shuddered. The lights swam up above them. Far below, way below the landing pad, was the dark, swirling water. The helicopter dropped lower. Three massive derricks towered above it. It dropped down and touched lightly on the deck and then came to a halt.

'Here we go,' Barker said.

The men surrounded them on all sides, were all wearing ordinary overalls, were all holding light automatic rifles and Sten guns and pistols. The lights washed across their faces. The faces looked white and featureless. Ricketts moved towards the door and they moved in, encircling the helicopter. The Prime Minister hesitated. He saw the surrounding white faces. Beyond them were the bright lights on the derricks, the stark, jet-black shadows. He saw Ricketts opening the door. Ricketts didn't hesitate. He jumped out and was followed by Barker as a cold wind rushed in. The Prime Minister stood up, felt as if he were dreaming, bent low and walked across to the door and looked down at the landing pad. The terrorists were all around him. They had weapons, but they seemed ordinary. The Prime Minister took a deep breath and jumped down and then stood beside Ricketts.

'Right,' Ricketts said. 'Where's McGregor?'

One of the terrorists stepped forward. He grabbed hold of Ricketts' shoulder. He jerked Ricketts around, threw him against the helicopter and then kicked his two legs apart. Ricketts put his hands up. He offered no sign of resistance. The terrorist ran his hands up and down Ricketts' body, then he stepped back and motioned to Barker.

'Okay,' he said. 'You next.'

Barker faced the helicopter. He put his hands above his head. He put his legs out and then glanced at Ricketts who had not moved a muscle. The terrorist frisked him. He did it quickly and professionally. He stepped back and then looked at the Prime Minister and nodded his head.

'You too,' he said quietly.

The Prime Minister straightened his shoulders. He stared straight at the terrorist. He pursed his lips and put his hands behind his back and then glowered ferociously.

'I am the Prime Minister of Great Britain,' he said. 'I do not carry weapons.'

The terrorist raised his Sten gun. It was aimed at the Prime Minister. 'I don't give a fuck,' he said clearly. 'Put your hands on that chopper.'

The Prime Minister bristled. He turned his face to the helicopter. He was frisked and then the terrorist stepped away and said, 'Right, turn around.' They all did as they were told. They saw the terrorists on all sides. The wind moaned and they saw the stark shadows on the steel of the deck.

'Where's McGregor?' Ricketts asked.

'In the radio hut,' the terrorist said.

'I know where it is,' Ricketts said. 'Are we going there now?'

'Right now. After you.'

The terrorist motioned with his Sten gun, the surrounding men made a path for them, and Ricketts, followed by Barker and the Prime Minister, walked towards the steel catwalk. The Prime Minister glanced around him. The barrels of the guns were pointing at him. He felt a tension that wasn't quite fear; more a heightened awareness. Ricketts was mounting the catwalk. Armed terrorists were walking ahead of him. Barker followed up his rear and then the Prime Minister stepped forward and felt the blast of an icy, numbing wind. He followed Barker across the catwalk. He glanced down and felt dizzy. The surging sea was two-hundred feet below, a dark pit flecked with silver lights. He took a deep breath, gripped the railings more tightly. There was nothing on either side but the sea and the sky, both black, both making strange lonesome sounds. The Prime Minister stopped once. He felt a gun probe his spine. He moved forward again, walking carefully down the catwalk, and finally found himself standing on the main deck, beside Ricketts and Barker.

'Keep going,' the leading terrorist said. 'You're not here for the scenery.'

The terrorists formed a circle around them as they walked across the main deck. There were more terrorists standing along the modules, looking on with some interest. Someone laughed and someone shouted. The remark was obviously derisory. They kept walking past the huge tanks and derricks, under cranes and catwalks. The deck was slippery underfoot, filmed with mud and oil, and they either walked through the dazzling brightness of the floodlights or through a stark, blinding blackness. It was very quiet here. The drilling floor had been silenced. They heard the wind and the murmuring of the sea, their boots banging on metal.

They came to a steel ladder. It led up to another deck. Some of the terrorists climbed up, Ricketts and Barker promptly followed, and then the Prime Minister himself did the same. It was a vertical climb, he wasn't used to such exercise, and when he reached the top he found himself gasping, felt the strain on his muscles. He saw that Barker was grinning at him. He saw that Ricketts' eyes were roaming. Following Ricketts' gaze, he saw the radio hut on the deck's right-hand corner. The front door was open, a bright light was pouring out, and there was a man silhouetted in the doorway, surrounded by bodyguards.

'Is that McGregor?' the Prime Minister asked.

'Yes,' Ricketts said.

'He obviously has a flair for theatrics,' the Prime Minister said.

They all walked across the deck. They stepped into the bright light. McGregor, unarmed, was in the doorway, a grin on his face.

'Hello, Ricketts,' he said.

'Hello, McGregor,' Ricketts said.

'Have I surprised you?'

'Yes, McGregor, you've surprised me. I just never suspected.'

McGregor's grin was not good-humoured. His brown eyes were obsessive. They flicked quickly from Ricketts to Barker, back across to the Prime Minister. McGregor studied the Prime Minister. The Prime Minister was unflinching. The Prime Minister's well-fed face was florid, but the blue eyes were steely. McGregor turned away, motioned the three of them inside, and they brushed past him and went into the radio hut which was small, bright and sweltering. McGregor stepped in after them. Two armed bodyguards were with him. One of them closed the door, the other moved up beside him, and the both of them levelled their Sten guns at the three waiting men. McGregor grinned and sat down. He was sitting beside the radio. He looked at his prisoners and he kept the tight grin on his face.

'I thought I'd make the radio hut my headquarters,' he said. 'Particularly since we'd so much to talk about.'

Ricketts didn't smile. 'All right,' he said. 'You've got us here, so just tell me one thing: Is there really a bomb?'

'Aye,' McGregor said.

'Where?' Ricketts said.

'Where do you think?' McGregor said. 'In a pontoon leg. Just like the first one.'

'Which leg?' Barker asked.

'Dinnae be daft,' McGregor said. 'You think I'd be dumb enough to tell you? Ask me another.'

'Would you really use it?' the Prime Minister said.

'Aye, Prime Minister,' McGregor said.

'You must be mad,' Barker said.

'No, I'm not. And damned well you know it.'

He suddenly stopped grinning. His dark eyes flashed at them. He looked at each one of them in turn, then looked directly at Ricketts.

'You're well armed,' Ricketts said.

'Aye, we are that. All the weapons came from Ireland via the States and the Middle East, and we just shipped them aboard as per normal.'

'Very neat,' Ricketts said.

'It took a long time,' McGregor said. 'It was eighteen months before we had our sixty men on board. We shipped the weapons in over the past three months.'

'And the bomb?'

'Easy. It's only the size of a tea-chest. It was shipped in in some crates containin' radio equipment, and stored as per normal in the storage space. A lot of my men were on the night-shift. They often had to check the pontoon legs. One night last week they simply took it out of storage and winched it down one of the pontoon legs. It's now restin' on a girder halfway down – and it's ready to go.'

He grinned at the three of them. They just stood there and looked at him. The floor was undulating from side to side, very slowly, hypnotically. Barker glanced at Ricketts. Ricketts was looking at McGregor. The Prime Minister coughed into one hand and McGregor looked up.

'What are your demands?' the Prime Minister said.

'I speak for the Clan,' McGregor said. 'I want you to understand that. These demands are on behalf of the People's Army for the Liberation of Scotland.'

'I don't wish to hear that nonsense,' the Prime Minister said. 'I just want your demands.'

'All right,' McGregor said. 'We want one million pounds sterling. We want four of our men out of jail. It's as simple as that.'

'What men?' the Prime Minister said.

'You mean you agree to the money?'

'I haven't said that,' the Prime Minister said. 'Now who are these men?'

'Dan MacKinnon,' McGregor said. 'William Burns and Robbie Turner. And last, but no' the least, Malcolm Ross.'

The Prime Minister looked at him. It was a hard, searching look. McGregor, to his credit, stared back, with just the hint of a smile.

'That's rather a large demand,' the Prime Minister said.

'Aye, Prime Minister, it is.'

'Those are your four most important men. It's taken a lot of time to find them. Besides which, I very seriously doubt that I could order their release.'

'Yes, you can, Prime Minister. You can dream up an excuse. They're political prisoners, there's already doubt that you can hold 'em, and we want 'em to be pardoned and set free. We won't settle for less.'

'It's impossible,' the Prime Minister said.

'Nothing's impossible,' McGregor said. 'We don't care what you say to the public; we just want their release.'

'I can't do it,' the Prime Minister said.

'Yes, you can,' McGregor said. 'They're in prison awaitin' trial. Their guilt hasn't been proved yet. They haven't actually been tried yet, your evidence hasn't been broadcast, so you can say that the evidence was all circumstantial and wouldn't have held up in court.'

'That will make fools of our intelligence.'

'That's part of our general plan.'

'And the million pounds. You want me to give you a million pounds so you can finance more terror?'

'Aye, Prime Minister, that's right. That's just what we want.'

The Prime Minister stared at him. The Prime Minister's eyes were cold. The Prime Minister scratched his chin with one hand and gazed down at the floor.

'And what then?' he said. 'You've already done all the damage. I can't see us recovering from the public knowledge that all this has happened.'

'That's right,' Barker said. 'You've done too much already. We'll lose international confidence when this gets out, and that will finish the North Sea.'

'It won't be public,' McGregor said. 'It dinnae have to be public. If you give us what we want, we'll pull out – and we won't even mention it. You just keep it quiet. The oil companies put out a statement. They say the loss of Eagle 3 was due to a sea-quake that also stretched as far as Charlie 2. It destroyed Eagle 3 completely. It devastated Charlie 2. You say most of the crew on Charlie 2 were killed and will have to be replaced. Naturally we'll be gone. You simply bring the new crew in. They'll take over and they'll never know this happened – nor will anyone else.'

'To your advantage,' the Prime Minister said.

'That's right,' McGregor said. 'We'll stay quiet as long as our men stay out of prison. We'll only talk if you touch 'em.'

The Prime Minister looked at him. He tapped his chin with his fingers. He pursed his lips and his shoulders were slumped, but he seemed very steady. The hut swayed from side to side. It was a slow motion; dreamlike. McGregor sat in his chair by the radio, looking at all of them.

'Okay,' Barker said. 'What if we agree? What guarantee do we have that the Prime Minister will then be released?'

'You have my word,' McGregor said.

'That would hardly be acceptable.'

'There'd be no reason to kill 'im,' McGregor said. 'It just wouldn't make sense.'

'Why not?' Barker said. 'Why the sudden display of sense? The Clan is notable for its killing of politicians, so why not the Prime Minister?'

'Because there's limits,' McGregor said. 'There's just so far you can go. Whether you like it or not there's a lot of British support for us, and most of it comes from the workin' classes. It's true we kill politicians. It's equally true that it's not haphazard. We select the targets carefully and we never hit men who're too popular.'

'I'm popular?' the Prime Minister said.

'Not particularly,' McGregor said. 'But they'd be outraged if we killed their Prime Minister. They'd think it was too much.'

'So,' Barker said, 'you let him go. That still leaves the bomb.'

'We wouldn't use it,' McGregor said. 'We'd be cuttin' our own throats. Bear in mind that the Clan are fightin' for an independent Scotland and rights of ownership on all oil in Scottish waters. Is it therefore in our own interests to destroy those same oil fields and lose the very thing we've been fightin' for? No, Barker, it isn't. It just dinnae make sense. We'll do it if there's no other way, but we'd rather avoid it. As for killin' the Prime Minister, it wouldn't do anything but turn the whole of Britain against us.'

'Then why demand his presence in the first place?'

'Yer smart,' McGregor said.

'I want an answer,' Barker said.

'Aye,' McGregor said, 'an' your going to get one – but yer not gonna like it.'

He glanced at each of them in turn. He wasn't smiling at all. He glanced briefly at the guards near the door and then he turned back to Barker.

'I thought you'd have guessed that the Clan couldn't have financed an operation of this size on its own. I won't give you the details, but I can tell you that we were approached by the spokesman for some overseas backers who wanted us to kill the Prime Minister. He didn't say why an' we didn't ask too many questions. We only had one meeting with this single representative, and he wouldn't say who his bosses were. He just said they were a group. He also said their funds were limitless. But since they specifically wanted the killing done during this visit to the oil fields, I think it's safe to assume they've some interests here.'

Barker felt a sudden chill. It was sliding down his spine. He was shocked by this fresh revelation, by the thickening plot. He felt the chill again. It was the chill of mute terror. What form of security could handle this monstrous conspiracy? He glanced across at Ricketts, saw the frozen granite features. Ricketts stood there and studied McGregor with a veiled curiosity. The Prime Minister hadn't moved, had merely furrowed his brow, was now scratching at his chin with one hand in unconscious bewilderment.

'Anyway,' McGregor said, 'this group wanted the whole thing to look like the act of a radical terrorist group; they didn't want it to be connected to anyone outside the U.K. They wanted the Clan to do the job. They wanted the Clan to take the blame. In return, they would finance the whole operation and pay a separate fee of two million pounds.'

He smiled a little at Barker. It was a tight, unfriendly smile. Barker simply stared down at the floor as if not quite believing it.

'Now,' McGregor continued, 'we'd no intention of killin' the Prime Minister and turnin' the whole of Britain against us – but we *did* need that money and we *did* want our men out of jail. We therefore accepted the job, receivin' full finance for the operation – and with the two million pound fee to be paid later. The first half of that fee was due to be paid in Aberdeen the minute you all stepped aboard this rig.'

'I don't get that,' Barker said. 'How would your backers know that the Prime Minister had actually boarded this rig? If the Prime Minister had never left Bravo 1, you could still *say* he had.'

'Because,' McGregor said, 'one of the men at the Prime

Minister's conference, one of yer men on Bravo 1, is actually in the employ of our backers. He'll know the Prime Minister's come here. He'll know everything that's happened. Right now, by private radio, he should be contacting the mainland and arrangin' for the money to be passed over. When my man rings through to say that it's been done, I'm to kill the Prime Minister.'

'But you won't,' Barker said.

'No,' McGregor said. 'And I've already told you why. I'm not gonna become a pawn in their game. The Clan hasn't forgotten that Scotland, at the moment, is useless without commerce with England; this again means that it's in our own interest to avoid doing anything *that* drastic. I dinnae know who our backers are, but totally alienating the British public is something I wouldn't do for their benefit. They offered two million pounds. I want you to offer more. Your million plus their million makes up my two million – but I also want our men out of jail.'

'You simply used them,' Barker said.

'That's right, I simply used them. They financed this whole operation and gave me my leverage.'

'So,' Barker said, 'if we give you what you want, the Prime Minister will go free and the oil fields will remain as they are.'

'That's right,' McGregor said. 'I want the million pounds in cash by tomorrow evenin'. I want the free pardons announced in the evenin' papers. After that, when the Prime Minister is officially due to fly back anyway, he can do so as if nothin' happened.'

'Wrong,' Barker said. 'There's no way we can possibly keep this quiet.'

'Why not?' McGregor said. 'The few survivors from Eagle 3 – apart from Ricketts here – dinnae even know that it was bombed. As a matter of interest, Ricketts, how many were there?'

'Me,' Ricketts said. 'And one other.'

'And does *he* know it was bombed?'

'No. He only knows it went down.'

'Right,' McGregor said. 'So that takes care of Eagle 3. As for this rig, there's only two of the original crew left – and I'm sure you can persuade 'em to keep their mouths shut. So, as I said, you announce that a sea-quake destroyed Eagle 3 and then travelled as far as here, where it almost destroyed the rig and killed twenty of your eighty man crew. That's yer official press release. It'll go down a treat. Then, when my men leave, you temporarily shut the rig down – for repairs, as it were – and then after a decent interval you put a whole new crew on board and work can proceed as per normal. No one but yourselves, and those jokers in your boardroom, will have the slightest idea that it ever happened.'

'And your mysterious backers?' Barker said. 'What about them? Wouldn't their man on Bravo 1 let the news out to make up for their loss?'

'No,' McGregor said. 'The bastard wouldn't dare do it. If the group he works for let the cat out of the bag they'd immediately expose themselves as the real villains. After all, *they're* the only other ones who could know. No, Barker, they won't do that. They'll burn with rage and they'll hate my guts – aye, they'll do that – but they'll just have to keep their mouths shut.'

'And your own men, McGregor? Won't *they* talk?'

'No,' McGregor said.

'We're talking about sixty men, McGregor.'

'They won't talk,' McGregor said. 'They have reasons beyond our discipline. As long as they aren't touched by yer security they'll keep their mouths shut. Your knowledge of who they are is what you've always got over 'em; their own silence is their guarantee of freedom. You have us by the balls and we have you by the cock – it's a draw.'

There was silence for a long time. They were trying to take it in. Barker felt as if he'd been on a jury and was pondering the evidence. The whole plot was very complex, was intricate and widespread; he tried to find a loophole and gave in, suddenly feeling exhausted. Then he looked across at Ricketts, almost sensed what Ricketts was thinking, felt that Ricketts was thinking of Bravo 1, of that aware, unknown enemy. Which one of them was it? Who the hell could it have been? Who the hell could have set up all this while being one of their own? Barker shivered with fatigue, felt old and strangely anguished. He looked around at the Prime Minister and saw that he was shocked and outraged. The Prime Minister was a tough man – the past hours had shown that much – yet tough as he was he was breaking into shocked disbelief. The Prime Minister returned his gaze. He then looked at McGregor. His blue eyes, with their cold, shrewd intelligence, were drowning in anger.

'I won't agree,' he said harshly. 'I think the price is too high. I will not release your men and sit back while they organize more of this. Nor will I give you money. I will not finance the Clan. To capitulate will just be a sign that you can do it again. Well, I won't do it. Nothing you say will make me do it. There are limits and I think you've just reached them: you won't go any further.'

'I will,' McGregor said.

'I don't think so,' the Prime Minister said. 'You said yourself that you depend on the North Sea. I don't think you'll destroy it.'

The minute he said it he felt horror, realized how wrong he was; he looked into the growing rage of McGregor's eyes and saw the truth of fanaticism. McGregor was getting out of his chair, was walking up to the Prime Minister. When he reached him, he looked directly at him with his eyes burning fiercely. He grabbed the Prime Minister by the collar and pulled him roughly towards him. His eyes were dark and they burned with that obsession that knows no normal boundaries.

'I'll do it!' McGregor hissed. 'Believe me, mister, I'll do it! I'll do anything that puts you bastards down, even if I go with you!'

He threw the Prime Minister aside, snatched a pistol from the table, pushed the two guards aside, kicked the door open, and walked out to the deck.

'Bring the bastards out here!' he bawled.

One of the guards grabbed the Prime Minister and threw him out through the door. He nodded curtly at Ricketts and Barker, and they both stepped outside. They were standing in the hut's light. The lights above blazed through darkness. The lights dazzled their eyes and they blinked and then they saw the survivors. It was Griffith and Sutton, the geologist and the driller, both on their knees on the deck, surrounded by terrorists. Sutton was badly beaten; his face was bruised and he was weeping. Griffith, kneeling beside him, was untouched, but his eyes shone with fear. McGregor didn't waste any time. He grabbed Griffith by the hair. He jerked his head back, put the pistol to his temple, and then glanced around wildly at the Prime Minister. The Prime Minister stepped forward. Two of the guards dragged him back. They twisted his arms behind his back and held him there while he looked on in horror.

'No!' the Prime Minister cried. 'No, McGregor. *For God's sake, you can't—*'

His voice was cut off by the explosion. Griffith's head split in two. His body jerked like a puppet on a string and then collapsed to the deck.

'*Do you believe me?*' McGregor hissed.

He whirled around and grabbed Sutton. He jerked Sutton's head back. Sutton shrieked and the Prime Minister cried, 'No!' and then the gun fired again. Sutton arched and hit the deck. His body shuddered and then was still. The blood dribbled from the shadows where his head was and touched the Prime Minister's feet. The Prime Minister started sagging. The guards pulled him back up. He shook his head from side to side as if dazed, and started shaking all over. McGregor walked up to him. His eyes were bright and obsessed. He waved the gun in front of the Prime Minister's face as if wanting to hit him.

'Do you believe me?' he hissed. 'Do you believe me? *Is that enough for yer conscience?*'

The Prime Minister did not reply. He simply gasped and shook his head. Barker bit his lower lip and Ricketts clenched both his fists as the two bodies were thrown overboard. They couldn't hear the splash. The sea was too far below. They glanced down and saw the blood on the deck, seeping out of the shadows. The Prime Minister shuddered. Barker continued biting his lip. Ricketts clenched both his fists and looked around him and fought to control himself. The huge derricks towered above him. The lights climbed up to the stars. He dropped his gaze when he felt the gun barrel sticking into his ribs. He was pushed back to the hut. He saw Barker and the Prime Minister. The Prime Minister was shuddering in the chair and Barker stood close beside him. Ricketts had to turn away. He saw McGregor in the door. McGregor told him they had one hour to decide, then he slammed the door shut.

CHAPTER TEN

THE Prime Minister raised his head and looked at them with shocked eyes. He shuddered and then he controlled himself and sat up in the chair. He covered his face with his hands, took a couple of deep breaths, removed his hands from his face, placed them lightly on his knees and looked at them as if praying for clemency.

'My fault,' he said softly. 'So stupid. God forgive me for that.'

'It wasn't your fault,' Ricketts said. 'I think he wanted to do it anyway. I think he wanted to put on a show, and he used you for that.'

The Prime Minister shook his head. 'I can't believe it,' he said. 'Like animals. They were shot down like animals. You always think men can't do that.'

'They can do it,' Ricketts said. 'They've been doing it for centuries. Let's forget it. Let's talk about something else. We've got one hour to stop it.'

'Stop it?' Barker said. 'How the hell can we stop it? We're locked in and they won't let us out. We just say yes or no.'

'Wrong,' Ricketts said. 'That bastard made one mistake. Of all the places on the rig to lock us up in, he picked the wrong one.'

Barker looked at him sharply. He then looked around the hut. The one window had a solid metal covering which the terrorists had locked.

'We can get *out*?' Barker said.

'That's right,' Ricketts said. 'We can get out. What happens then, I don't know.'

He looked down at the Prime Minister. The Prime Minister was looking at him. The Prime Minister's blue eyes were clearer, and he seemed to be steadying.

'Are you all right?' Ricketts said.

'Yes, lad, I'm all right. I don't feel good, but that can be lived with. Apart from that, I'm all right.'

'They forgot something,' Ricketts said. 'They probably don't even know about it. This hut has a trapdoor in the floor, practically under your feet.'

The Prime Minister glanced down. He saw nothing but solid steel. He looked back between his legs, under the console, and he saw a steel plate. He looked back up at Ricketts.

'That's it,' Ricketts said. 'It leads down to the drilling floor. This hut's above one corner of that floor, well away from the moonpool. The corner's filled with large crates. They're filled with spare parts and antennae. If anything goes wrong with this communications unit, the spare parts are passed up through that trapdoor. We can get down to that floor. The packing crates will give us cover. That corner of the floor rests on top of a pontoon leg, and an exit door leads out to the catwalk. Ladders run down the pontoon legs. They run straight down to the sea. I happen to know that there's a supply barge anchored beside the rig, and since they always unload from this side that's where it will be. We can climb down the pontoon leg. There'll be no one in the barge. If we go down the inside of the leg, there's no way we'll be seen.'

'And once there,' Barker said. 'What happens then? Do we just hide and wait?'

'No,' Ricketts said. 'We don't have to do that. The barges are towed out by small boats, so we'll take one of those. They're not fast, but they'll do. We'll have to time it pretty well. McGregor's left the radio open to let us ring Bravo 1 because he thinks we can't get away anyway. So, we'll ring Bravo 1. We'll tell them to send a helicopter. We'll tell it to hover about five miles from here and be ready to pick us up from the boat. It's not much, but it's something.'

'We can't just leave,' the Prime Minister said. 'I don't think we should do that.'

'The bomb,' Barker said.

'That's right,' Ricketts said. 'We have to dismantle the bomb and kill their radar and cameras. If we manage that, we can return. We can launch an assault on this rig. With their cameras out of action, we can come under the sea and get to the rig before they see us. In short, we have to leave them paralysed.'

'It's impossible,' Barker said. 'It can't be done. We don't know where the bomb is.'

'I think I do,' Ricketts said. 'I think McGregor said too much. He said the bomb was inside a pontoon leg – halfway down a pontoon leg.'

'You're going to search for it?' Barker said.

'That's right,' Ricketts said. 'The support legs are hollow, they're laced with steel ladders, and if I don't find the bomb in the first leg I'll climb through to the next.'

'You haven't time,' Barker said. 'There are *four* main pontoon legs. Those legs are a quarter mile apart. You haven't time to check all of them.'

'I won't have to,' Ricketts said. 'At least I might, but I doubt it. I think the bomb is on this side of the rig, and probably right down below us. McGregor's made this hut his headquarters. He wants to be near the radio. I suspect he'd automatically place the bomb in the leg nearest to him. There's another reason for thinking this. The off-loading is done this side. When McGregor brought the bomb aboard, whether it was well hidden or not, I think he would have wanted it stored in the nearest available spot. The closest spot is beneath this hut; it's the first storage space you come to. Come to think of it, he said that the bomb was packed with some radio spares – and all the radio spares are stored beneath this hut. I think that's where the bomb is. I'm almost sure of it. I think the bomb's hidden in the pontoon leg directly below us.'

Barker gave a low whistle. 'You might be right,' he said. 'And that just leaves the radar and cameras. How the hell can you kill them?'

'I'm not sure,' Ricketts said, 'but if I dismantle the plutonium bomb, I might be able to make more modest explosives. I suspect the terrorist bomb is an implosion type weapon, which means that the plutonium metal core is surrounded by a large quantity of ordinary, conventional high explosive.'

'You mean dynamite?'

'Yes.'

'*Sticks* of dynamite?'

'Yes. And if it's that kind of bomb – and I think it would have to be – I'll use the dynamite on the antennae and driller's room.'

'You'll never get there,' Barker said. 'The terrorists are bound to see you.'

'Will they?' Ricketts said. 'I'm not sure that they will. There are sixty terrorists aboard, they've arrived separately over three months; they all worked with the regular crew, and they all worked in shifts. Given the size of the rig, and the nature of shift work, I think it's safe to assume that one half has never seen the other half. A lot are probably meeting for the first time; a lot probably haven't even met yet. I'm in overalls and I look just like the rest, so they may not give me a second glance. True, McGregor knows me, and a lot of those men out there have seen me. But I think that those men are all stationed on this deck, so if I can manage to keep out of McGregor's way I've a fairly good chance.'

Ricketts' grey eyes were bright and held a hard, driving light. They were staring directly at Barker, and then they turned to the Prime Minister. The Prime Minister was standing up. His large body wasn't shaking. The colour had returned to his face and he gave a small smile.

'I don't believe this,' he said.

Ricketts grinned. 'It's a long shot,' he said. 'We don't really have another choice, so I think we should try it.'

'Yes,' the Prime Minister said. 'So do I.'

'There's no time,' Barker said. 'We've only fifty minutes left. That gives us time to get off this rig. There's no time for the rest.'

'You want to leave them with the bomb?'

'No, Ricketts, I don't. I just think fifty minutes is too short. There's no way you can do it.'

'If the bomb's below I can.'

'It might not be below. It might be in the leg at the other end. It might be over the other side.'

'At least we can try.'

'I agree,' the Prime Minister said. 'But what happens if you don't get off in time?'

'Then the both of you leave me.'

The Prime Minister looked at Barker. Barker shrugged and turned away. He stared at the bolted steel door and then turned back again.

'If you don't get off, they're going to find you.'

'Not before I get their bomb.'

'Then they'll kill you. They'll definitely kill you. They won't like what you've done.'

'It's the only way, Barker.'

'No. Let's call their bluff.'

'No, Barker, we can't call their bluff. You know they're not bluffing.'

Barker looked at him. He knew that Ricketts was determined. He shrugged and then he gave a small grin.

'Okay,' he said. 'Let's go.'

'Can you work the radio?' Ricketts said.

'Of course,' Barker said.

'Right. You get in touch with Bravo 1 while I remove the trapdoor. Tell them we want a helicopter. Say we want it right now. Tell them to make sure that they fly by the chart route and that they stay at low altitude all the way. We'll be in a small boat. We'll be five miles from the rig. Tell them to keep their eyes peeled because we'll want picking up. They should have the harness ready. They should search around that area. If we see them we'll send up a flare and they can come down and get us.'

'I've got it,' Barker said. 'Now what about this radio? I think we should knock this out as well.'

'No,' Ricketts said. 'They can't detect us with a radio. And we'll still need communication with the terrorists when we get back to Bravo 1.'

'*If* we get back,' Barker said.

'Yes, *if* we get back.'

They went to work. Barker turned on the radio. Ricketts crawled under the operative's console and reached out for the steel plate. It had a small, buried handle, it lay flush with the steel plate, and Ricketts tugged and the steel plate came out and he pulled it aside. It made a harsh, grating sound. The Prime Minister looked at the door. There was no sound of movement, so he assumed that they hadn't been heard. Meanwhile Barker was on the radio. He was in touch with Bravo 1. He had the volume low and they heard him whispering into the microphone. Ricketts crawled from under the console, pulled the steel plate out, stood up and wiped his hands on his overalls and then grinned at the Prime Minister. The Prime Minister was watching Barker, was listening to what he was saying. Barker was talking in nautical terms and arranging the pick-up. The Prime Minister felt strange, very bright but unreal. He looked at Ricketts as he walked across the hut and put his ear to the door. There was obviously no panic. Ricketts put his thumb up. Barker finished his conversation and turned the radio off and then joined them in the middle of the hut.

'It's all set,' he said.

Ricketts went to the table. He picked up a box of matches. He put the matches in the pocket of his overalls and then joined them again.

'All right, Prime Minister,' he said, 'now please listen carefully. Barker here knows the rig well, so he's going to guide you. You'll go through that trapdoor. You'll find a steel ladder. I want you to go down that ladder and wait at the bottom. It's about twenty feet down. You should be hidden by the crates. Barker will be going down first, and then he'll lead you out. It's pretty simple, but it's dangerous. There's a door right by the steps. It leads to the outside of the rig just beneath the main deck. That ladder drops down to a catwalk. It's on top of the pontoon leg, running down two-hundred feet to the loading barge. Don't look down or you'll get dizzy. Don't let go for a second. You'll be hanging on the outside of the pontoon leg, and the wind there is rough. The deck stretches out above you. That means the terrorists won't see you. They might see you when you jump on the loading barge, but I think it's too dark. You'll both wait for me there. Give me forty minutes from now. If, by that time, I don't show up, just get in a small boat. Barker knows how to operate them. He'll take you out about five miles. The helicopter should be hovering in that area and it'll pick you both up.'

'Fine, lad,' the Prime Minister said. 'And then what about you?'

'If I don't show up, I've been caught. You'll find out soon enough. The terrorists are bound to ring Bravo 1 and give you the good news.'

'And what can we do then?'

'You can go back to square one. You can either give in to their demands or let them blow up the rigs.'

The Prime Minister looked at him. He saw the grey, driven eyes. He looked at Barker, and Barker just nodded and they went to the console. Barker crawled under first. He slithered down through the trapdoor. He kicked until his feet found the ladder, and then his head and hands disappeared. The Prime Minister looked at Ricketts. He smiled bleakly and knelt down. He crawled under the console, put his legs through the hole, found the ladder and started lowering himself down. He looked up once at Ricketts. Ricketts was waiting to follow him down. The Prime Minister, with his eyes at floor level, glanced up and then waved.

'Good luck, lad,' he said.

He disappeared through the hole. Ricketts stood on a moment. He looked around the hut, listened carefully at the door, and then went to the console and dropped low.

He disappeared through the hole.

CHAPTER ELEVEN

RICKETTS stood on the ladder. He was just beneath the radio hut. He reached up with one hand and pulled the steel plate back over the trapdoor. It dropped back into place and Ricketts checked that it was secure. There was a chance that when McGregor entered the hut he wouldn't notice the trapdoor. Then Ricketts looked around. He saw the ceiling of the drilling floor. He was twenty feet above the floor, just above the packing crates. He looked beyond them at the large cluttered workshop, the pipes and chains of the moonpool. It was very quiet out there. There was no work going on. He saw some terrorists wandering lazily back and forth, weapons hanging down loose. They seemed very far away. Their conversation echoed dully. The lights blazed and the machinery cast great shadows that swallowed whole areas.

Ricketts climbed down the ladder. The drilling floor disappeared. The packing crates were piled high above his head when he stood on the floor. The floor rose up and fell. It was a very gentle swaying. The Prime Minister was about five feet away, standing close to the wall. There was a steel door beside him. The handle squeaked when Barker turned it. Barker winced and glanced over his shoulder and nodded at Ricketts. Ricketts nodded back. He gestured for Barker to continue. Barker slowly pulled the large handle down until it locked into place. The sound of the lock echoed. It seemed louder than it was. Ricketts turned and peered through the packing crates at the huge, silent drilling floor. None of the terrorists had noticed. They continued wandering back and forth. They moved in and out of shadow, talking lazily, bored by their vigil. Ricketts turned back towards Barker, saw him pull the door open. He stepped outside and waved to the Prime Minister, and the Prime Minister followed him. Ricketts waited till they had gone. He checked the drilling floor again. There was no sign that anyone had noticed, so he walked through the door.

He was slapped by an icy wind. The wind beat and moaned around him. He was on the catwalk of a circular deck that was thirty feet wide. It was the top of a pontoon leg. The main deck loomed above it. The leg plunged two-hundred feet to the sea where reflected lights danced. It was dark on the catwalk. The surrounding night was black with clouds. The wind moaned and rushed in from the sea and he heard the waves hammering. They were smashing against the pontoon leg. The leg groaned and reverberated. Ricketts turned around and closed the door behind him, making sure it was locked.

'I can't do it,' the Prime Minister said. He was looking down through the catwalk. He was looking at the ladder that was fixed to the huge leg and dropped vertically two-hundred feet to the sea. It just plunged straight down. It was totally exposed to the elements. He would have to climb down two-hundred feet, and he just couldn't face it.

'Don't look,' Ricketts hissed. 'Just forget it. Just get on and climb down.'

The wind howled around the catwalk, whipped the Prime Minister's grey hair. The Prime Minister was holding on to the railing and shivering with cold. He was looking down at Robert Barker. Barker was already on the ladder. He was hanging in an all-embracing darkness with nothing below him.

'*Get down!*' Ricketts hissed.

He grabbed the Prime Minister's shoulder, shook him violently and pushed him down. The Prime Minister blinked his eyes and licked his lips and then murmured, 'Oh, God!' He turned his back to the sea, took hold of the railings, put his right foot on the step just above Barker's head, and Barker started to descend and he followed him. Ricketts watched him go down. He was going down very slowly. He was hanging in a black, howling void without shape or dimension. The sea wasn't really visible. The darkness just fell down and deepened. The grey head of the Prime Minister was bobbing in the middle of nothing. The wind howled around the ladder. Ricketts heard the ladder rattling. He looked down and saw the head disappearing, saw it melting in darkness.

Ricketts dropped to one knee. He was kneeling in front of another trapdoor. He grabbed the handle and pulled the door open and looked down a black pit. The pit had no bottom. The darkness rumbled and echoed. The pit, which was the interior of the large pontoon leg, was circular and thirty feet wide. Ricketts lowered himself in. The icy air clamped around him. His right foot kicked the side and found the ladder, then his other foot followed. He climbed down a bit lower, reached out for a switch. He turned the lights on and looked down and saw the dizzying depths.

The pontoons were filled with water. The water rose halfway up the leg. It was splashing up and down as the tapering leg swayed from side to side. The circular wall was webbed with ladders. They plunged down below the water. They seemed to taper off into single lines before they finally disappeared. Ricketts almost stopped breathing, felt dizzy and claustrophobic. The water outside the leg made a hollow drumming sound; the water inside, in that shadowed pit below, splashed and sent up its echoes. Ricketts looked to his right, saw a black, three-foot hole. It was the entrance to one of the support legs, and it echoed as well. Ricketts looked into that leg, saw the glint of steel through darkness. The knowledge that he would have to crawl down there made him feel slightly ill. He reached up above his head. He pulled the trapdoor down. It clanged shut and the noise echoed all around him, up and down the main leg.

Ricketts started to descend. He did it slowly and carefully. He heard the echo of his footsteps on the ladder, watched the wall rise above him. He didn't look up. He only looked left and right. He closed his eyes when he passed the dimmed lamps, moved through shadow and light. The leg was swaying from side to side. The curved wall creaked and shuddered. The waves outside the leg pounded dully; the waves inside were splashing. Ricketts kept going down, kept looking from left to right, passed girders that formed shelves around the wall, red with rust, strewn with debris. The divers often came down here. They left cups and bits of wire. Ricketts felt a brief annoyance when he saw this, but he kept going down. He was looking from left to right. He was convinced the bomb was here. He was sweating fifty feet above the water when he finally saw it.

The bomb was sitting on a narrow girder. The girder circled around the wall. The bomb was resting on the girder beside the ladder, about two feet away. It was the size of a tea-chest, had a slotted iron frame, and was attached to the base of the girder with two cast-iron clamps.

There was no dynamite.

Ricketts cursed at his own ignorance. Of course there wouldn't be dynamite. The plutonium metal core would be surrounded by TNT and packed tight inside the sealed explosive shell. Ricketts cursed again. His voice echoed all around him. He gripped the ladder as it swayed from side to side, as the shadows fell over him. Still, he had found the bomb. Now at least he could dismantle it. He reached out and nearly fell off the ladder, so he grabbed it again.

Cursing, he just hung there. The ladder swayed with the pontoon leg. The shadows darted up and down the rusted steel, changed their shapes, crept around him. He clung to the ladder, heard the water far below. He knew that the men who worked here were normally tied on with safety straps. But he had no safety straps, he had nothing to hold him on. He would have to climb up on that girder and do it from there.

Ricketts briefly closed his eyes and pressed his forehead against the ladder. He felt it swaying gently from side to side, heard the water below. He didn't want to look down there. That vertical tunnel was terrifying. The tunnel plunged down to the water and the water seemed much darker than the sea. Ricketts opened his eyes, felt the sweat on his brow. He heard the rumblings of the sea all around him, then he moved up the ladder.

He climbed on to the girder. It was eighteen inches wide. On his knees, he pressed himself against the wall and tried not to look down. The glint of water caught his eye. His eyes were drawn against their will. He looked down past the bomb, down that spiralling fifty feet, saw the round pool of water far below, very black, very cold. Ricketts knew how cold it was. He knew he couldn't survive in it. He knew that if he fell, and if he couldn't find a ladder, he would freeze to death in five minutes flat.

He fixed his eyes on the bomb.

The dismantling was easy. He was surprised at his own

116

skill. He had picked up this skill in the army, but not for plutonium bombs. Still, he managed to do it; the basic principles were the same. He only needed his pocket screwdriver and his own past experience. He pulled the connecting wires loose, unscrewed the explosive lenses. It seemed like a child's toy in his hands and it didn't take long. He threw the pieces in the water, heard them splashing far below. When he had finished, he loosened the clamps and tried to push the bomb over. He couldn't budge it; it was too heavy to move. He smacked it lightly with the palm of one hand, and then grinned and just left it.

Ricketts looked at his watch. He had twenty minutes left. He felt a cold, sneaking panic, and it made him crawl back to the ladder. He reached out with one hand, grabbed the ladder and swung down. He kicked out with his feet and found the rungs and then hauled himself up.

He felt better as he ascended. He saw the roof of the leg above him. It was swaying from side to side and creaking loudly, but this didn't concern him. He simply kept going up. He felt a warm exultation. It was born of his need to escape from this round, chilly prison. This mood carried him upward; refired him with energy. Then he reached the narrow entrance to the support leg and the panic returned.

The support leg was three feet wide. It was merely part of a larger web. The support legs crisscrossed beneath the decks, then plunged down to the pontoons. Ricketts had to go down there. He really didn't want to do it. He wanted to climb out of this leg and breathe the fresh air. Yet he had to cross the rig, had to reach the driller's room. The driller's room was in a module on the drilling floor, just beyond the moonpool. He couldn't get to the drilling floor; he simply had to go under it. He could do so by going down this support leg until it joined with another. That was sixty feet down. From there he could climb the other leg. It was another sixty feet and it would bring him out on to the lower deck, not too far from the driller's room. Ricketts clung to the ladder, looked down the support leg. It was narrow and its ladder fell steeply and disappeared into darkness.

He started down the support leg. He didn't really have a choice. His footsteps echoed as he went down the ladder, and he heard his own breathing. It seemed to take a long time. In fact, it took no time at all. Conscious only of the ringing of his boots, he soon started climbing. The climbing was worse. He kept straining to see the top. He looked up and he heard increasing noise, a dulled cacophony of movement. It was the rattling of chains, the clanging of pipes, the general background noise of a rig that was no longer working. The noises got through to Ricketts. They made him think of the world up there. They made him think of the terrorists on the deck, and of the time he had left. Yet eventually he reached the top. He reached a catwalk and a door. He opened the door carefully and looked out and was blinded by light.

He was on the storage deck. All the wall lights were on. They blazed down on the crates and the crates themselves shadowed the floor. Ricketts looked left and right. There was no sign of movement. He stepped out and walked across the steel deck until he came to another door. He opened the door and walked through. He climbed up some steel steps. There was a low, narrow corridor at the top, leading out to the drilling floor. Ricketts didn't go out there. He turned left near the exit. He went straight up another flight of steps and walked into a module. It was just above the drilling deck. Looking down he could see the terrorists. They were wandering back and forth past the moonpool, laughing and talking. The deck was cluttered with equipment, the bright lights cast stark shadows, and the men were all carrying weapons, wandering lazily back and forth.

Ricketts entered another corridor. It was bright and low-ceilinged. A man stepped out of a door just ahead and nodded curtly and brushed past. Ricketts walked to that door, heard the sound of the television, looked in and saw a man in a chair, looking up at the screen. The cameras were scanning the sea-bed, scanning over the anchor chains. The sea-bed was four-hundred feet down and the whole view was murky. The man had his back to Ricketts, his feet up on the desk. He seemed bored and he coughed into his right hand and gazed up at the screen. His weapon was leaning against the desk, a MAS Combat Rifle. There was a pile of hand grenades on the table close beside the man's feet. Ricketts looked down at the floor, saw some magazines for the gun. The man coughed again into his hand, clearing phlegm from his throat.

Ricketts walked up behind him. He only had to walk six feet. He brought the edge of his hand down on the man's neck, at the side of the throat. The man didn't cry out, simply grunted and slumped down. Ricketts checked that he was dead and then he turned around and closed the room door.

Ricketts looked at the television and saw the murky sea-bed. He looked out through the window, at the floor twelve feet below, and saw the terrorists gathered around the moonpool. They were smoking and drinking beer, their weapons scattered all around them. They appeared to be having some sort of break, and he didn't like that. He turned the television off, then switched its mains supply off. He opened a box in the wall and saw the fuses, a collection of bright wires. Ricketts pulled some of the wires out, quickly tied the wires together, then pushed the wires back against the wall and closed up the box. He knew what would happen now. The television was turned off. The terrorists, finding the television off, would turn it on at its power supply. That's all Ricketts wanted. The crossed wires would do the rest. The whole system would ignite and burn out beyond hope of repair.

Ricketts had to move the dead man. The corpse would only cause suspicion. He wanted the terrorists to find the room empty, think the man had just sneaked off. But first he looked at the grenades, which were in fact not hand-grenades. They were grenades for the MAS Combat Rifle, which was just what he needed. The grenades were clipped on to a belt. Ricketts put the belt on. He then opened the room door and looked out and saw no sign of movement. Ricketts went back to the dead man. He pulled him out of the chair. The man was heavy and Ricketts just dragged him out into the corridor. He looked up and down, saw that no one was coming, dragged the man along the corridor to the next door, a small storage room. He bundled the corpse into the room, returned quickly to the driller's room, picked up the MAS Combat Rifle and then casually walked out.

Ricketts looked at his watch. He had ten minutes left. He walked down the steel steps and turned left and went into the drilling deck.

The terrorists were lounging around the moonpool, still smoking and drinking beer; other terrorists were wandering

119

back and forth, in and out of the shadows. Ricketts simply started walking. It was a trick he had learnt somewhere. He knew that total lack of self-consciousness made people ignore you. He walked across the drilling floor. A few passing men nodded. They looked at him as if they hadn't seen him, without lengthy inspection. He kept walking across the deck, passed through shadow and light, climbed up some steel steps and walked out of the drilling hut and emerged into the cold air of the main deck.

The derricks towered above him. The lights tapered up into nothing. There were floodlights beaming down on the deck, illuminating the terrorists. They were wandering back and forth, carrying rifles and grenades, walking under the massive cranes, past the stacked pipes, with the darkness beyond them. Ricketts walked to the end of the deck. He was parallel to the radio hut. He saw the two guards standing outside the door, looking bored and lethargic.

Ricketts looked at his watch. He had five minutes left. He started walking along the edge of the deck, towards the radio hut. The sea murmured far below, the wind howled right across him. He walked along to the radio hut and then slipped in behind it. It was very dark in there. He saw the corner of the rig. He looked down and saw the huge pontoon leg, disappearing in darkness. He thought of Barker and the Prime Minister. They should both be down there. They should both be hiding down there in the barge, checking their watches. Ricketts turned and looked up; looked beyond the radio hut, saw the radar antenna thrusting skyward, halfway down the deck.

There was a sling on the rifle and Ricketts put his arm through it. With the rifle hanging down from his shoulder, he climbed the ladder before him. He reached the roof of the radio hut, slithered across it on his belly, stopped crawling when he got near the edge and could see the whole deck. Ricketts made himself comfortable. He pulled the rifle off his shoulder. He unclipped the attachment for the grenades and placed it quietly beside him. The guards below made no sound. Ricketts looked along the deck. The radar antenna was about halfway along the deck, soaring up towards the sky.

Ricketts looked at his watch. He had one minute left. He

checked the rifle's magazine, put the change lever to single-shot, then crawled forward to the edge of the roof. The two guards were just below him. The other men were far away. Ricketts aimed at the guard to his left and then fired his first shot.

There was a sharp, cracking sound. It really wasn't all that loud. The guard's head seemed to spin in a circle and then he went down. The other guard whirled around, was trying to pull his rifle up, was shadowy and unreal in the gloom as Ricketts aimed for his head. The rifle cracked in his ear. The guard's arms flew out sideways. He spun around but had not yet hit the deck when Ricketts rolled from the edge.

He heard shouting and running feet, heard the roaring of guns. He knew they were confused as he reset the rifle and fixed a grenade to the barrel. The sound of running feet was louder. He heard the roar of a machine-gun. He rolled around on his stomach and aimed his rifle at the radar antenna. He didn't have much time. He heard the shouting and the shooting. He took aim at the base of the antenna and fired the grenade. It seemed to take a long time. He saw the shadows running towards him. Guns flashed and then he saw the white explosion, heard a roar, shrieking metal.

He didn't wait to check the damage, attached another grenade, took aim and squeezed the trigger and felt the recoil as the butt punched his shoulder. The second blast seemed louder. The metal shrieked in a fierce white glare. The men near it started spinning and falling, ran backwards and forwards. The antenna groaned and started bending, swayed wildly back and forth. Ricketts put another grenade on the rifle and fired at the running men. The grenade exploded in the darkness, flared up and died away. The antenna swayed to and fro and caved in before the wind and crashed down over the deck and the running men. Steel exploded in all directions, a shower of sparks geysered skywards, and Ricketts slithered back across the flat roof and climbed down to the deck.

He was behind the radio hut, was on the corner of the rig, looked down and thought he saw the sea below, a black mat in the nothing. The wind was pushing him against the wall. He fought his way to the catwalk. A steel ladder pointed down past the decks, to the top of the pontoon leg. Ricketts

121

started climbing down it, heard gunfire and shouts. He thought he heard the door of the radio hut banging, McGregor's voice bawling angrily. He had no time for McGregor. He kept climbing down the ladder. The wind howled and tried to sweep him from the rungs, but he didn't dare stop. He finally reached the pontoon leg. The wind howled around the catwalk. He found the hole in the catwalk, put his feet on the ladder, and started to climb down once more. It took a very long time. He passed under the lower deck. He looked through the silvery web of the supporting legs and saw the darkness beyond. The wind here was fierce. It was blowing under the rig. He looked up and saw searchlights beaming down, exploring the sea below.

Ricketts didn't dare stop. He went down as fast as possible, heard the firing of guns above his head, very high up, and muffled. Then he felt the ladder shaking, heard the clanging of boots above. He heard shouting and the ladder vibrated and he knew they were following him. Ricketts climbed down even faster, forgot the wind and the height, heard the beating of the sea against the legs, a dull metallic cacophony. That made him move faster. He heard the men above shouting. He climbed down and heard the roar of a boat and knew that Barker was leaving. He heard himself bawling crazily, bawling out Barker's name, the rifle slung over his shoulder and pummelling his ribs.

Ricketts jumped from the ladder, fell down through dark space, dropped on to the barge and rolled over and crashed into some crates. Barker called his name out. He heard the sound very clearly. He jumped up and stumbled blindly across the deck, hitting boxes and cables. Then he suddenly saw Barker. He was not too far away. He was silhouetted against the cloudy night, at the prow of the loading barge. Ricketts lurched towards him, Barker disappeared from view, and Ricketts got to the prow of the loading barge and saw the boat just below him. Barker was at the wheel. The Prime Minister was waving at him. The sea was rough and the engine was roaring and Ricketts jumped down. He almost hit the Prime Minister. He crashed into the cabin wall. Barker shouted and the engine roared louder and the boat started moving. They pulled away from the loading barge, saw the rig high above them, saw searchlights beaming down on the water, and then heard the gunfire. Wood exploded all around them. Barker screamed and threw his arms up. They saw the whites of his eyes, an awful incomprehension, then he jerked back and seemed to somersault and went over the side.

There was no point in stopping.

CHAPTER TWELVE

RICKETTS took the boat out. It made a deep, muffled roar. The sea was rough and it sloshed across the deck and drenched him up to the waist. He heard the louder roar of the guns. The terrorists were firing from the loading barge. He heard shouting and another engine roared and he knew they would follow him. He glanced over his shoulder. The Prime Minister was at the stern. He was fully exposed to the gunfire, looking into the water.

'Get down!' Ricketts shouted. 'Get your head down! They're trying to kill you!'

An automatic rifle roared. He heard the whipping of the bullets. Wood exploded all around him and he dropped down and the wheel started spinning. He cursed and looked up, saw the rig's lights flashing over him. The boat was turning and he saw the huge rig, the lights blazing from darkness. He looked at the Prime Minister. The Prime Minister was crouching down. He was peering over the stern of the boat, his eyes probing the darkness.

'Keep down!' Ricketts bawled.

'What about Barker?' the Prime Minister shouted. 'I can see him! He's floating out there in the water! I'm sure I can see him!'

The boat was spinning around, the waves sloshing across the deck, then it rose and plunged down into the sea and just kept on turning. Ricketts cursed and jumped up, reached out for the spinning wheel. The guns roared and wood exploded around him as he pulled the wheel back. The boat started straightening out. It was heading away from the rig. There was a roar from behind them and he heard the other boat ploughing forward.

'What about Barker?' the Prime Minister shouted.

'It's too late!' Ricketts bawled.

'We can't leave him!'

'There's no choice!' Ricketts bawled. 'Keep your head down!'

Ricketts opened up the engine, gave it full throttle, and the boat roared and jumped up and plunged down and the waves washed across it. The Prime Minister yelped, stumbled back towards Ricketts; he was drenched and he was looking at himself as if not quite believing it. 'It's freezing cold!' he shouted loudly. Ricketts didn't respond. He held the wheel and headed into the darkness, the rough sea and the cutting wind. The boat rose and fell, the Prime Minister grabbed a rope, and from behind they heard the rumble of the other boat, the shouting of men.

'They're following us!' the Prime Minister shouted.

'Damn it!' Ricketts shouted. 'I know that!'

'Is there anything I can do to help?'

'No, there isn't! Just keep your head down!'

There was the chattering of guns. The bullets whistled all around them. The Prime Minister dropped down behind Ricketts and mumbled something inaudible. Ricketts glanced across his shoulder, was almost blinded by a spotlight. The light passed across the boat and then wavered, started coming back towards them. Ricketts cursed and looked down. The Prime Minister was crouching low. Ricketts grabbed him by the shoulders and pulled him up and put his hands on the wheel.

'Hold it steady!' Ricketts shouted. 'Don't let it move! Don't let the boat change direction!'

The Prime Minister's eyes were wide, staring at Ricketts as if stunned, but he took the wheel and then looked straight ahead at the dark, surging sea. Ricketts unslung his rifle. The boat tossed and threw him sideways. He heard the roar of an automatic rifle and he dropped to the deck. The sea growled and washed over him. He crawled along to the stern. He looked up as the spotlight turned towards him, filled the boat with a glaring light. The Prime Minister was exposed. There wasn't really any time. Ricketts put the rifle on to automatic and aimed right at that white haze. He could hardly keep his eyes open, the boat was pitching and rocking wildly, but he fired off a short burst, fired another, then another, heard the roar of the rifle in his ear, saw the darkness rush in.

He had knocked out their light. It was a temporary respite.

He knew that the boat would have flares and emergency lights. It continued to roar behind them, was a distant, muffled sound. It was gaining and Ricketts felt a keen dread as he rushed back to the wheelhouse. The Prime Minister was still there, was still holding the wheel firmly. He looked at Ricketts and offered a shy smile, as if almost embarrassed.

'I'm no good at this,' he said.

'You're doing fine,' Ricketts said.

'I don't think I'll ever manage to forget this.'

'Don't worry. You'll live with it.' Ricketts took the wheel. 'Can you fire a rifle?' he said.

'No,' the Prime Minister said. 'I'm no good at that either.'

The darkness howled all around them, the boat bucked and plunged down, the water sloshed across the deck to their rear and poured back out again. Ricketts held a steady course. He knew just where he was going. He glanced briefly over his shoulder and saw the lights of the distant rig, soaring up to the sky, a diamond web, illuminating the darkness. The other boat was still behind him, was gaining every minute. It was racing up behind them, growing larger, a black threat in the darkness. Ricketts heard the shouting men, saw the lamps flickering on, saw the light beaming down on the water, silver lines on the surging waves. The boat was coming closer. The men were shouting with excitement. The boat loomed large to the stern and cut around him and ran parallel to him.

'*They've caught up!*' the Prime Minister shouted.

'Not for long!' Ricketts hissed. He reached down and grabbed a rope from the deck and started tying the wheel up. 'Get into the cabin!' he bawled. The Prime Minister just looked at him. The guns roared and Ricketts grabbed the Prime Minister and threw him down to the deck. 'In the cabin!' Ricketts shouted. 'Go down to the cabin!' The guns roared and wood exploded all around them and Ricketts dropped low. He grabbed the Prime Minister by the shoulder, threw him towards the cabin steps, and the guns roared as the Prime Minister crawled forward, made his way down the steps. Ricketts looked up at the wheel. The rope was holding it steady. The window of the wheelhouse framed the sky, a dark sheet sliding over them. The guns roared again. The bullets were stitching the whole boat. Wood

126

exploded as Ricketts crawled forward, dragging the rifle behind him. He went to the starboard side, huddled up there and waited, heard the rumbling of the other boat as it came closer, running parallel to them. The terrorists were all shouting. They were firing semi-automatic rifles. He could hear the boat crashing through the waves, coming closer each minute. Ricketts still didn't move. The sea hissed and poured over him. The guns roared and stitched the deck near the stern and streams of water shot up. Ricketts cursed. The boat was punctured beneath the water-line. He heard the shouting of the terrorists, heard the growl of their engine, and knew that they were coming in broadside. They were practically on top of him; they would ram him any moment. Ricketts unclipped a grenade, pulled the pin out, then stood up and threw it.

The boat filled his whole vision. The men were silhouetted in pale light. They seemed startled and Ricketts dropped down again and pressed himself to the side. The grenade exploded, made a deafening, jagged roar. He heard shrieks and the sound of tumbling bodies and he jumped up immediately. He fired his rifle without looking. He had it set to automatic. He saw white flame spitting out through the darkness, the silhouettes dancing crazily. He just kept on firing, swung the gun from left to right. Men screamed and tumbled over the sides, threw themselves to the deck. The boat was pulling away from him. It was obviously out of control. The white flames were leaping over the cabin, turning blue, edged with black smoke. The grenade had exploded their spare petrol. The flames were hissing and crackling. A silhouette was jerking up and down the deck, flapping arms, blazing furiously. Ricketts fired his gun again. The burning man twitched and fell. Something winked and Ricketts dropped back to the deck and heard the roar of the gun. He crawled back to the wheelhouse, reached up and untied the ropes. He opened the engine and let the boat go slowly forward, then he turned it to starboard.

The Prime Minister's face appeared. He was looking up from the cabin steps. Ricketts told him to stay down, but the Prime Minister pointedly ignored him. He emerged from the cabin, crouched down beside Ricketts, glanced over the side and saw the burning boat, falling behind them. The Prime Minister stood up. He was fascinated by the burning boat. The flames were leaping up and casting shadows on the sea's glowing surface. The Prime Minister heard some screams. The blazing boat was simply drifting. Their own boat was now circling around it, cutting across to the other side. The Prime Minister glanced at Ricketts. He didn't know what Ricketts was doing. He looked back at the blazing boat, at the bright fire, saw it drifting and bobbing. It was now to their right, drifting very close to them. An inflatable dinghy fell into the sea, and some terrorists climbed into it. Another scream came from the deck. It was someone burning to death. The terrorists in the dinghy started rowing, the wall of flame dancing over them.

'Take the wheel,' Ricketts said.

The Prime Minister took the wheel, did it almost automatically. Ricketts had turned the engine off, and the boat was just drifting. The Prime Minister held it steady, saw Ricketts bending down, saw Ricketts standing up with the gun, taking aim at the terrorists. '*No, Ricketts!*' he shouted. '*You can't do it! For God's sake, lad, you*—' But Ricketts was ignoring him, was taking careful aim, and the Prime Minister left the wheel and rushed at him and tried pushing the gun up. Ricketts cursed and grabbed his shoulder, threw the Prime Minister away. 'Damn it, let me go!' he hissed harshly. '*I won't let them go back!*'

The Prime Minister just stood there. He was shocked by Ricketts' venom. He glanced across at the choppy, freezing sea, at the men in the dinghy. Then Ricketts fired. It was a short, decisive burst. Someone screamed and a man threw his arms up and splashed over the side. Ricketts put the gun down. They heard the hissing air clearly. The men shouted and waved their arms wildly as the dinghy collapsed. The Prime Minister closed his eyes, heard them screaming for help, opened his eyes and saw them splashing in the water, swimming over towards him. Ricketts went back to the wheelhouse, turned the engine on, and the boat growled and the water boiled around it and then it moved off. It went past the swimming men. Their cries for help were very clear. Ricketts turned the boat around the other boat and headed into the darkness. The Prime Minister looked back, saw the terrorist boat blazing, heard the pleas of the men in the water, fading out, disappearing.

'They'll freeze to death,' the Prime Minister said.

'That's right,' Ricketts said. 'But at least they won't go back to that bastard and help him tomorrow.'

Ricketts headed out to sea, kept the boat on an even course, while the Prime Minister sat down on the deck, feeling stunned and exhausted. The darkness was all around him. It swallowed up the burning boat. The lights of the rig had long since vanished and the clouds hid the moon. The Prime Minister shivered, was drenched and very cold, was tired and gave way to a fear that could not be controlled. Ricketts' venom had startled him. He understood it, but it had unnerved him. He had never been touched by violence before, but now it seemed almost natural. Of all his fears, that was the worst. He was actually becoming adjusted to it. Now alone in the North Sea, stripped of rank and the need for manners, he was forced to see the animal in himself that lived just for survival. The real world seemed far away. All he had gained was briefly lost. He looked around at the dark, surging sea and tried to find his old skin.

It didn't take very long. They soon heard the helicopter. It was flying from east to west just ahead at a very low altitude. Ricketts promptly stopped the boat. He walked back to the stern. The deck had been shot full of holes and the water was pouring in.

'We were lucky,' he said. 'Another mile and we'd sink. We'd have frozen to death just like the terrorists. Try not to forget that.'

He threw the anchor overboard, walked back to the wheel-cabin, rummaged around on the floor of the cabin and stood up with a flare-gun. He aimed the gun at the sky. There was a small, dull explosion. The flare burst in the sky high above, turned the darkness bright crimson. Ricketts fired off another. The crimson streaks formed an umbrella. They raced out and then curved down to earth, died above the dark sea. The helicopter had seen them. They heard its comforting approach. It was soon hovering just above the boat, its props causing a whirlwind.

A searchlight cut through the darkness, beaming down from the helicopter. The helicopter hovered thirty feet above

them, rising up and down rhythmically. Its engine was very
loud. In fact, the roar was almost deafening. The spinning
props whipped the air up and made the sea swirl and soar.
The waves rushed across the deck, drenched Ricketts and the
Prime Minister. They both held on to the side of the boat and
blinked against the bright searchlights. Then the harness fell
down. It blew crazily on the straps. The Prime Minister,
looking up at the helicopter, immediately felt dizzy. He
glanced numbly at Ricketts. Ricketts was shouting and waving at him. The Prime Minister looked down and saw the
water creeping over his ankles.

The boat had started sinking, was going down fast, and the
Prime Minister reached out for the harness and it flew from
his grasp. The helicopter roared. The waves rushed up and
drenched him. Ricketts reached out for the harness and
caught it and then waved at the Prime Minister. The Prime
Minister stepped forward. He was holding the side of the
boat. The boat was rocking in the violent, surging water,
sinking down at the stern. Ricketts indicated the harness. He
was holding it up to the Prime Minister. The Prime Minister
saw two loops for his arms, an encircling belt. He held his
arms out. The boat rocked and he nearly fell. He saw Ricketts' mouth opening, but he couldn't hear what he was
saying. Ricketts put the harness on him, tightened the belt
around his chest. The helicopter roared and the wind was
beating wildly around them. Ricketts stepped back a little.
He waved up at the helicopter. The Prime Minister felt the
pounding of his heart, an absurd, childish dread. The belts
above him went taut, the Prime Minister held his breath,
then he was picked up and he flew out on the wind and was
swinging in space.

The Prime Minister held the straps, gasped for breath and
closed his eyes. His stomach heaved and he suddenly felt
hollow and he opened his eyes again. He heard the roar of the
helicopter, felt himself swinging freely, glanced down and
saw the sea far below, the dark waves growing flatter. He
kept swinging to and fro. The straps were jerking him
upwards. The roar of the helicopter grew louder, and the
wind beat about him. Suddenly he was exhilarated, he
experienced an incandescent warmth; he understood that he
was finishing his child's dream of adventure, and that life

would never be this keen again. The Prime Minister swung in space, saw the dark sky and the sea, felt the wind and tasted the salt in the air, and then the feeling was gone. The helicopter's roar deafened him. He was jerked up and in. A pair of hands grabbed his shoulders and pulled him in and he saw metal walls. It was the inside of the helicopter. A pair of nervous eyes studied him. The Prime Minister suddenly realized who he was; that he *was* a Prime Minister. He said his thanks to the nervous eyes. He smiled kindly as he did so. The young man smiled and unclipped the harness and threw it back out.

The Prime Minister looked down, saw the dark, surging sea. The boat below seemed too small to be real, its stern buried in water. Ricketts stood on the prow. The prow was pointing towards the sky. Ricketts swayed to and fro as if falling, then reached out for the harness. The sea washed across the boat. Most of the boat disappeared. The prow suddenly jumped up and fell back and Ricketts jumped into space. He swung away from the sinking boat. The boat sank beneath the waves. Ricketts swung to and fro on the harness, and the straps pulled him up.

It seemed to take a long time. The wind howled through the helicopter. Ricketts floated far below in the blackness, moving up, coming closer. Then his head came through the floor. The young man hauled him in. Ricketts turned around and looked back through the hole at the black void below. There was no sign of the boat. The sea was merging with the darkness. Ricketts gasped and rolled onto his back and just lay there and smiled.

'Now we've got them,' he said.

CHAPTER THIRTEEN

'THE situation is this,' Ricketts said. 'The terrorist bomb is now inoperative. We've knocked out their radar. That means we can get close to the rig without being detected. I suggest that we do so. I suggest we do it this morning. I think we should do it while it's dark, before the dawn breaks.'

Ricketts stood at the end of the table, wearing fresh overalls. The Prime Minister was sitting at his right hand, wearing a new suit. The boardroom was very smoky, the rest of the men looked tired and pale; there were numerous cups and tumblers on the table, and the ashtrays were full. The men were all looking at Ricketts. They were trying to take the news in. They hadn't slept and their whole world had exploded, leaving them dazed. Keith Turner rubbed his beard, Sir Reginald drummed his fingers nervously, while Paul Dalton, the American, chewed a pencil and seemed quite bemused. He glanced across at the Prime Minister. The old man was looking healthy. He was wearing a shirt and tie and a grey suit, his blue eyes bright and vigorous. Keith Turner rubbed his beard, feeling grubby and dishevelled. He glanced around him and then he looked at Ricketts, trying to order his thoughts.

'I'm worried,' he said. 'Who the hell backed the terrorists? You say they've got a man aboard this rig. Which one of us is it?'

'It doesn't matter,' Sir Reginald said. 'We can sort that out later. What matters at the moment is Charlie 2. We have to get that rig back.'

'I disagree,' Paul Dalton said. 'I think Turner has a point. If McGregor says they have a man on board, then that man could be dangerous. McGregor said he was one of us. He happens to be sitting in this boardroom. If, as McGregor says, he has a radio, he could contact the terrorists. If he did, we couldn't surprise them. They'd just be sitting there wait-

132

ing. I don't think we can make that assault if they know that we're coming.'

There were twenty men around the table and they started looking at one another. Suddenly they all seemed very uncomfortable, self-conscious and edgy.

'One of us?' a Frenchman said.

'That's right,' Ricketts said. 'The terrorists' backers have a man on this rig, and he's a top-flight executive.'

There was another brief silence. The men fidgeted and coughed. The Under-Secretary put his chin in his hands and looked extremely annoyed.

'Incredible,' he said. 'It's more incredible every minute. This whole situation defies belief, and it's really quite sickening. First the terrorists sink one rig. Then they casually take over another. Now we find that one of your top-flight executives has tried to kill the Prime Minister. I find the whole thing appalling.'

'We've been through that,' Sir Reginald said. 'I see little point in continuing it. Let's stick to the issue at hand and sort this mess out.'

'It's your mess,' the Under-Secretary said. 'It's a damned disgusting mess. The lack of security throughout your whole organization is utterly scandalous.'

'I agree,' the Prime Minister said. 'I'm still appalled by the whole thing. If word of this ever got out the repercussions would be terrible.'

'We'd be laughing-stocks,' the Under-Secretary said.

'Precisely,' the Prime Minister said. 'Worse: we'd lose international confidence in the whole of the North Sea.'

'I agree,' Paul Dalton said. 'I'm afraid my side would pull out. I don't see the Americans staying on if this mess is made known to them.'

They all slumped back into silence. There was a spasm of nervous coughing. More cigarettes and cigars were lit up, and the smoke made the air blue.

'He had a radio,' Turner said. 'Whoever he was, he had a radio. We'll just search every cabin in the rig and make sure that we find it.'

'No,' Ricketts said. 'I don't think we can do that. For one thing, he's possibly gotten rid of it already; for another, such a search would arouse the crew. We don't want that to happen. We want this kept as quiet as possible. If, as McGregor says, the man is here in this boardroom, then let's just make sure he stays here. We'll attack the rig immediately. It'll all be over by dawn. Until then, we won't let anyone leave the boardroom. That should solve the problem.'

Ricketts glanced around the table. Most of the men seemed in agreement. The Prime Minister had a slight smile on his lips as he stared at Sir Reginald.

'And what then?' Dalton said. 'We've still got to know who he is. If he can pull this stunt, he's gonna pull others, and that isn't acceptable.'

'Tomorrow,' Ricketts said. 'We can worry about that tomorrow. Right now our major worry is that rig.'

'I agree,' the Prime Minister said. 'We must get the terrorists off. We must get them off and hush this thing up. That's all there is to it.'

'But why attack?' Turner said. 'I don't see the point in that. An attack like that will need a lot of men, and a lot will be killed. Why not just sit tight? They haven't got their plutonium bomb. Why attack when we can just leave them there until their food is all gone?'

'We can't do that,' Ricketts said. 'It would take far too long. Fresh supplies went out to Charlie 2 yesterday. That gives them four weeks.'

'So,' Turner said. 'Sweat them out.'

'No,' Dalton said. 'I back Ricketts on this. If we let them sit for four weeks on that rig they'll start using their radio. They'll talk to the press. They'll talk to the whole damned media. Before we know it, the whole world will be informed – and we've got to avoid that.'

'They'll know anyway,' Turner said. 'If we capture the terrorists, they'll talk. You can't keep a thing like this quiet. It's just too big for that.'

'I disagree,' Dalton said. 'Nothing's too big for silence. If we capture the terrorists we'll rush them straight to maximum security and allow them no access to the press. This is a matter of national security. You can have the trial behind closed doors. We'll write up our own press-release version of the events, the terrorists will each be given twenty years to life, and by the time you let the dumb bastards out this will be ancient history. It won't matter at all then. Old scandals are merely titillating. Besides which, the North Sea will be drained dry and we'll be drilling elsewhere.'

'That's important,' the Under-Secretary said. 'A total lock-up is vital. The only people who know about this are the terrorists and us – and we've got to make sure it remains that way.'

'The terrorists' backers know,' Turner said.

'They won't talk,' Ricketts said. 'As McGregor most kindly pointed out: they wouldn't dare let their knowledge out.'

'He really screwed them,' Dalton said.

'That's right,' Ricketts said. 'He really screwed them and now they have to sit tight and keep their mouths shut.'

'So,' Sir Reginald said, 'we attack the terrorists immediately. We launch a full-scale assault and we get them off that rig and we throw them all in jail and forget about them.'

'That's right,' Dalton said. 'McGregor's already given us our story. We say it was an earthquake on the sea-bed. We put that out as our press-release.'

'It's rather dicey,' Sir Reginald said. 'That attack will need a lot of men. I can't see how we're going to keep it quiet with so many men knowing.'

'We do it ourselves,' Dalton said. 'We keep your army and navy out of it. This is an oil company affair, so let's keep it that way. We have our own security forces, and they're disciplined and well-trained. They're sworn to secrecy and we know they won't talk; they never have in the past.'

The Prime Minister raised his eye-brows. 'In the past?' he said quietly. 'Are you telling me you've had this in the past? Is that what you're saying?'

Dalton grinned at him. 'Nothing quite this ambitious. But the oil fields, especially on shore, have always had lots of trouble.'

'We've never heard about it,' the Prime Minister said.

'You wouldn't hear about it,' Dalton said. 'We tend to keep a low profile in these matters. We don't upset the shareholders.'

The Prime Minister looked at him, his eyes hard and perceptive. He turned and glanced briefly at the Under-Secretary, then he stared at Sir Reginald.

135

'The more I hear about these oil companies,' he said, 'the more disturbed I become.'

'We need to protect ourselves,' Sir Reginald said.

'The government's supposed to do that for you.'

'We feel we can do it quicker ourselves. We don't like complications.'

'Incredible,' the Under-Secretary said. 'You simply need to protect yourselves. So you finance and train your private armies, unbeknownst to us all.'

'Something like that,' Dalton said.

'It's bloody monstrous!' the Prime Minister said.

'It's also illegal,' the Under-Secretary said. 'It's illegal and it's utterly appalling.'

He glared at Paul Dalton. The American merely smiled gently. 'These are multi-national conglomerates,' he said. 'You have no jurisdiction.'

'I beg your pardon?' the Prime Minister said. 'You say we've no jurisdiction? I thought these rigs belonged to British United Oil.'

'No, Prime Minister. These rigs are *rented* by British United. The rigs are hired from drilling companies, and the majority of those companies are multi-national. Likewise with the North Sea. The North Sea's been parceled out. You auctioned it off in lots to companies bearing British names, but all those companies depend on international backers. What's British United Oil? It's an internationally financed company. It's merely part of a conglomerate that includes about six other companies. Where's your jurisdiction? It only covers a few oil fields. But the conglomerates own fields everywhere, and those fields need protecting. You can't protect us in Saudi Arabia. You can't protect us in the Persian Gulf. You can only make a formal complaint about your own British waters. That might cover British United. It doesn't cover the whole conglomerate. The conglomerate, or conglomerates, are much too big to be controlled by one country. You don't have jurisdiction. You wouldn't know where to apply. The conglomerates, existing for and by themselves, now look after themselves.'

The Prime Minister sat back. He couldn't believe what he was hearing. He had only flown out to this rig twelve hours ago, and already it seemed like twelve years. He had been involved in a terrorist war, had been imprisoned by those same terrorists, had seen men shot to death, had made his escape, and now, with midnight just passed, he had to listen to this. It was incomprehensible; it was shocking beyond belief. He wondered what the role of government might be in the years still to come. The Prime Minister glanced around him, saw his Under-Secretary's face. The Under-Secretary had gone very pale, and he was shaking with rage.

'So,' Paul Dalton said, speaking calmly and carefully. 'We will use our own men, we will take back our rig, and then we'll put out our own press-release and replace the whole crew. I think that solves the matter.'

He looked at the Prime Minister, but the Prime Minister turned away, stared balefully across the table at Sir Reginald, his blue eyes cold with rage. Sir Reginald didn't look up; he merely glanced once at Paul Dalton. The American smiled casually and glanced around him, finally focused on Ricketts. Ricketts stared through the portholes, saw the dark Forties Field. He thought of Barker standing up in the boat, his look of stunned disbelief. Now Barker was dead, was drifting somewhere out there; he was drifting out there with all the others, and those bastards had done it. Ricketts glanced at the Under-Secretary, saw the handsome, shocked face. He knew that the Under-Secretary didn't think of the dead; that his hatred of the oil companies had totally erased the dead from his mind. Ricketts knew it was all politics. In the end it was always politics. He knew it and he didn't give a damn – he just wanted revenge.

'All right,' the Prime Minister said. 'You do it yourselves.'

The telephone rang. Turner quickly picked it up. 'I've got Charlie 2,' the operative said. 'They want to speak to the boardroom.' Turner frowned. 'Anyone special?' he said. 'No,' the operative said. 'It's McGregor. He just wants the boardroom.' Turner felt a great fear. It shook him loose and passed away. He glanced up and then he dropped his eyes again and said, 'Okay, I'm listening.' McGregor came on the line. He sounded angry and wild. 'All right,' he said, 'you bastards got my bomb; but I'm no' finished yet.' He demanded to speak to Ricketts. Ricketts saw Turner's glance. He stood up and then walked around the table and picked up the other phone.

'This is Ricketts,' he said.

'Yer a smart bastard, Ricketts.'

'Yes,' Ricketts said, 'I know that. Now what do you want?'

'I want yer hide,' McGregor said.

'You won't get it,' Ricketts said.

'I just might,' McGregor said. 'I'm no' finished yet. Not by a long way.'

Ricketts closed his eyes and just stood there, saying nothing. He opened his eyes again and glanced around him, a dead look, lethargic.

'What is it?' he said.

'You think I'm dumb?' McGregor said. 'You think you've fucking beat me, is that it? Well don't think too quickly.'

'What do you want?' Ricketts said.

'I want what I've always wanted. I want one million pounds, and I want those four men out of jail.'

'You're too late,' Ricketts said. 'You've got nothing to offer. You can't even offer your plutonium bomb. I took that away from you.'

'Aye,' McGregor said. 'You managed to do that. But that dinnae mean I'm sittin' here stranded. Not by a long way.'

'No?' Ricketts said.

'No,' McGregor said. 'If you weren't so fucking dumb you'd have guessed. I can still sink this rig.'

Ricketts didn't respond. He simply glanced around the room. The men around the table leant forward, looking tense and confused.

'We came prepared,' McGregor said. 'We've got plastic explosives. We can't blow up the whole fucking field, but we *can* sink this rig. I'm gonna blow a leg off, Ricketts. You know just what that means. This whole bloody rig'll go down – and that isn't good news.'

Keith Turner groaned audibly, covered his face with his hands, and the Prime Minister sat up in his chair with his broad forehead wrinkling. The other men looked at each other, some visibly turning pale, while the Under-Secretary stared straight at Sir Reginald, who seemed slumped in despair. Paul Dalton stood up, walked slowly around the table, stood beside Ricketts and looked at him with his eyes narrowed slightly.

'Plastic explosives?' Ricketts said.

'Aye,' McGregor said. 'Enough plastic explosives to blow a hole in one leg. And that, Ricketts, is what I'm gonna do if we dinnae agree now.'

Ricketts said nothing. He simply looked hard at Dalton. The American shrugged his shoulders and nodded, put his hands on the table.

'All right,' Ricketts said. 'How do we do it?'

The Prime Minister stared at Dalton. The American shrugged and put his hands up. Turner groaned with his face in his hands while Sir Reginald sighed.

'You've got t' dawn,' McGregor said. 'I dinnae need the Prime Minister. I've already stolen a million from our backers; I'll take the rest from you bastards. You'll deliver it by dawn. You'll make the delivery by helicopter. You'll personally fly the helicopter, Ricketts, and then we'll have words. That leaves my four men. I want them out by tomorrow. I want one of them to ring me as soon as they're all free, and I want the pardons announced in the evenin' papers.'

'And then?'

'Then we'll leave. We'll fly out by helicopter. We'll land on a private airstrip and we'll simply disappear and we'll keep our mouths shut while we're free. If you touch us we'll talk, if you don't we'll keep quiet, and as long as no Clan member's bothered, yer secret is safe.'

'Anything else?' Ricketts said.

'No,' McGregor said. 'You've got till dawn to fly over with the money; if you don't, the rig sinks. And don't try a sneak attack. That wouldn't please me at all. At the first sign of an attack we'll blow the leg. That's all there is to it.'

There was a very long silence. Ricketts stared all around him. His gaze came to rest on the portholes, on the darkness beyond. Eventually he sighed, did it loudly and deliberately. He coughed and then he took a deep breath and his voice was subdued.

'Okay,' he said. 'Dawn.'

McGregor cut him off. Ricketts put the phone down. His grey eyes scanned around the boardroom table, took in the dazed faces. The Prime Minister sat forward, scratching abstractedly at his chin. He looked at Ricketts and Ricketts stared back and then smiled just a little.

139

'Yes?' the Prime Minister said.

'No,' Ricketts said. 'We're going to take that rig back tonight. We'll start the whole thing right now.'

'We can't do that,' Sir Reginald said. 'We all heard what the man said. The minute he sees a sign of an attack, he'll blow a hole in that leg.'

'What does that mean?' the Under-Secretary said.

'The rig will sink,' Turner said.

'Can we afford to lose another one?' the Prime Minister said. 'Can we sacrifice that much?'

'No,' Sir Reginald said. 'I really don't think we can. Charlie 2 is the most crucial rig we've got, and we can't let it go.'

'Why crucial?' the Under-Secretary said.

'It's a refinery,' Turner said. 'It's a floating refinery and it controls the flow of all oil north of Beryl.'

'I don't understand,' the Under-Secretary said. 'It's only one rig. Surely at least one rig is replaceable.'

'One rig we can afford,' Turner said. 'But not Charlie 2.'

'Why?' the Under-Secretary said.

Turner stood up and went to a map of the North Sea. He put his finger on Forties Field, moved it north to Beryl Field, then moved it farther north until it passed Eagle 3 and came to rest well above the whole Frigg Field.

'More than half of our oil – by which I mean all the oil in the British sector – now flows from a single undersea pipeline linking the five major oil fields to Peterhead. As you can see, that single pipeline connects every major field north of Forties. The oil from *all* the fields north of Frigg flows down through Frigg, from Frigg down to Beryl, through Beryl to here, and then goes from here back to Peterhead. Charlie 2 is a sort of refinery. It controls the speed of the oil flow. If McGregor blows that leg, Charlie 2 will certainly sink, but to sink, it first has to topple over. That might tear out the extractor pipes. We'd be very lucky if it didn't. It'll tear the extractor pipes out and thus split the main pipes. We'll lose the oil then. The pipes will just break apart. The oil will pour into the sea and miles of pipe will be lost. We won't be able to repair that. It'll take years to repair such damage. And in the meantime, all the oil north of here will be lost, and that amounts to over half of our total output.'

'You mean *Britain's* output,' the Prime Minister said.

140

'Yes,' Turner said. 'Britain's output.'

'And what if we can't avoid this?' the Prime Minister said. 'Just how bad would this be?'

'*Very* bad, Prime Minister,' the Under-Secretary said. 'Oil is our primary machine-driving fuel. We also need it for power stations and domestic fuel. It's also the raw material for all kinds of substances, such as plastics, and without it the petrochemical industry would die. As of this moment, Britain is dependent on oil for almost two-thirds of its fuel needs. To lose over half now, for the length of time envisaged by Mr. Turner, would certainly be catastrophic in the extreme.'

'All right, Mr. Turner,' the Prime Minister said. 'Just how long *would* it take to repair the damage?'

'One to two years,' Turner said, 'depending on weather conditions.'

'Also,' Sir Reginald cut in, 'since government taxation and British labour have forced us to have the rigs made in France and Norway rather than at home, they, seeing our predicament – and already annoyed by Britain's continuing concentration on American and Middle East markets – will doubtless get their own back by charging the earth for future rigs and by enticing foreign investors to deal with Europe. In short, Prime Minister, it will be disastrous.'

The Prime Minister knotted his hands, cracked his knuckles, flexed his fingers and looked at Sir Reginald, his blue eyes cold with anger.

'Laying the blame on this government,' he said icily, 'is scarcely appropriate.'

'So,' Ricketts said. 'We attack them tonight.'

Everyone looked at him. He was still by the telephone. He was standing at the end of the table with Paul Dalton beside him.

'If we attack them,' Sir Reginald said wearily, 'they will sink Charlie 2.'

'No,' Ricketts said. 'They won't sink it. They'll just blow a hole in it.'

'And that won't sink it?' the Prime Minister said.

'It'll take time,' Turner said. 'It'll take a good twenty minutes. It depends on how big the hole is, but we would have *some* time.'

'That's right,' Ricketts said. 'And they won't know we're

coming. They won't know until we're on that rig, and that gives us a head start.'

'The submersibles,' Dalton said.

'That's right,' Ricketts said. 'We'll use the submersibles. The submersibles are miniature submarines. They're normally for two men, but we can squeeze three men in each, and that will still leave a lot of room for weapons. We'll leave from Peterhead. The boats will take us close to Charlie. About five miles from Charlie we'll go down in the submersibles, and we'll surface right beneath the main deck. We can climb up the ladders. They probably won't be waiting for us. A lot of the terrorists will be asleep, so that should be an advantage. Another advantage is the weather. There's a storm due in three hours. If that makes our climbing difficult, it's also certain to make the terrorists more lethargic. So, we get on board. The first wave attacks the terrorists. While they're doing that, the second wave goes down the damaged leg and blocks the hole up before the rig sinks.'

'And they won't see you?' Sir Reginald said.

'I don't think so,' Ricketts said. 'I knocked out their radar and their undersea cameras, so at least they won't see us coming in. They might see us on the ladders. That's a chance we have to take. But even if they *do* see us there, we can fight our way up. They'll blow the leg up when they see us. That gives us twenty minutes or more. If our men can get down that leg on time, we should save the rig.'

'It will be damaged,' Sir Reginald said. 'It will be damaged in the fighting. You said the terrorists were very well armed. They'll do as much as they can.'

'That's true,' Ricketts said. 'I'm afraid we'll have to accept that. But at least if we can keep it afloat, we'll be able to fix it. Besides,' he continued, 'that rig's *supposed* to be damaged. It's supposed to have been damaged by an earthquake, so I think it should look that way.'

'He's got a point,' Dalton said. 'We're going to report it as an earthquake. As soon as that press-release goes out, you'll see planes flying over. The media will want to see it. They'll want to see a damaged rig. So *let* the terrorists knock the hell out of it; we're committed to that anyway.'

The Prime Minister sat back. He looked at Dalton and

Ricketts. He put his hands flat out on the table, shook his head with amazement.

'I don't believe this,' he said.

'Let's do it,' Ricketts said. 'Let's do it right now. We have to hit that rig while it's dark, and it's two o'clock now.'

'I agree,' Dalton said. 'Let's get going. We've no time to waste.'

'Who's going?' Sir Reginald said. 'It's a small point, but I'd like to know. I'd like to know who's leading this wonderful raid. I do not want a cock-up.'

The Prime Minister glared at him. Sir Reginald picked at his fingernails. He glanced at the Prime Minister for a moment, then he looked at the floor.

'You go, Ricketts,' the Prime Minister said. 'You obviously have the experience for it. I've read your records and they're somewhat impressive. You also know that whole set-up.'

'Right,' Ricketts said. 'I wanted to go anyway. I've got a few scores to settle there – not least with McGregor.'

'I'll go as well,' Dalton said. 'I don't think I should miss it. And I want to have a talk with that McGregor. I want to know who his backers are.'

'I don't agree,' Sir Reginald said. 'I don't think you should go at all. This isn't the work for an executive. I think you should stay here.'

'No,' Ricketts said. 'I'd like Dalton to come along. He knows more about security and terrorist warfare than anyone else in this room. We can do it between us.'

'Right,' Dalton said.

'I'd like to come,' Turner said. 'I couldn't bear waiting here. I can't fight, but I do know that rig and I can organize something.'

'That's right,' Ricketts said. 'You can lead the maintenance men to that leg. You can make sure they find it double-quick and get down there and block it.'

'Fine,' Turner said.

They all looked at each other. The boardroom suddenly seemed quiet. The light seemed very bright and it cut through the haze of cigarette smoke. There were rumblings outside, distant shouting and banging. As usual, work was going on through the night, the men oblivious to all this.

143

Ricketts looked at his watch. He looked down at the Prime Minister. He saw the blue eyes and the shrewd, florid face, the large hands on the table.

'I'll stay here,' the Prime Minister said. 'We'll all stay here until it's over. I'll make sure that no one leaves this room until you give us a call.'

Ricketts smiled at him, then he looked down at Turner. Turner stood up and yawned and stretched himself as if no longer nervous. Ricketts glanced around the room. It was very bright and filled with smoke. The realization that it was two in the morning suddenly made him feel tired. He shook his head and blinked, feeling weak and unreal. He glanced at Dalton and Dalton smiled wearily and walked to the door. Dalton opened the door. Turner just walked on out. Dalton held the door open, but Ricketts nodded and Dalton also walked out. Ricketts glanced around him, saw the men around the table. All the men around the table looked guilty as he walked from the room.

CHAPTER FOURTEEN

WALKING with Dalton and Turner across the enormous platform, feeling the cold wind at his face, seeing the lights of the derricks tapering up to the dark sky where the clouds formed a low brooding ceiling, Ricketts experienced a real feeling of elation, a fresh inflow of energy. He walked quickly and impatiently. Dalton and Turner raced behind him. Ricketts cut around the cranes and the mountains of wooden crates, heard the hammering of the sea against the legs, saw the wide, shielding darkness. He didn't want to waste any time; he wanted to hit them before dawn. He knew the boats would take a few hours to get out, and he wanted them organized. Dalton and Turner raced behind him, could barely keep up with him. Ricketts reached the end of the deck, quickly climbed up a ladder, then walked rapidly across a smaller deck to the cramped radio hut. The door was closed, but Ricketts opened it and walked in. The bright light stung his eyes and he blinked and looked down at the operative.

'Okay,' Ricketts said, 'take a break. Close the door when you leave.'

'What?' the operative said.

'I want you to leave,' Ricketts said.

'I'm not supposed to do that, Mr. Ricketts. You know I can't do that.'

Dalton walked in behind Ricketts and jerked his thumb towards the door. The operative, recognizing him as one of the top American men, stood up and looked a little confused and then walked out the door. He then stuck his head back in. 'Do I wait here?' he said. 'That's right,' Ricketts said. 'You wait there. When we want you, we'll call you.' The operative's head disappeared as Turner walked into the hut. He closed the door behind him and stood there, blinking his eyes.

Ricketts sat down at the radio, got on-shore security, and

told them to put Blackburn on the line as quickly as possible. The line was crackling. The storm was obviously brewing. After what seemed a very long time, Blackburn came on the line.

'Ricketts?' Blackburn said.

'Yes,' Ricketts said.

'What's up?' Blackburn said. 'I was sleeping. This better be good.'

'It's an emergency,' Ricketts said. 'Do you have a pen and paper? I want you to listen very carefully, and to take all this down.'

'Sure,' Blackburn said. 'Fire away.'

'I want six submersible-carrying ships to leave Peterhead straight away and sail directly for Beryl Field. I want thirty assault-trained security troops to go with the submersibles. They're all to be equipped with full combat packs, including hand-grenades and light automatic rifles. I also want a crack six-man maintenance crew equipped with spare plates and emergency welding equipment; these men are all to be on the same ship.'

'Hey, hold on,' Blackburn said. 'That's emergency A1. I can't take that sort of directive from you, Ricketts. Only Barker can order that.'

'Barker's dead,' Ricketts said.

'*What*?' Blackburn said.

'Barker's dead,' Ricketts said. 'He was shot a few hours ago. I'm in charge of this whole operation, and I don't want an argument.'

'Jesus, Ricketts, what the hell's going on?'

'Never mind,' Ricketts said. 'This is absolute top security. I want everyone involved to be stamped; they're to keep their mouths shut. I want them to move out immediately. I don't want them to be seen. And I want them at Beryl Field as soon as possible – something like yesterday.'

Dalton moved up behind Ricketts, leaned over towards the microphone. 'This is Mr. Dalton,' he said. 'I'm your author-ization.' There was a very brief silence. 'Yes, sir,' Blackburn said. Dalton grinned and stepped away from the table and nodded at Ricketts.

'Right?' Ricketts said.

'Right,' Blackburn said.

'Okay,' Ricketts said. 'Listen carefully.' He coughed once, then put his hand back on the table. 'I want the ships to leave immediately. I want them to go at top speed. I want them to rendezvous five miles east of Charlie 2 and just sit there until I arrive. Launch the submersibles while you're waiting. Put three men in each one. You can tell them that they're going to make a forced landing on Charlie 2, and that I'll give them further instructions when I arrive. Put the maintenance team on *Victory*. I'm going to come down on *Victory*. Don't let them get into the submersibles until I arrive.'

'It'll take four hours,' Blackburn said.

'That's too long,' Ricketts said.

'The ships just can't travel any faster.'

'It's too long,' Ricketts said.

'How soon?' Blackburn said.

'Three hours maximum,' Ricketts said. 'I can't launch the assault later than six, so that gives me four hours.'

'It'll take me an hour to get organized.'

'That's why I'm giving you three hours to get there.'

'The Shetland Islands,' Blackburn said. 'We've got all we need in Lerwick. That cuts the distance down by over half, so we'll just about make it.'

'Right,' Ricketts said.

'You want a reading?' Blackburn said.

'Yes,' Ricketts said.

'I'll check the chart.'

Ricketts sat back in his chair, glanced at Turner and Dalton. The American was leaning casually against the wall, smoking a cigarette. Then Blackburn came on. He gave Ricketts a grid location. He gave a rendezvous time of 0500 hours and then he rang off. Ricketts turned to the intercom, flicked a switch and asked for surgery. A sleepy doctor answered his call, sounding rather disgruntled.

'Dr. Seymour?'

'Who else?'

'This is Ricketts.'

'I gathered.'

'How's that cute American, Jack Schulman?'

'He's okay, but he's sleeping.'

'Where?'

'In the surgery.'

'Drugged?'

'No, just sleepy. He had a couple of beers and fell asleep, so I just let him lie there.'

'Wake him up,' Ricketts said. 'Send him up to the bar. Tell him to be there in half an hour. I want to have words with him.'

He turned the intercom off, then yawned and stretched himself. When he had finished, he looked up at Dalton and gave a small grin.

'Here we go,' Dalton said.

They all walked out of the hut. The operative was standing there. He was shivering with cold and slapping his arms vigorously around his body.

'Can I go in now?' he said.

'You can go in,' Ricketts said. 'But don't let anyone make a call out. I don't care who it is.'

'I'll authorize that,' Dalton said. 'Any arguments, use my name. And if anyone tries to make a call, I want to know who they are.'

'Right, sir,' the operative said.

He disappeared into the hut as Ricketts turned and walked away. He was followed by Dalton and Turner, and they climbed down the ladder. The wind was growing stronger, was moaning around the derricks. The whole platform was a quiltwork of bright lights, of white space and shadow. They walked across the main deck, were surrounded by working men. The men were ants beneath the structures of the platform, rushing backwards and forwards. Ricketts climbed another ladder, and Dalton and Turner followed him up. They all entered the modules and walked along the narrow corridors, and then finally went down some more steps and walked into the restaurant. Some of the shift-workers were eating, were cutting up huge steaks. Ricketts and Dalton put their elbows on the counter while Turner ordered some coffees.

'When do we leave?' Dalton said.

'As soon as we can,' Ricketts said. 'Just as soon as Schulman gets his chopper ready. I don't mind being early.'

'Do you think the boats will make it?'

'Yes, I do,' Ricketts said. 'That storm isn't due until six, so they should have a smooth trip.'

'Coffee,' Turner said.

'Just what I need,' Dalton said. 'I don't know; I'm still worried about this storm. I don't think we need that.'

'It'll be rough,' Ricketts said. 'It won't make the climbing easy. But it'll certainly put the terrorists off their guard; they just won't be expecting us.'

'Thirty men,' Turner said. 'We're just thirty against sixty. I don't see that as very good odds.'

'To hell with it,' Ricketts said. 'We're just going to have to risk it. We've only got six ships in each port, so that's all we can take. Besides, the odds aren't that bad. Half their men will be asleep. We can hit the fucking bastards real hard before they get their eyes open. That should bring their numbers down, that should even the odds a little, and with the storm and the element of surprise, they'll be really confused.'

'I hope so,' Dalton said.

'So do I,' Turner said.

'What the hell,' Ricketts said. 'We've no option. It's all up for grabs now.'

They drank their coffee, kept glancing at their watches. The roustabouts and roughnecks at the tables were talking and laughing. In a way it was incredible, was more than fantastic: all that had been happening had occurred in twelve hours, and these men had continued working right through it. They still didn't know about it, would probably never know about it, would read about a seaquake and the deaths of some rig-workers, and would put it down as part of the job, the normal risks of the North Sea. Ricketts grinned at the thought of it. He just couldn't believe it. He drank his coffee and put his cup down and saw Schulman walk in.

'Hi ho,' Schulman said.

'You look tired,' Ricketts said.

'I *am* tired,' Schulman said. 'I'm fucking tired. What the hell's going on?'

'We need you,' Ricketts said.

'At *this* hour?'

'At this hour.'

'Don't tell me another goddamned rig's sunk. I still haven't recovered.'

'No,' Ricketts said. 'It's nothing like that. We just want

you to fly us out to Beryl. We have to fly there immediately.'

'Charlie 2?'

'Five miles east.'

'What the hell's five miles east?'

'You'll find out,' Ricketts said, 'soon enough. Now go and get ready.'

'I don't believe this,' Schulman said.

'You better believe it,' Ricketts said.

'It's two-thirty in the morning, for chrissakes. What the hell's going on?'

'It's an emergency,' Ricketts said.

'Jesus Christ, not another.'

'The same one in a sense,' Ricketts said. 'Eagle 3 was a seaquake.'

'A seaquake?' Schulman said.

'That's right,' Ricketts said. 'The sea-bed cracked open right beneath Eagle 3 and then it ran on as far as Beryl.'

'That's what sank Eagle 3?'

'That's what sank it,' Ricketts said.

'And now it's run as far as Beryl Field?'

'That's right,' Ricketts said.

'Here,' Turner said. 'Have a coffee.'

Schulman took the coffee. He drank it down and it was hot. He put the cup back on the counter, wiped his lips with one hand.

'What's happening on Beryl?' he said.

'It's Charlie 2,' Ricketts said. 'Charlie 2's been badly damaged and we're launching a rescue operation.'

'From five miles east?' Schulman said.

'That's right,' Ricketts said. 'We don't want to land the chopper because we think it might be sinking, so we're going to move in slowly with boats.'

'I'm gonna drop you on the boats?'

'In a nutshell,' Ricketts said. 'You drop us down and then you fly back to Forties and wait for our call.'

'If you get on, I'll pick you up?'

'If we save the rig, you'll pick us up.'

'And what if you don't save the rig?'

'Then we might go down with it.'

Schulman glanced around the room, saw the men at the tables. 'Okay,' he said. 'What time do we leave? I could do with a meal.'

'We leave yesterday,' Ricketts said. 'We're a day late already. I want you to go straight up to the deck and call us here when you're ready.'

'Jesus,' Schulman said.

'Take a sandwich,' Turner said.

'Thanks,' Schulman said. 'That's a thought. I mean I like the high life.'

He picked a sandwich from the counter, jammed it into his mouth, started chewing and waved his left hand and walked out of the restaurant. Turner ordered more coffees. The man behind the counter served them. They stood there and sipped at their coffee, checked their watches methodically.

'You're pretty smart,' Dalton said.

'So I'm told,' Ricketts said.

'When this is over,' Dalton said, 'give me a call. I think we're wasting your talents.'

Turner looked at his watch. 'Two forty-five,' he said. 'Those boats should have pulled out by now. They'll be well on their way.'

'I hope so,' Dalton said.

'They'll be moving,' Ricketts said. 'That Blackburn is pretty well organized. He knows what he's doing.'

'I don't like it,' Turner said. 'I don't like this hanging around. I wish to hell that kid would get moving. I want to get out of here.'

'You take the maintenance men,' Ricketts said. 'You know all about that business. When we hit the deck, you go straight for the leg and have them fix up that hole.'

'I might not get there,' Turner said.

'You'll get protection,' Ricketts said. 'I'll make sure you're covered all the way. I'll make sure you get there.'

'I want McGregor,' Dalton said.

'So do I,' Ricketts said.

'I want him alive,' Dalton said. 'I want to talk to that bastard.'

'Who backed him?' Turner said. 'I'd really like to know that. It beats me who the hell would have done that. That McGregor, he knows.'

'That's right,' Ricketts said. 'That bastard knows. And we'll make sure he tells us.'

The telephone rang. The man behind the counter

answered it. He was hot and he wiped sweat from his forehead as he put the phone down.

'The helicopter pad,' he said to Ricketts. 'They want you all up there.'

They walked out of the restaurant and climbed to the main deck. The lights on the structures beamed down, cutting swathes through the darkness. Ricketts heard the wind, moaning mournfully through the derricks; it was stronger than it had been before, and that made him feel good. They walked across the catwalk. The wind was very strong there. It came out of the North Sea and blew straight across them and out again. The sea was very far below. It was too dark to see it. They heard it smashing into the concrete legs as they passed over space. Then they were on the landing pad. The helicopter was already roaring. It whipped the wind around and hurled it at them as they hurried towards it. They bent low beneath the rotors. They didn't need to, but they did. Two men in yellow overalls were pulling the blocks away as they climbed up and into the helicopter.

It was a six-man helicopter. The whole interior was vibrating. It made a hell of a noise and it seemed very cluttered and dark. Schulman closed the door behind them, grinned broadly and waved one hand, and they sat down and strapped themselves in as he went back to the cockpit. Ricketts took the seat beside him. They both strapped themselves in. Schulman took the controls and the engine roared louder, then the helicopter rocked from side to side and rose up in the air. The deck fell far below them. The darkness surrounded them. The helicopter lurched and turned around and headed north towards Beryl Field.

Ricketts studied the darkness, saw moonlight on the clouds. It was a faint light that rippled and bent, gliding over that dark field. He looked down to his right, saw the winking lights of Maureen; he couldn't see a single oil rig, but he could see the lights. Ricketts sat back in his seat. He felt uncomfortable with the straps on. Only the moonlight flitting through the black clouds showed that something was actually out there. The helicopter rose and fell, fought against a strong wind. The wind was blowing down from the north, between the Shetlands and Norway. He was very pleased at that. It was just what he wanted. Let the sea rise up and smash the whole rig; let it give them their cover. The helicopter kept going, kept fighting the growing wind, and Jack Schulman was chewing some gum and glancing vaguely around him. Ricketts grinned at the sight of him. He was comforted by Schulman's presence. He closed his eyes and put his head back on the seat and tried to let the time pass.

'What time is it?' Dalton asked.

'Four-thirty,' Schulman said.

'What time do you think we'll get there?'

'About five,' Schulman said.

The time seemed to pass slowly, the helicopter bucked and swayed, and Ricketts opened his eyes and looked left and saw lights far below. It was the lights of Piper Field. They winked fitfully in the darkness. He couldn't actually see the rigs, but he knew that the work was going on down there. Ricketts shifted in his seat, watched the lights moving backwards, falling behind and leaving nothing but darkness, that chilling black void.

'What time is it?' Dalton said.

'Four-forty,' Turner said.

'Jesus,' Dalton said, 'it's a time-warp. We're just going backwards.'

'We're nearly halfway there,' Schulman said.

'Good,' Turner said.

'It's a bitch of a night,' Schulman said. 'There's a storm coming up.'

They said nothing after that, simply looked out at the darkness, saw the moonlight rippling over the clouds, that black painted on blackness. Jack Schulman chewed his gum. Turner checked his watch constantly. Dalton seemed to be lost deep in thought, his face hidden in shadow. The helicopter kept going, roared all around them, shuddered and jumped up and down, heading into the growing wind. Ricketts emptied his mind. It was a trick he had learnt somewhere. He went down through himself and found rest, slowly rose up again. He opened his eyes, looked down and saw the lights. They were winking in the black mat of the night, and he knew it was Beryl Field.

'There she blows,' Schulman said.

'Just keep going,' Ricketts said.

'She's still afloat,' Schulman said. 'You want to look?'

'No,' Ricketts said. 'Later.'

They flew over Charlie 2, recognized it by the lights. The lights passed below and behind them, and then there was darkness. Schulman studied his chart: he wanted the rendezvous point. He snapped his fingers and said, 'Here we go!' and started dropping down lower. They dropped to a thousand feet, passed through some thin clouds. Looking down they saw nothing but darkness, a black void flecked with grey light. Schulman flew back and forth, circled around in the void. He was looking for the lights of the ships, but there was nothing below them.

'We're too early,' Ricketts said.

'I gathered that,' Schulman said.

'Head direct for Lerwick,' Ricketts said. 'We're bound to pass over them.'

Schulman did as he was told. He kept at low altitude. The helicopter rocked crazily and shuddered and then steadied again. Ricketts looked at the sea below. It was one with the darkness. The clouds above had cut off the moonlight, which was just what he wanted. Still, he kept looking. He wanted to see those damned lights. If he didn't see the lights pretty soon, they'd be too far away. He heard the roar of the helicopter. A black mass passed overhead. The helicopter was fighting the wind and flying under the clouds. They flew for five minutes, keeping dangerously low. Finally, far below and ahead, they saw the lights of the ships.

'There they are,' Schulman said.

'Thank Christ for that,' Ricketts said. 'I thought they might be still in Lerwick, bottled in by the storm.'

'I'm going down,' Schulman said.

'Right,' Ricketts said. 'Get down there and drop us on *Victory*. That should be the first ship.'

The helicopter dropped lower and the lights ahead raced towards them. The lights were like candles in a black room, just floating in space. Then they grew larger, illuminated the ploughing ships. There were six ships and they formed a triangle, the tip pointing towards Beryl Field. Schulman dropped lower, dropped towards the first ship. The helicopter dipped forward and nosed down and rocked roughly from left to right. It dropped lower and lower. The ships seemed to separate. They were spread out in the darkness in triangular formation, their dimmed lights illuminating the sunken decks.

'The first ship?' Schulman said.

'The first ship,' Ricketts said.

'Okay,' Schulman said. 'We're right on top of it. I'm going down now.'

The helicopter started falling, a perpendicular fall, and as it fell it rocked wildly from side to side, up and down on the howling wind. Ricketts looked down at *Victory*. The deck was widening beneath him. It was a quiltwork of dim light and shadow, rising up, falling down again. It didn't seem very large, it bobbed about in the blackness, and the helicopter started hovering above it as the waves washed around it. The waves were ribbons of white and black, forming circles around the hull. The circles closed in and rippled and exploded and reformed and moved in again. The helicopter didn't move, merely shuddered and rocked wildly. It was thirty feet above the forward deck and the ship had dropped anchor.

'Right,' Ricketts said. 'We're on our way.'

He took off the strap, stood up and moved back, saw Dalton and Turner climb out of their seats and move towards the emergency hatch. The hatch was in the floor. The rescue winch was beside it. Dalton knelt down and jerked at the hatch door and pulled it away. A blast of cold air rushed in. They heard the roar of the helicopter. Dalton waved a hand at Turner and made him put on the leather halter. Turner did as he was told, did it quickly and expertly. He put his legs over the side of the hatch and then let himself slide out. The straps went taut behind him. Dalton operated the winch. It turned around and Turner disappeared from view and Ricketts went to the hatch. He looked down through the hole, saw Turner swinging out. He went out on the wind and swung back, but he kept dropping lower. The deck of the ship rose up and down. There were deck hands looking up. Their white faces matched the white of the sea as it swirled around the ship. Turner swung above the deck. He was spinning slowly around. He dropped lower and the deck hands reached up and pulled him aboard.

Dalton went down next. He spiralled down into the darkness. He was swung to and fro by the wind, but he kept

155

dropping steadily. Schulman worked the winch. The helicopter was on automatic. Ricketts looked down through the hole and saw the deck hands grabbing Dalton and releasing the straps and waving up at him. Schulman winched the harness in. Ricketts quickly put it on. He slithered over to the hole and put his legs through and saw Schulman grinning.

'Adios,' Schulman said. 'Give me a call. Don't get too wet down there.'

Ricketts dropped into space. He heard the roar of the helicopter. The wind howled and picked him up and threw him out and then the straps took control of him. He was lowered to the ship, saw the black sea and white foam, saw the white faces staring from the blackness, a pair of hands reaching up to him. Ricketts felt the icy spray. It poured over him and drenched him. He felt the wind and heard the roaring all around him, and then the waiting hands grabbed him. He rolled on the deck, stood up and released the harness, saw Dalton and Turner beside him, the deck hands around him. Then the harness was drawn up. It vanished inside the helicopter. The hatch was shut and the helicopter started climbing, then it disappeared quickly in the darkness.

CHAPTER FIFTEEN

THE ship was tossing from side to side. The sea roared and smashed over it. The other ships had stopped also, and were spread out in a vague, bobbing circle. Ricketts fought to keep his balance as an icy spray showered over him. He looked around and saw the lights of the other boats, illuminating the water. The boats were rising and falling, their lights dancing across the waves. The wind howled and made the sea hiss and swirl and then explode into white spray.

'That sea's rough,' Dalton said.

'It's only starting,' Turner said. 'I wouldn't like to see it in an hour. Those waves will be murder.'

Ricketts looked at the men around him, at the deck hands and divers, and saw six other men on the deck at the stern, clambering over the three pinioned submersibles. The stern was open to the sea. A steel frame formed a bridge. The three submersibles were connected to the frame, all set to be lowered. The stern rose and fell, a white spray exploded into it, and the men at the submersibles were in wet-suits as black as the night.

'Are those the maintenance men?' Ricketts said.

'Yes, they are,' someone said. Ricketts turned and saw a rough seaman's face, a peaked cap on the head. 'Cap'ain Cabot,' the man said. 'Those six men are the maintenance men. They've already put their gear in the submersibles. Are you Ricketts by any chance?'

'Yes,' Ricketts said.

'I was told to see you,' Cabot said. 'Blackburn said you were in charge of this show, said you'd know what was happening.'

'I want us dropped,' Ricketts said. 'Then your boats go back to Lerwick. You don't need to know anything but that. Now just where the hell are we?'

'Ten miles from Charlie 2. You said five, but you came early. We only stopped to let you aboard. Shall I start up again?'

'Will the submersibles go that far?'

'Of course. And a lot farther.'

'Okay,' Ricketts said. 'This will do. We'll all set off from here.'

The ship rose up and fell, there was a roar and they were drenched, the water swept around their feet and poured out through the holes in the sides. Ricketts looked at the other boats. He saw them rocking in the sea, their lights dancing in the hollows between the waves and racing backwards and forwards.

'Are they ready?' Ricketts said.

'They should be,' Cabot said. 'They won't be in the submersibles right now, but that can soon be arranged.'

'Weapons?'

'Full packs.'

'Instructions?'

'A bit vague. Blackburn said you'd be filling them in when they took off for Beryl.'

'What do they know about Charlie 2?'

'They know they're making a forced assault. They know commencement time is 0600 hours, but they don't know much else.'

Ricketts looked at his watch. It was 0530 hours. He didn't have much time to play around with; they would have to go now.

'Are they in contact?' he said.

'Absolutely,' Cabot said. 'All communications systems are open. Just give me the word.'

'Right,' Ricketts said. 'I want the men in the submersibles. I want the submersibles launched straight away. What's the system for that?'

'It's pretty simple,' Cabot said. 'It's a lot simpler in better weather. A large lift-line picks the submersible up off the deck and then lowers it away just above the water. A diver stands on the casing and disconnects the lift-line and lets the submersible half sink in the water. It's held up by a tow rope, we tow it out to its diving position, and then, when you're all set to go, the diver disconnects the tow rope. You sink down to whatever depth you require and then switch on the engines. It's as simple as that.'

'What kind of submersibles are they?'

'Vickers Pisces III,' Cabot said. 'Battery operated.'

'Charged up, I hope?'

'Jesus Christ,' Cabot said.

'Communications?'

'Marconi Modular systems with thryster control circuits, sub to sub, no interference at all.'

'Right. So your ships pull away, we float on the end of the tow ropes, I give my instructions while we're drifting, and then we cast off.'

'That's about it,' Cabot said. 'Then you're all on your own.'

'Will we get there in half an hour?'

'Those little bastards are fast.'

'Okay,' Ricketts said, 'let's get started.'

He looked around him. The wind howled and the sea roared. The waves were growing higher each minute, exploding over the deck. Ricketts looked up at the sky. It was black and unrelenting. He looked across at the other bobbing boats, saw their lights through the flying spray.

'I'll get in contact,' Cabot said. 'I'll order them into the submersibles. I'll have them all over the side in five minutes from now.'

'Okay,' Ricketts said. 'Let us drift for five minutes. That'll give me enough time to brief the men. You can cast us off then.'

The captain nodded and walked away. Ricketts walked to the stern. He was followed by Dalton and Turner, and they had to be careful. The sea was roaring all around them, sweeping viciously across the deck, pouring over the other side while the ship rose and fell and plunged down through more oncoming waves. They finally reached the submersibles. The maintenance men were waiting to board. The launching deck looked like a car ferry, and the wind howled right through it. The ship was rolling from side to side, the sea roared and sprayed over them, but the submersibles were firmly pinioned to the deck and Ricketts studied them carefully.

They were miniature submarines, about twenty feet long.

They were eleven feet high from the sail to the skids, and they looked like huge insects on skis. There were lights above the ports. The ports comprised three round windows. It was these windows, on the nose of the machines, that made them seem like large insects. On each side there were propellers. The submersibles had no rudders; they were steered by simply increasing the drive on the relevant propeller. Squat legs joined up to the skids, which were for movement on the sea-bed. Beneath the ports, at the base of the prow, there was a mass of equipment. This was the manipulator assembly, a complete set of steel arms, the robotic manipulating devices for manual work on the sea-bed.

Ricketts looked at the six men. They had grenades around their wet suits. They were windblown and their faces were drenched and they swayed with the ship.

'Who's in charge?' Ricketts said.

'I am,' a blond giant said.

'What's the situation with the men?'

'You got all you asked for.'

'Thirty-six men?' Ricketts said.

'That's right; thirty-six. There's three submersibles here, two on each of the other five boats, and we've ordered three men to each sub.'

'Good,' Ricketts said. 'I want two of you to each sub. One of us will make up your third man and we'll meet up at the rig.'

'What's happening?' the blond giant said.

'It's terrorists,' Ricketts said. 'They've taken over Charlie 2 and they've threatened to blow a leg if we attack. Well, we've got no choice. We're going to attack. The job of this team is to mend the leg before the rig sinks.'

'We'll have to fight our way to it.'

'That's right,' Ricketts said. 'You and I can be taking care of that while Turner leads the men down. That's it. Now let's go.'

Dalton and Turner split up, they each took a separate submersible, and Ricketts climbed up the side of the third submersible and grabbed hold of the metal sail. He had to fight to keep his balance since the ship was rocking crazily, and he looked at the ship's open stern and saw the dark, surging sea. The waves exploded and sprayed over him. He wiped the water from his eyes. The first man was lowering himself down the hatch, inside the curved metal sail. He dropped into the submersible, then Ricketts swung his legs over, sat briefly on the edge of the steel sail and carefully lowered himself down.

His feet landed on a wooden deck. Beneath the deck were pipes and pumps. The inside of the submersible was small and very cramped, with curved walls of steel and a low ceiling. Ricketts had to stoop low. The hatch was directly above his head. He saw two curved wooden benches around the side of the sphere, facing the three windows at the front. There was more equipment beneath the benches, there were controls everywhere, and every available space in the sphere was covered with gauges and valves.

The other man was at the pilot's console, sitting on a wooden bench. A pair of boots dropped down above Ricketts' head and he had to move back. He bumped his head on the low ceiling, and he cursed and sat down. The blond giant had dropped on to the deck and was shutting the hatch. He grunted as he turned the wheel. The wheel made a grating sound. The noise reverberated around the tiny sphere and then the wheel locked. The blond giant muttered something and knelt down between the benches. He seemed incredibly large in that enclosed space, grinning casually at Ricketts.

'They're pretty small,' he said to Ricketts.

'Too small,' Ricketts said.

'I don't like to be under the sea in these fuckers. At least not for too long.'

The submersible suddenly shook. They heard the sound of ringing steel. Ricketts looked up and wondered what it was, and then he heard clanging chains.

'It's the diver,' the blond said. 'He's standing on top of the submersible. He'll stay there while we're lowered over the stern, and then he'll disconnect the lift-line. The ship will pull away from us. We'll float out on the tow line. Then, when we're ready to cast off, he'll disconnect that as well.'

The man's voice had an echo. Everything echoed inside the sphere. The lights were on and they shone down the curved walls, illuminated the pipes and valves. Ricketts felt claustrophobic, thought of being trapped in here, thought of himself under the sea in this hot, tiny prison. The very thought made him shiver. He blinked his eyes and checked himself. He saw the other man facing the pilot's console, checking gauges and dials. Ricketts looked at his watch. It was 0540 hours. They would reach the rig shortly after 0600 hours, and then the real business would start.

The submersible started vibrating, shook violently and broke loose, jumped up and then swung from side to side as if hanging in space. That's exactly what was happening. It was swinging over the launching deck. It had been picked up by the lift-line and was now swinging over the sea. Ricketts held on to the bench, felt light and disorientated. The rig shook and he felt it dropping down and then he heard a loud drumming sound.

'That's it,' the blond man said. 'We're in the sea.'

Ricketts kept his head low, clambered along to the pilot's console, brushed the shoulder of the first man and looked out through one of the windows. He felt like a goldfish. He saw the dark, heaving sea. It stretched away at eye level, seemed to rise up above him, and then was swallowed totally by the darkness. They were half sunk in the water. The waves crashed against the ports. The submersible rose and fell, swayed left to right, in a sickening fashion.

'We're drifting out,' the first man said. 'The ship's pulling away. When we stop drifting out, the tow rope's tight. Your five minutes start then.'

Ricketts gazed through the window. The sea climbed up to the darkness. The waves rolled up and rushed down through valleys and then rolled up again. The sea was really very rough. It was like being on a big dipper. Ricketts felt his stomach heave as they climbed up and then plunged back down again. He looked out through the window, saw a dark, swirling void; the void rushed up towards him, swirled around him, threw him up towards the black sky. This movement was continuous. It was sickeningly repetitive. Ricketts crawled from the window and sat down on the bench facing the console. Then he felt a jerking motion and was almost thrown sideways. He heard the drumming of the sea against the hull and then the sphere seemed to steady.

The radio was crackling. The man at the console had turned it on. The voice of Captain Cabot came through the speaker like the voice of a robot.

162

'*Victory* to *Josephine*. *Victory* to *Josephine*. You are now in position in tow drift. We will launch in five minutes.'

'*Josephine* to *Victory*. *Josephine* to *Victory*. Message received. Roger and out.'

The pilot turned around. He had left the radio open. He waved his right hand at the console and then nodded at Ricketts.

'It's all yours,' he said. 'I've already signalled the other subs. They'll all be on receive when you talk, so just pick up the mike.'

Ricketts crossed to the other bench as the submersible swayed from side to side. It nosed forward and then started tilting down as he sat by the console. He picked up the microphone, heard the drumming of the sea outside, suddenly realized how warm the sphere was, how suffocating it felt.

'*Josephine* to all subs. *Josephine* to all subs. We are now in tow drift and will be casting off as soon as I finish. We will be heading for Charlie 2. Charlie 2 has been hijacked. The normal crew have all been killed, and it is estimated that sixty terrorists are aboard. We have to take back the rig. We have to rout the terrorists. We are not concerned with damage to the rig; nor with the lives of the terrorists. Once aboard, you will shoot to kill. You will get aboard by climbing the pontoon legs. You will commence firing as soon as you reach the deck or as soon as they fire. We are casting off now. We will go down to three-hundred feet. We will follow the chart route to Charlie 2 and surface under the deck. The pilots will open the hatches. They will check with the other pilots. No one is to move to the ladders until all hatches are open. There's to be no noise down there. We will move when *Josephine* signals. When I signal, you will go up the ladders with your weapons engaged. Take the ladder closest to you. Shoot on sight of the terrorists. Don't stop until the whole rig is cleared and the terrorists mopped up.'

Ricketts stopped talking, wiped sweat from his brow, heard the drumming of the sea against the hull, felt the sub pitch and toss.

'Instructions for *Auk* and *Huk*. Repeat: instructions for *Auk* and *Huk*. You are not to engage the terrorists unless absolutely necessary; your mission is to get to the damaged leg.

You will stay with the crew of *Josephine*. The crew of *Josephine* will give you cover. You will go down the damaged pontoon leg and temporarily repair it. Take full diving equipment. Take wet-welding equipment. The only weapons you can take along are pistols; you'll have to carry the replacement plates. Repeat: stick with *Josephine*. We will give you covering fire. Your mission is to fix that damaged leg. I want no deviations.'

Ricketts looked at his watch. It was 0550 hours. They could get to Charlie 2 by 0630. It would still be dark then.

'We're casting off now,' Ricketts said. 'Good luck to all of you. Over and out.'

He switched off the microphone, stared around the curved steel walls. The walls curved up and met above his head where a bright light was shining. Ricketts blinked his eyes, heard the drumming of the sea, looked at the three small round windows, saw the dark waves beyond. Then he heard the diver's feet. The diver was walking along the hull. There was a dull metallic sound from the stern as the tow line dropped off. This was followed by a splash and a scraping along the hull. The diver's face, grotesque in the breathing mask, appeared at the window. He stuck up one thumb. The pilot waved his right hand. A white foam bubbled over the window as the diver swam off.

The pilot switched on the power. The engine made a humming sound. He switched on the outside lights, and they beamed over and into the dark waves. Then the pilot opened the vent, water hissed into the tanks, and the sea rose up above the three windows and eventually covered them. The submersible sank steadily, vibrating and humming quietly. Ricketts went to a window and looked out and saw the murky dark water. It gave him a chill. He sensed the silence of those cold depths. The beams of the lights cut through the murk about six or eight feet. It was not very far. Beyond that was total darkness. The only matter in the dulled beam of the lights was a drifting, grey-green mass.

The depth gauge registered a hundred feet, inched around to two hundred, and after what seemed a very long time they reached three-hundred feet. The pilot closed the vent. He turned on the radio. He checked that the other submersibles were all down and then he turned the propellers on.

The submersible moved forward, its lights cutting through the murk. The sea seemed to part around the windows and they glided on through it. The submersible vibrated slightly, made a low, humming sound, and the hands on all the gauges were quivering, recording their movements. The pilot switched on the sonar set, kept his eyes on the small screen, then he checked the gyro compass and settled back, watched the lights through the windows.

'What's your name?' Ricketts said.

'Roy Walters,' the pilot said.

'And you?' Ricketts said to the blond giant.

'Hubbert. Ralph Hubbert.'

Ricketts glanced around the sphere. It was terrifyingly small. The walls were covered in gauges, the benches hid more equipment, and the space between the floorboards of the deck was filled with grey pipes and pumps. Ricketts couldn't stand up, could scarcely put out his arms; it was more comfortable sitting, so he sat there and studied the weapons. There were Sterling Light Automatic Rifles and 20-round magazines. He saw a pile of tear-gas canisters and grenades, some clubs and handcuffs.

'You're well equipped,' Ricketts said.

'That's what you wanted,' Hubbert said.

'That's right,' Ricketts said. 'That's what I wanted. I got just what I wanted.'

Hubbert grinned laconically. He was sitting on the bench facing Ricketts. His blond head was scraping the ceiling and his huge hands were folded.

'You think we'll get them?' he said.

'We've *got* to get them,' Ricketts said.

'It's a tough nut to crack,' Hubbert said. 'Those Clan guys, they're all psychos.'

'You think so?' Ricketts said.

'Yeah, I think so,' Hubbert said. 'They're all psychos. They're all fucking suicidal. It's part of their rules.'

'You've fought them before?' Ricketts said.

'No,' Hubbert said. 'I haven't fought them but I've read all about them, and they're all fucking freaky.'

'They're just fanatics,' Ricketts said.

'Fucking right,' Hubbert said. 'And they won't stop until we kill them all. We'll have to just burn right through them.'

It seemed to take a long time. They kept travelling through silence. The submersible was vibrating and humming, but it moved forward smoothly. Ricketts went up to the front, heard the pinging of the sonar set, saw the pinpoints of light on the screen, saw the beams of light outside. He looked through a window. The beams of light cut through the darkness. The darkness parted and let them pass on, but spread its wings all around them. It was quiet out there; it was the silence of the deep. In the lights, in the swimming grey-green murk, he saw translucent fish. Ricketts sat beside the pilot. The pilot was watching the gyro compass. The needle of the compass was quivering, but it didn't move much.

'How long?' Ricketts said.

'About ten minutes,' Walters said. 'We'll have to start climbing in five minutes. I think the sea's pretty rough.'

'How rough?' Ricketts said.

'Bloody rough,' Walters said. 'Those waves might be fifty feet high. I'm not sure, but they could be.'

'The rig?' Ricketts said.

'The rig's out,' Walters said. 'If we try to get under that bloody rig, we'll just get smashed to pieces.'

'We'll have to surface,' Ricketts said.

'That's right; we'll have to surface. We'll have to come up well away from the rig and then put on our diving masks.'

'That's not practical,' Ricketts said.

'Yes it is,' Hubbert said. 'We'll just have to put the weapons in bags and drag the buggers behind us.'

'And the replacement plates?' Ricketts said. 'What about them? You can't drag those plates through the water; they're too heavy for that.'

'That's right,' Walters said. 'We can't take the plates with us. But we *can* take the welding equipment. We'll find plates on the rig.'

Ricketts licked his lips, thought of fifty-foot waves, thought of the men swimming through the water, beneath the sea's killing surface. They would come up under the pontoons. They would find the base of the pontoon legs. They would climb up to the surface on the ladders and the waves would then find them. The waves could be fifty feet. The men would have to be strong. No doubt more than one would be lost before he reached the top deck. Ricketts licked his lips. He knew what Hubbert had meant. This would be a tough nut to crack, and they might not succeed.

'Okay,' Ricketts said. 'I take your point. Let's do it your way.'

He turned on the microphone and spoke to the other submersibles. He gave them their instructions, then he sat back and glanced at the floor. The floor was vibrating. The humming noise had changed slightly. Ricketts heard the tanks ejecting their water and he knew they were going up.

'Bless us all,' Walters said.

Hubbert slid off the bench, pulled out a rubber bag, put two rifles and extra magazines in the bag, added tear gas and hand grenades. He then zipped the bag up and attached a small chain to it. He jerked it and the bag didn't move and he nodded his head.

'It'll do,' he said quietly.

The submersible was rising. It was beginning to rock from side to side. Hubbert sat down on the bench and held on, let the chain trail away from him. Ricketts glanced through the window, saw the light in the murk. The separate beams were rising up and down, splaying out, disappearing. The submersible kept rising, was rocking more and more, and they heard the drumming noise from outside as the waves grew in strength.

'Okay,' Hubbert said, 'here we go. Help me on with the cylinders.'

He didn't stand so much as kneel, but he put on the large flippers and then he waited patiently for Ricketts. Ricketts held the cylinders up. Hubbert's arms went through the straps. Ricketts buckled the strap around his chest and then held out the oxygen mask. Hubbert put it on. He did all this crouching over. When he had finished he nodded at Ricketts and put up his thumb.

The submersible was still rising, was rocking more violently; it was coming to the surface of the sea, and the surface was stormy. Ricketts put on his flippers, then picked up the oxygen cylinders, but Hubbert stepped forward awkwardly and took the cylinders out of his hands. Ricketts turned around as Hubbert held the cylinders out. Ricketts slipped his hands and arms through the straps and buckled the belt at his chest. Then he put on the oxygen mask. His breath made the shield misty. He felt hot and suffocated, and he noticed that his vision was limited. He clipped the breathing tube in, turned around and looked at Hubbert, and they glanced at one another through their masks and then turned on the oxygen.

The submersible was still rising. It was rocking badly from side to side. Ricketts turned around and blinked through his mask and saw Walters before him. Walters was putting on his flippers. He was sitting beside the console. He put on the flippers and stood up and then reached for his cylinders. Hubbert helped him to put them on. The two men rocked with the submersible. The submersible was rocking to and fro, drifting up to the surface. Ricketts watched the two men. They both moved in total silence. The only sound Ricketts heard was his own breathing, the rhythmic hiss of the oxygen. Finally Walters was also ready. He pressed his hands against a wall. Hubbert followed his example and Ricketts did the same and then waited.

The submersible broke the surface. It soared up and fell back down. It was swept along the trough between waves and then was hurled up again. Ricketts timed the rise and fall, braced himself beneath the hatch. The submersible swept along the next trough and Ricketts reached up above him. He turned the wheel viciously. He felt hands holding him up. The submersible reached the crest of a wave and started racing on down again. Ricketts wrenched the hatch open, grabbed the grips at the top, held on as the submersible plummeted down and spun around and rushed sideways. It suddenly shot up again, climbing up a huge wave, and Ricketts took a deep breath and jerked his arms and pulled himself up.

He flopped over the steel sail. A monstrous wave towered above him. It roared and then curled above his head and then exploded all over him. Ricketts clung to the steel sail. The water swirled all around him. It poured back down the sides of the submersible and the wind started beating. The noise was incredible. He heard it even through the mask. He glanced up and saw the sea's rise and fall, the huge waves soaring skyward. Ricketts clambered over the sail, took the grip in one hand. He reached down with the other hand, and Hubbert reached up and took hold of it. Ricketts started pulling. A wave picked the submersible up. Ricketts felt the wind and heard the roaring wave and saw a valley of darkness. The water down there was black. It poured down and swept back up. Ricketts held the grip tight and plunged down and then flew up again. He tried not to look around him, tried to ignore the roaring sea, took a deep breath and pulled Hubbert up and knew that Walters was pushing him. Hubbert flopped across the sail, wriggled around and lay flat out. He took hold of the other grip, and he and Ricketts pulled the bag up between them. The sea roared and swept across them, sweeping Hubbert off the hull, and the submersible rose up on a wave and Ricketts plunged into empty space.

He didn't know what was happening, saw distant lights spinning, saw a huge wall of darkness rising up and blocking out the whole world. Then there was the void, streams of light through the black, and he kept spinning, turning slowly upside down, bereft of sense of direction. His head broke the surface. He was rising up on a roaring wave. He saw the lights of the rig straight ahead, soaring up to the sky. It didn't seem real, was too fierce to be real. He was carried through the air, felt the wind, and then was hurled down again. He knew he wouldn't come back up, didn't want to come back up, saw a distant submersible spinning around, saw dark forms in the monstrous waves. Ricketts blinked and looked below. He saw a black, concave void. He was plunging down towards it, and it roared and then swallowed him whole.

CHAPTER SIXTEEN

RICKETTS didn't go back up. He kicked his flippers and
went down. He went down through the dark, silent depths, to
where the waves could not reach him. A grey murk filled his
vision, he felt light as a feather, and he went down and
levelled out and kicked his legs, heading straight for the rig.

There were other men around him. They looked like
strange, primordial fish. They were kicking their legs and
blowing bubbles, dragging bags on long chains. Ricketts was
amazed. He felt a fierce exultation. It was miraculous that
these men had actually made it and were still going forward.
Ricketts kicked his legs harder. It was calm and quiet down
here. He saw the shadows in the murk all around him,
coming closer, increasing. A lot of the men had obviously
made it. They were obviously well-trained men. They were
now swimming silently all around him, and they still had
their weapons. Ricketts kicked and glided forward, heard the
hissing in his ears. It was the soft, rhythmic hissing of the
oxygen; it was all he could hear. He glanced left and right,
saw streams of small bubbles, streaming back and upwards
in silence, a dance of air and trapped light.

Ricketts felt incorporeal, felt divorced from his own body;
he was numb and he couldn't hear a sound but his own
steady breathing. The gloom ahead was unrelieved. Beyond
the gloom was pure darkness. The men ahead, the drifting
bags, the kicking flippers, were swallowed up by this darkness. Ricketts headed straight towards it. It always moved
back and eluded him. The gloom parted and swept by on
either side and the darkness receded. Ricketts kept swimming towards it. His own breathing hypnotized him. He
started dreaming, drifting out of himself, and then he saw
something moving. Ricketts moved forward cautiously, saw
some shadowy figures. He saw a black wall that was darker
than the depths, and the shadows were touching it. Ricketts

swam forward, heard the hissing of the oxygen, and the black wall, what had seemed like a wall, was the huge, round pontoon.

Ricketts went into that darkness. The men were spiralling around him. They were above him and below him and beside him, drifting up and down slowly. Ricketts swam even closer. The huge pontoon curved above him. He went under it and swam out around it and went up to the top. He saw the base of the pontoon leg. It was vague in the murk. It was thirty feet wide and it dwarfed the swimming men and soared up and disappeared into darkness. Ricketts swam across and touched it. A pair of flippers kicked above him. He glanced up and saw the base of the ladder, stopping short at the pontoon.

Ricketts took hold of a rung, started pulling himself up. It was difficult, so he took off his flippers and used his bare feet. The water was icy. He felt his feet growing numb. Nevertheless, other men were doing the same, and flippers drifted down past him.

Ricketts pulled himself up. He tried not to go up too fast. He knew that he would have to be holding the ladder when he broke through the surface. He kept moving upwards, saw the kicking feet above him, and the water, cold and black, moved around him, filled with bubbles of trapped light. Ricketts heard his own breathing. He felt the tugging of the sea. The darkness weakened and let in some light and then the black became grey. Ricketts felt a sudden tension. It passed away and he kept climbing. He felt the swirling of that icy, grey-green mass, and then he broke through the surface.

The noise exploded around him. He gripped the rung of the ladder. The sea roared and swept between the pontoon legs and then roared out again. Ricketts clung to the ladder, saw men on the other legs, saw the thinner support legs thrusting up and crisscrossing above him. The noise was appalling. The sea roared and hammered the legs. It exploded and shot upwards and out, poured back down the support legs. Ricketts held the ladder tightly. The waves roared and swept across him. He was punched by the fist of a giant, nearly torn off the ladder. He clung desperately to the rung, saw men lying on the support legs; they had steel clamps attached to their belts, and these were fixed to the ladders. The clamps kept them from falling off, let them manoeuvre with their hands. The men were clamped tight to the rungs of the ladders, and they were helping each other. The sea roared and exploded, echoed under the deck above. The men were opening the waterproof bags and taking out all the weapons. They slung the rifles across their backs, clipped the grenades to their belts. The spare magazines were in small bags which hung down from loops around their necks. Ricketts climbed up the ladder. He stretched out on a support leg. He took the clamp that was chained to his waist and snapped it over a rung. The sea roared and swept across him. His body jerked away and stopped. The chain on the clamp was only six inches long, and it kept him from falling off the support leg. The sea roared again, its white foam streaked the darkness, and it was roaring up and clawing at the men and rushing back out again.

The men were starting to move up. They moved up when they had weapons. They snapped the clamps open and climbed up the ladders and then locked the clamps around the nearest rung when they had to do something. The sea roared and swept across them. Some of the men disappeared. The sea rushed away and took the men with it, leaving no trace at all. The other men kept climbing, only stopping to help each other. Ricketts saw them disappearing in the darkness, climbing up to the main deck.

Someone kicked Ricketts' shoulder and he looked along the support leg. The sea roared and poured across him and drowned him, then he saw a pale face. The man was shouting something at him. He was passing a rifle down. Ricketts took it and slung it across one shoulder, then reached up for the magazines. He put the bag around his neck, clipped grenades to his belt, and when he had finished, he waved to the man and snapped the clamp loose. The sea roared and rushed at him. He clung tightly to the ladder. The sea pummelled him and poured all around him and then fell away. Ricketts slithered back down the leg, reached the main pontoon leg, stretched out with one hand and took hold and then swung across. He landed on the other ladder, heard the roaring of the waves. They were fifty feet high, towering high above his head, and they roared with an indescribable loudness and exploded around him. He clung to the ladder, felt the jolting of his arms, as the waves roared past and rushed beneath the rig and poured out through the other side.

Ricketts started climbing. He had to rest more than once. When he did so, he used the steel clamp, snapped it over the nearest rung. The other men were all around him, were above him and below him, were climbing up the ladders of the other legs, stretching along the support legs. They were vague in the gloom. They were fighting the roaring waves. They were using the short breaks between waves to move up even farther. Sometimes they failed, they clamped themselves on too late, and Ricketts saw the waves crash down upon them and sweep them away. Yet the other men kept climbing. They climbed up into the darkness. They were swallowed by the black mass of the deck that loomed high above Ricketts.

Ricketts kept climbing. He fought the wind and the roaring sea. He was now above the waves, but he felt the icy sting of the spray. The men above were disappearing. The deck's shadow was swallowing them. Ricketts wondered if the first men were on deck, and if so, what was happening. The storm was very rough. The rig was creaking and swaying. Ricketts hoped that the terrorists would be indoors, hiding out from the elements. He kept climbing the ladder. The wind howled and tore at him. The waves thundered below and the spray swept up to him and drenched him.

He glanced back down the leg, saw the men on the support legs, throwing off their cylinders and masks, unwrapping weapons and magazines. Ricketts saw the snarling waves. They swept over the swarming men. They rushed away and the men kept on moving, dark ants on a silvery web. They stretched along the support legs. They were climbing the four pontoon legs. They climbed out of that black, swirling pit and came up the steel ladders.

Ricketts looked up again. The bottom of the deck spread out above him. It was close and it was swaying up and down, the steel groaning in protest. Then Ricketts heard gunfire. It was coming from the main deck. It was the sound of light automatic rifles, dominating the howling wind.

Ricketts reached the catwalk. It was directly above his head. It was dark and the wind howled across it, raced back out to sea. The sound of gunfire was now louder, rising above the howling wind, and the catwalk was moving up and down as the massive deck rolled. Ricketts reached up through the hole, grabbed the grips at each side. He took a deep breath and pulled himself up and then he rolled on the catwalk.

The wind howled all around him, the sea roared and hissed beneath him, and he glanced down and saw white waves in darkness, climbing high, smashing inwards. More gunshots rang out. There was a muffled, deep explosion. Ricketts felt the blast jolting up his legs, and he grabbed for the railing. He glanced down the pontoon leg. The sea was boiling up around it. Someone screamed and was grabbed by a white claw and dragged into the darkness. The whole leg reverberated. The massive platform tilted slightly. The boiling water fell back and gave way to monstrous waves, and Ricketts knew that the leg had been blown and that he stood right on top of it.

Ricketts cursed and shook his head, suddenly ran around the catwalk. He was unslinging his rifle as he ran, and then he came to a ladder. He went up the ladder quickly. He remembered the ladder well. He reached the top and then went through an open door and a bright light washed over him. He was on the drilling floor, right behind the stacked crates. The noise of the gunfire echoed wildly, and he saw men in wetsuits. They were kneeling behind the crates, firing into the drilling room, and Ricketts looked beyond the crates and saw the terrorists, racing backwards and forwards. They seemed small and far away. The drilling floor was very bright. The light fell across the crates and machines, and cast large, bizarre shadows.

Ricketts knelt beside his men, released his safety-catch, heard a roaring from the far side of the deck as wood exploded around him. The men beside him returned the fire. The noise was harsh and almost deafening. Ricketts saw a terrorist throw up his arms, spin around and fall down.

'*Ricketts!*' someone shouted. '*Over here!*'

Ricketts jerked his head around, saw Turner near the door. Turner still had his cylinders and breathing mask, the mask strapped to his belt. Ricketts went over to him. The guns roared behind his back. He dropped to a crouching position and moved up beside Turner.

174

'We're in luck!' Turner shouted. 'They've blown the leg beneath us!'

'I know!' Ricketts shouted. 'Where are the other maintenance men?'

'Outside! I've got two men out here! We're going to do it between us!'

The guns continued roaring, someone screamed and fell down, and more men were rushing through the open door, crouching low, weapons ready. Ricketts looked back at the crates. A man was throwing a grenade. He jumped up and his arm swung in a blur and then he dropped down again. Ricketts saw the grenade spinning. It seemed suspended in space. It was far out above the drilling floor and then it curved down again. The explosion came immediately, made a hell of a noise, and through the roar there was the sound of a scream and bits of debris flew everywhere. Ricketts looked back at Turner. Turner's eyes were excited. Someone shouted and the men behind the crates broke apart and ran forward.

'—the leg!' Turner shouted. 'We've got to fix that leg! Let's get going!'

Ricketts looked past the crates, saw the massive drilling floor, saw his own men darting backwards and forwards, falling down, jumping up again. They were firing as they ran, were answered with more gunfire, and a grenade curved through the air and exploded and a crate fell apart. A man writhed on the steel deck. He was wearing a wet-suit. He was kicking his legs and screaming loudly, his hands on his stomach. Another man rushed towards him. The guns roared and cut him down. His rifle clattered to the deck and he shuddered and spun around and fell down. Another grenade went off. It exploded near the moonpool. Metal shrieked and a standing pipe buckled and crashed down on some terrorists. The men in the wet-suits ran forward, firing as they ran, and the guns roared on both sides and the shouting of the men echoed wildly.

'—now!' Turner shouted, slapping Ricketts on the shoulder, and they both jumped up and rushed through the door and felt the blast of the wind. Ricketts ran around the catwalk, saw the door in the floor opening. The head of a terrorist emerged and the man looked up, startled. Ricketts saw the wide eyes, saw the brief, scalding panic. He kicked the man's head and it jerked back and thumped on the catwalk. It bounced back up again. It rolled around on shaking shoulders. The man vomited and dropped back through the hole, leaving blood on the deck. Ricketts dropped to his knees. He looked down the pontoon leg. He saw a splash far below and then he saw another face staring up. The man was hanging from the ladder. The water boiled far below him. The man shouted '*No!*' and Ricketts fired and saw blood and stripped bone. The face just cracked open, the hands slid from the ladder, the body curved back and the arms waved above it, and then it plunged down the hollow leg and disappeared in the water. Ricketts had another look. There were no more terrorists down there. He glanced up and saw Turner with two men, and they all had full diving gear.

'We're okay!' Turner shouted. 'I know this rig well! There are spare plates on the catwalk down the leg! I don't think there's a problem!'

'Where's Dalton?' Ricketts shouted.

'I don't know!' Turner shouted. 'He probably came up one of the other legs! He's probably at the other side of the rig! *Come on! Let's get going!*'

Turner shuffled across the catwalk. His flippers were tied around his neck. He untied them and put them on his feet and then he untied the oxygen mask. The catwalk rose and fell, the wind howled and the sea roared; they heard the sound of gunfire from inside, heard more gunfire above them. Turner put on the oxygen mask, then he waved at the other men. They were wearing full diving equipment and they walked forward awkwardly. There was a pack on one man's back. It was the welding equipment. The other man was carrying an electric hammer and more bits of equipment. The rig suddenly tilted farther; the leg they stood on sank lower. Turner sat on the edge of the hole and then slid down and disappeared.

The second man took up position. Ricketts heard a sound behind him. He turned to face the door and saw a silhouette framed in the light, a gun pointing towards him. Ricketts fired immediately, raked the rifle to and fro, heard the roar and then saw the man dancing and falling back in. Another terrorist appeared. Ricketts shot him and he fell. Ricketts tugged a grenade from his belt and then ran to the door. He threw the grenade in, flattened himself against the wall; the grenade exploded and the whole wall vibrated and then Ricketts rushed in. A man was sliding down the crates, another man rolled on the floor, and a third man was stumbling and screaming with his hands at his bloody face. The rifle roared in Ricketts' hands. He felt it jolting against his arm. The three men jerked and shuddered along the deck and then they were still.

Ricketts rushed back outside, saw the hole in the catwalk, looked in and saw the three men on the ladder, climbing down towards the water. The water was far below them, over a hundred feet down, boiling and climbing up towards them, coming in from the sea. Ricketts closed the trapdoor. He heard the wind and the sea. The storm was not as strong as it had been; it was gradually fading. Ricketts looked all around him, saw a grey light in the darkness, turned and went back through the door and walked into the drilling deck.

The dead men lay at his feet. There was blood streaked down the crates. Ricketts walked past the crates and looked out at the vast drilling floor. His men were still fighting. They had reached the moonpool. They were hiding behind the stacked pipes and chains, firing up at the driller's room. Ricketts ran across the floor, his bare feet slipping in mud; he was drenched and he felt very cold and there was sweat on his brow. The guns roared and bullets whistled, ricocheted all around him. He kept running and he came to a forklift and dropped down behind it.

Bullets whipped past his head, he heard the roar of a grenade, and glass shattered and he heard a piercing scream and then he looked at the moonpool. His men were stretched out around it, were hiding behind what they could find, were shouting and waving arms and firing up at the raised driller's room. Ricketts looked up at the driller's room, saw the terrorists at the window. The glass was shattered and the terrorists were firing down at the men in the wet-suits. Then a grenade sailed towards the window, disappeared amongst the terrorists. It exploded in a blinding flash of light and more shards of glass rained down.

Ricketts' men darted forward. A terrorist flopped through

177

the window. The men raced across the floor and up the stairs and disappeared from his view. Ricketts jumped up and ran, saw a terrorist at the window, saw the barrel of the terrorist's gun and then heard a loud roar. Ricketts kept running. The terrorist plunged down to the floor. Ricketts ran through the door and up the steps and rushed into the driller's room. He saw the men in the wet-suits. They were examining the terrorists. The driller's room was wrecked, and the terrorists, all dead, were drenched in blood.

'Anyone seen Dalton?'

'Who's Dalton?' someone said. 'If he's in a wet-suit he's one of us. That's all we're concerned with.'

Ricketts turned and walked out, went along a narrow corridor; the lights were bright and the ceiling was low and he felt his eyes stinging. It was quiet in the corridor. He heard the sound of distant gunfire. He kept walking and he turned a sharp corner and then came to more steps. He saw a pair of dark overalls, raised his gun and heard it roar. The overalls flapped like a flag and then the man started falling. His rifle clattered down the steps. He pitched forward and followed it. His head thumped on a step and split open and his body flipped over. His boots banged on the floor, his spine cracked on the steps, and he sprawled there, propped up by the steps, as Ricketts jumped over him.

Ricketts went up to the main deck, stepped out and felt the wind. He noticed that the storm had abated, but the wind was still icy. The sound of gunfire was loud here; it echoed and ricocheted. There were men running backwards and forwards, through the light and the shadow. A hand grenade exploded, the flash illuminated the darkness, and silhouettes spiralled up and fell down and rolled over the deck.

The deck itself was tilting. It was covered in mud and oil. The guns roared and men shouted and ran backwards and forwards, exposed in bright lights, lost in shadows, skidding over the deck.

Ricketts saw the sea, far below the tilting deck, saw flashes of white through the gloom, the black void turning grey. Another grenade exploded. Ricketts heard the shattering blast. He was picked up and smashed against a wall and found himself on the deck. He looked up at a towering derrick, saw lights winking from the platforms, heard a scream and then saw a man falling, plunging down through the moonpool.

Ricketts jumped up and ran. He saw the base of the derrick. There were terrorists huddled up within the web of the girders, firing down from the roof of the drilling floor, their guns winking and roaring. Ricketts ran across the deck, saw a man in overalls, jumping out from behind a large crate with a gun in his hands. He didn't have time to shoot. Ricketts just bowled right into him. They both tumbled to the deck and rolled over, one on top of the other. Ricketts saw the man rising, still holding his Sten gun, and Ricketts kicked out at his knee and he went down, his head thumping the steel deck. Then Ricketts jumped up. The man was rolling away from him. Ricketts took a step forward and kicked him, in the ribs, on the head. The man grunted and shuddered. Ricketts kicked his head again. There was a dull snapping sound and the man's whole body twitched and then froze. Ricketts picked up his rifle. Splinters of wood flew off the crate. He heard the whipping of bullets and he turned and ran towards the towering derrick.

His men were scattered around the deck. They were firing up at the derrick. The base of the derrick rested on the roof of the drilling shed, and the terrorists were firing down from there. Ricketts' men were trying to storm it, were rushing forward and falling down, and a tear-gas bomb had fallen near the shed, and the smoke spiralled skywards. The sky itself was turning grey, drifting beyond the towering derrick, and the guns roared and a hand grenade exploded and some more men fell down.

Ricketts saw the blond giant, pointing up at the shooting terrorists, drenched like the rest of the men, his pale face now flushed. Ricketts crouched low and ran, skidded crazily in the mud, fell down and slithered over the deck and then crawled up to Hubbert. The blond man looked at him. He seemed startled and then he grinned. He poked a finger into one ear, turned it slowly, then smacked his own head.

'I'm half deaf!' he shouted.

'What happened to Walters?' Ricketts said.

'I don't know!' Hubbert shouted. 'I haven't seen him! I don't think he made it!'

There was another loud explosion, lumps of metal flew

179

through the air, and the head of a man rolled across the deck, pumping blood from the severed neck. Ricketts turned and saw the body. It was standing beside some pipes. One hand flapped in the air and the legs shook and then it collapsed. There was another explosion, they heard the whistle of flying shrapnel, and it subsided and the guns continued roaring, the noise fierce, almost deafening.

'Those fucking bastards!' Hubbert shouted. 'They've just holed up on that roof! There's nowhere they can go, but they're staying there and cutting us to pieces!' He suddenly stood up, fully exposed to the terrorists, and he looked at the men all around him and then waved his rifle. 'The hell with it!' he bawled. 'Let's go get 'em! Let's wipe out the bastards!'

The men roared and jumped up and started running across the deck; the guns of the terrorists cut them down, but still they kept running. Ricketts couldn't remember much. He suddenly found himself near the shed. He heard screams and saw men falling down and rolling over the sloping deck. A hand grenade exploded, tore the running men apart; another flew down from the roof of the drilling shed and the noise was demonic. Ricketts looked up and blinked, saw the guns of the terrorists. The terrorists were looking down, he saw the guns winking, then the bullets ricocheted off the deck. A grenade exploded above his head, making a jagged, fearsome roar; he heard screams and saw a man flying out and plunging down to the deck.

Then Ricketts saw Hubbert. The blond giant was on a ladder. He was clambering up the side of the drilling shed, his gun swinging from one hand. Ricketts followed without thinking, saw Hubbert disappearing, kept climbing and felt almost numb from the roaring and shouting. He climbed on to the roof, saw a mass of milling men. The roof was large and the terrorists were in the middle, around the hole of the drilling shaft. The men in wet-suits fired at them. Some of the terrorists fell down. A few screamed and fell back against the shaft and plunged down the moonpool. Then Ricketts saw the dynamite, piled up around one leg. The sticks of dynamite were all tied together and a long fuse was burning.

'*Get down!*' Ricketts shouted.

He threw himself to the deck, slithered back towards the ladder, grabbed the ladder and flung himself over and hung down by his arms. He saw white light and flames, his whole head seemed to explode, then he dropped down through a roaring cacophony of pressure and heat. The sky above seemed to split, there was a rainfall of debris, and Ricketts crawled across the deck on hands and knees, shook his head, fell face down. The thunder imprisoned him. He was pummelled and scorched. He shook his head and heard a ringing in his ears, and then he tried to look up. The deck was spinning around, he saw a smoky grey sky, and he rolled on to his back and looked up and saw the whole derrick crumbling. The huge legs were bent, were buckling and breaking; the tiered platforms started shrieking and splitting, then they plunged down the centre. The roof of the drilling shed collapsed, flesh and steel poured down through it, and the noise was demonic and the black smoke billowed up from a wall of flame. Then the derrick fell, toppled over to the right, suddenly exploded in a mass of wood and steel and crashed over the main deck. Ricketts heard the screams of men, saw the steel girders bouncing. They bounced over the deck, smashed through men and machines, and then plunged into space and disappeared. Ricketts climbed to his feet. He felt dizzy and unreal. He turned around, picked up a Sten gun, then he saw the blond giant.

Hubbert was crawling towards him. His blond hair had been burnt off. His face was blistered and his wet-suit was in tatters and he seemed to be smouldering. Hubbert crawled right up to Ricketts. He looked at him with wide eyes. He raised one hand and then he rolled over, coughed blood and died.

Ricketts felt a searing rage. He cursed and looked all around him. He saw the grey light pouring over the sea – but he did not see McGregor. Ricketts wanted McGregor, wanted to have that bastard's guts. He stepped forward and tripped on a dead man and cursed and walked on.

The air was filled with smoke, there was gunfire everywhere, and he heard the clatter of feet across the catwalks, heard shouting and screaming. A terrorist flopped across a railing. Another man swung his legs up. The terrorist screamed and fell down through the air and thumped on to the deck. Ricketts just kept walking, smelt smoke and cordite. There was a flash and then he heard the explosion and he dropped to the deck. The blast pummelled his body; he felt scorched and suffocated. It subsided and he got to his feet and saw a huge wall of yellow flame. One of the spare tanks had exploded, the petrol poured out as fire, and a man rushed from the blaze screaming crazily and beating his body. He spun around and fell down. His body twitched and then was still. He was still burning and smoking as Ricketts stepped past him and walked to the landing pad catwalk.

The wall of flame roared beside him, the smoke threatened to choke him, and he moved away from the flames and stepped on to the catwalk and saw the grey sea far below. The huge waves had subsided. The storm had dissipated itself. Ricketts looked down that two hundred feet and saw a sea strewn with debris. There were men drifting down there. There were weapons and oxygen cylinders. Farther out, but drifting in towards the rig, were the empty submersibles. Ricketts walked across the catwalk. It sloped up to the landing pad. Ricketts heard the sound of gunfire and shouting and it made him start running.

He jumped on to the landing pad, saw the helicopter at the far side, sliding along the badly tilting deck towards the edge of the landing pad. McGregor was going with it. His right arm was stretched above him. The sleeve of his overalls had caught on the door handle and he was being dragged backwards along the deck. McGregor was screaming wildly. He was covered in blood. Paul Dalton, looking angry, was walking towards him with a gun in his hand.

'You cheated us,' Paul Dalton said clearly. 'You won't do that again.'

The helicopter slid towards the edge, McGregor screamed and went with it, and Ricketts suddenly realized what was happening, and he ran towards Dalton. Then he knew it was too late. He saw Dalton raise his pistol. McGregor was being dragged backwards along the deck and Dalton aimed for his head. There was no need to shoot him; he was going over the edge. Ricketts saw Dalton aiming at McGregor, and he knew it was vengeance.

'*No!*' Ricketts shouted.

Dalton whirled around towards him. He saw Ricketts and he knew that he had heard, so he aimed with the pistol. Ricketts didn't think about it. He pressed the trigger of the Sten gun. There was a roar and Dalton flung his arms out and staggered back like a drunken man. The helicopter slid forward, McGregor screamed and kicked furiously, and Dalton fell to the deck and rolled over, still clutching his pistol. McGregor screamed again. His heels were dragging along the deck. The tail of the helicopter shot into the air and the nose pointed down towards the sea. The wheels caught on the edge, the helicopter turned over, and McGregor flew up and somersaulted with it, seemed to hang in the air. Then the helicopter fell down, plunged down towards the sea. McGregor's screaming grew faint and then stopped, and Ricketts heard a loud splash.

Ricketts walked across the deck. He saw that Dalton was dead. He then walked to the edge of the landing pad and looked down at the sea. The water boiled up and bubbled, rushed in circles and formed a whirlpool. The tail of the helicopter disappeared and then the sea settled down.

Ricketts went back to the catwalk. He looked across the main deck. The deck was sloping down to the right, but it was no longer sinking. The gunfire had stopped. There were dead men everywhere. A few prisoners were being herded towards the modules, their hands on their heads. The whole deck was strewn with debris, was covered with drifting smoke. A wall of flame was rising up from the petrol tanks, being fanned by the wind. Ricketts crossed the catwalk, saw the sea far below, saw bodies and pieces of equipment and the bobbing submersibles. He walked across the main deck. He saw Turner walking towards him. He had taken off the cylinders and mask, but he still wore his wet-suit. Turner tugged his beard and grinned. He stuck his thumb up. Ricketts waved and then turned and looked out at the choppy grey sea. He saw a distant rig. It was burning off its waste gas. It was close to the horizon and it seemed very small and remote. Turner walked up beside him. He put his hand on Ricketts' shoulder. They both stood there and looked at the sea, and they didn't say anything.

CHAPTER SEVENTEEN

RICKETTS and Turner, both wearing dry clothes, stood on a catwalk on Bravo 1 and looked out on the Forties Field. The sea was quite calm, the sky above it was grey, and the distant rigs, scattered along the horizon, seemed fragile and lonesome.

Ricketts and Turner looked down. The landing pad was just beneath them. They heard the roar of the helicopter, saw the massive rotors spinning, and kept looking as the bodyguards emerged from a module nearby. The guards fanned out across the deck. They were burdened down with weapons. The Prime Minister emerged and walked between them, bent against the strong wind. His grey hair was blowing wildly, his heavy body seemed tired, but he reached the helicopter, walked up the metal steps, and then turned around and waved up at the catwalk. Ricketts and Turner waved back. The Prime Minister dropped his hand. He looked at them for what seemed like a long time, and then he went inside.

'He's bloody angry,' Turner said. 'It was our mess and yet it trapped him. He had to give us our twenty-five per cent, and he won't like us for it.'

'I'm surprised,' Ricketts said. 'I thought he had us by the nuts. I thought he could have used all this against us, and made us settle for less.'

'It doesn't work that way,' Turner said. 'You can't fight the oil companies. With the loss of Eagle 3 and the virtual destruction of Charlie 2, Sir Reginald threw up his hands and said we couldn't go on. The Prime Minister was flabbergasted. He couldn't believe what he was hearing. But Sir Reginald just looked him in the eye and pointed out what our losses were. He mentioned the cost of rebuilding the rigs, mentioned how long it would take to do, pointed out that British United couldn't possibly survive all that without a full twenty-five per cent return. The Prime Minister was outraged. He said Sir Reginald was blackmailing him. He said his government wouldn't pay for the mistakes of incompetent oil companies. Sir Reginald just smiled at him. It was a hell of a smile. He said that the oil companies simply couldn't afford to do it if they weren't given twenty-five per cent. He said if they didn't do it, the world would ask why, and then word of this whole affair would just slip out. He pointed out what that would mean: it would mean the loss of international confidence. He said if British United Oil didn't handle it, then no one else would—and at that the Prime Minister surrendered.'

Ricketts smiled and glanced down at the landing pad. The Under-Secretary was going into the helicopter, stooping low at the door. The guards followed him in. They went backwards up the steps. The last one glanced around the landing pad and then slid the steel door shut.

'You were right,' Turner said. 'It was Dalton. It was him all along. Blackburn phoned through confirmation. He said he didn't have any doubts. He had interrogated some of the people who were listed in McGregor's notebook, and they said that McGregor had been seeing Dalton. They first met in Bahrain. Dalton called McGregor over. They met later in Los Angeles, and we think they made the final deal there.'

'I don't figure it,' Ricketts said. 'That means one of our own overseas backers was behind the whole thing.'

'That's right,' Turner said. 'It certainly seems that way. We can assume that someone in the conglomerate ordered the whole operation.'

'Why? It just doesn't make sense.'

'Yes, it does,' Turner said. 'It certainly does if you think in international terms. The conglomerate must have known that if the British Government reduced North Sea oil taxes, all the revenue we were giving to their overseas interests would have gone instead back into Britain. The conglomerate knew that it was the exorbitant British taxes that had forced the British subsidiaries to cut back on drilling and invest their capital in the conglomerate's tax-free havens; it was therefore in their own interests to get rid of the Prime Minister, discredit the British oil fields, and thus ensure that future British oil revenue continued to be dependent on the

185

conglomerate's tax-free, and therefore more lucrative, overseas markets.'

'But it backfired,' Ricketts said.

'That's right; it backfired. It backfired because of McGregor. They didn't think for a minute that McGregor would stop short at killing an English prime minister. They also forgot that it was not in the Clan's own interests to instigate the total destruction of North Sea oil. Fanatics or not, despised by the Scottish Nationalists or not, the Clan in its own way was nevertheless fighting for an independent Scotland that would be supported by North Sea oil. If McGregor hadn't wanted that, and if he had killed the Prime Minister, the North Sea would now be finished and Britain would have to invest overseas. As it stands, by what is almost pure chance, we've been given the winning hand.'

They looked down at the landing pad. The helicopter was roaring. The spinning rotors had whipped the air up and this wind lashed the roustabouts. The landing pad vibrated, the men pulled the blocks away, and the helicopter roared even louder and then climbed slowly upwards. It hovered a few feet above the deck, was framed by the grey sea, shuddered and swayed from side to side and then climbed up higher. Ricketts and Turner heard the roaring, were lashed by the swirling wind. They stood two-hundred feet above the sea, staring up, squinting painfully. The helicopter climbed higher, hovered briefly above the derricks, turned around like a huge, crippled bird and then headed west.

'So,' Ricketts said. 'What do we do?'

'Do?' Turner said. 'We do nothing.'

Ricketts looked at him. 'What the hell do you mean?' he said. 'We don't try to find out who ordered it? Is *that* what you're saying?'

'Yes,' Turner said. 'That's what I'm saying.' He tugged at his beard, ran his fingers through his hair, looked out across the desolate sea and then gave a small shrug. 'What can we do?' he said. 'There's not a thing we can do. Dalton was with the conglomerate for years and he knew lots of powerful men. Which one of them gave the order? Which office most stood to gain? Was it the Americans or the Germans or the French or the Middle East sultans? We'll never find out. The conglomerate's too big to investigate. Like most of the conglomerates, it's a multi-national affair, divorced from any single jurisdiction and removed from morality. And what if we mentioned Dalton? What if we accused the conglomerate in general? We would just receive a letter, an immaculately typed letter, denying all knowledge of Dalton's political activities. They have us whipped, Ricketts. There's not a thing we can do about it. We'll just have to get on with the job and forget that it happened. There's no evidence of their guilt. There's no power that can find the truth. The politicians no longer rule the world – the conglomerates do.'

Ricketts sighed, looked up at the grey sky, and saw the helicopter in the distance, flying over a lonely rig. It flew towards a grey haze. It dwindled to nothing and disappeared. Ricketts stared and saw only the grey sky, the rigs in the flat sea.

It was all like a dream. It might never have happened. Twenty-four hours had passed and the world was as it had been before. It just didn't seem real.

Ricketts sighed again. 'Well,' he said slowly, 'for the moment at least we've still got our oil.'

'Yes,' Turner said. 'Let's hope it stays that way.'

UNCLASSIFIED

1. On August 18, 1982, at approximately 1430 hours, an earth tremor travelling from north to south along the bed of the North Sea caused considerable devastation to some of British United Oil's major fields. Shock waves from the earth tremor caused extreme turbulence on the sea's surface with winds of approximately 150 miles per hour and waves as high as 120 feet. Due to this, Eagle 3, the main semi-submersible rig on Frigg Field, was sunk with all hands. The tremor then travelled on a south-westerly course until it reached Beryl Field where, before dissipating itself, it caused considerable damage to the main rig, Charlie 2, and led to the unfortunate deaths of twenty crew members who were trapped beneath a collapsed section of the drilling floor.

2. Since Eagle 3 (Frigg Field) was being prepared for shut-down and towing to another site no plans for reconstruction are envisaged.

3. Charlie 2 (Beryl Field) has been shut down temporarily for extensive repairs and the surviving crew members repatriated for medical examination and subsequent transfer to other rigs.

4. Since many of the crew members are suffering from severe shock it is felt by this company that their names should be withheld from the press and general public. Private settlement of compensation for the dependants of the deceased is currently being negotiated.

5. A full investigation into the nature of the earth tremor has been ordered, and a complete, top-classified report will be submitted in due course to the Under-Secretary of the Department of Energy. For reasons of internal security British United Oil has agreed with the Department of Energy that no further information regarding this matter should be released.

THE END

THE REPORTER BY PETER MAY

FIFTY OILMEN ESCAPE DEATH AS EXPLOSION
DESTROYS RIG!

The headline screamed the news of the latest in a string of North
Sea disasters, this one was unusual only in that nobody had died.
The Government claimed they were simply unfortunate 'accidents'; but to Colin Anderson, investigative reporter for THE
STANDARD, the 'accidents' turned out to be leads to one of the
biggest international sabotage stories of all time – a hell-raising
exclusive that was to endanger not only his life but the life of
Janis Sinclair, his attractive young research assistant who'd
somehow ingratiated herself into both his work and his feelings.

Based on the BBC television series 'The Standard'.

0 552 10692 5   85p

FIRESPILL BY IAN SLATER

FIRESPILL . . . 600 million gallons of high-octane fuel poured
on the windswept waters of British Columbia.
    Flashpoint . . . one match will ignite a raging inferno.
    Firestorm . . . burning with the fury of hell. Nothing will stop it.
    Firespill . . . a blazing inferno of terror, totally out of control,
threatening thousands of lives. An environmental disaster torn
from today's headlines. A gripping, shockwave novel of total
suspense, horror – and surprise.

0 552 10611 9   85p

THE NINTH MAN BY JOHN LEE

In 1942, eight Nazi agents were captured soon after landing in America. One was not ... Dietrich is The Ninth Man – a lone wolf, a trained assassin who knows neither love nor compassion, whose top secret missions are carried out with speed and ruthless efficiency. His mission in America is a vital one, known only to the highest echelons of the Reich, one which will shatter America's faith in her ability to win the war: he is to assassinate Roosevelt!

Only one man suspects his existence, but can he get anyone to believe him before it is too late?

Based on historical fact, John Lee's chilling novel builds up the suspense page by page, culminating in a devastating climax which will leave you breathless.

0 552 10396 9   85p

911 BY THOMAS CHASTAIN

When one of the enormous balloons exploded at the height of the Thanksgiving Parade along Broadway, terror hit the streets of New York. The nightmare began for Deputy Chief Inspector Max Kauffman when he became aware that this was not an isolated act of terrorism. For a call had come into the special police number 911 announcing that a second bomb was set to go off in Radio City – and the Music Hall was packed for the holiday show.

The call to 911 was followed by an anonymous note. 'This is only the Second Day of Christmas'. And Kauffman realised the full horror facing Manhattan in the midst of the Christmas shopping spree – an apparently motiveless maniac at large ... and a bomb for each of the Twelve Days.

0 552 10596 1   85p